CAGE OF BONES

JENNY O'BRIEN

Storm
PUBLISHING

This is a work of fiction. Names, characters, business, events and incidents are the products of the author's imagination. Any resemblance to actual persons, living or dead, or actual events is purely coincidental.

Ebook ISBN: 978-1-80508-393-1
Paperback ISBN: 978-1-80508-395-5

Cover design: Henry Steadman
Cover images: Shutterstock

Published by Storm Publishing.
For further information, visit:
www.stormpublishing.co

For Micky and Jane Underdown

Bone by Bone.

Emily Dickinson

ONE

Monday 4th September, 6 a.m.

Barney Mulcahy was in his usual spot in the wheelhouse, a navy fishing cap perched on top of his bald head and a roll-up squashed between the thumb and forefinger of his left hand. There was no wedding band on his ring finger, nothing to herald his approaching thirtieth wedding anniversary apart from a flurry of thoughts in his head about the up-and-coming party Deirdre had been planning since Easter. His other hand was coiled round the wheel as he manoeuvred the boat over the loops and swells of the waves, one eye on the sounder in front of him, the other on the lookout for other boats, not that he'd be likely to find anyone else fool enough to check their pots for brown crab with the threat of a force six on the horizon.

Howth Harbour wasn't the place it should be in September. A popular tourist spot when the sun was high in the sky and the sea millpond smooth instead of the freezing, swirling mass of crashing surf, ripping and rolling up against the rocks in a crescendo of musical chords akin to an orchestra stretching out towards the finishing line.

If Barney could be anywhere in the world right now, he'd be exactly where he was, as far away from the missus as he could get with her talk of menus and the like. The sea was both his playground and his passion. His livelihood and his place of work. Thirty years with the wife, thirty-one if he counted the one they'd spent walking out together – a smile touched his lips at the quaint term finding purchase in his matter-of-fact mind. He loved his wife, probably more than if they'd been able to have a brood to fill the empty rooms of their home and their hearts but not enough to spend hours pondering the benefits of lobster tails over Dublin Bay prawns for a party he didn't want but would end up paying for anyway.

With the harbour now a speck in the distance and the boat engine in neutral, he grabbed the boat hook from where it lived propped up in the corner of the wheelhouse and headed out, his yellow oilskins slapping round his legs, his cap pulled low over his ears. He'd lost too many caps in the past not to be wary of losing another.

He slipped the hook through the knot of the yellow buoy, one hand holding onto the rail as he dragged the swirling mass of slimy green rope towards him, the thrill of the unknown causing his heart to thump. It had always been that way, ever since he was a small lad fishing off the end of Dun Laoghaire Pier with his da. The thought of the biggest fish, the fattest, juiciest and heaviest. It made no difference as to the species. Money in the piggybank and with a little left over for the table except now the piggybank was more bank than pig and the table meant fifty friends wining and dining at his expense instead of something fishy to show off to his brother.

Muscles bunching, arm over arm until he had enough rope to wrap round the winch and start the motor. Long gone were the days when he'd relished bringing up the pots without mechanical assistance. Fifty-seven next birthday and with arthritic hips and knees to show for it. His heart was willing, it was the rest of him that saw the sense in letting machinery take the brunt of the work from out of his hands.

The winch screeched into action, the sound alerting his flying followers to the possibility of food up ahead. Wherever there were fishing boats trying to earn an honest crust there were a battalion of herring gulls happy to relieve them of it, but he'd been fishing so long that he barely heard their squawking and shrieks. His attention was on the first of the string of pots rising through the air, water streaming through the black netting, his gloved hands reaching out to pull it aboard, his greedy gaze landing on the couple of lobster in the bottom with annoyance. Undersized and as useless as if the pot had been empty.

It took seconds to rip open the trap door and fling the lobsters back into the sea, in the hope that he'd catch them when they were large enough to be any good to him. Re-baiting the pot with a selection of fish frames came next, a task quickly accomplished before restarting the winch and repeating the process all over again. Two more pots followed and both a waste of time. He engaged the winch to follow the line, annoyed at having left the comfort of his home for the pleasure of freezing his whatnots off in a blistering wind.

The winch creaked and groaned, the boat tipping under the weight as the fourth pot rose out of the sea in a shower of undersized brown crab, the netting invisible under their squirming, heaving bodies, their claws clutching onto the sides, the air quickly filled with the sound of sharp plops as their little bodies landed in the water.

He stepped back, a thick frown descending at the sight of what looked like thousands of baby crab, but in all probability was only a few hundred. He'd never seen the like and chances were he never would again.

Stripping the outside of the pot of its remaining unwelcome passengers was fast and furious, crab flying around the air in a hailstorm of squirming legs and bodies. He didn't expect to see the same again inside the pot, his tongue clicking against his teeth in annoyance at the sight. The same but different because the crabs inside weren't squirming. They were dead and already starting to blacken. Time was against him as was the weather and he still had two more strings to check before thinking of returning to shore. He also wasn't expecting to see the layer of bones wedged inside, their gleaming white surface picked clean of flesh.

Barney had been messing about in boats as long as he could walk and, in all that time he'd never been sick. He'd never felt the urge even after a bellyful of beer the night before or when the sea was at its roughest like today. It was his greatest shame that the vomit propelled up his neck in such a burst that he didn't have the time to reach the side, instead spraying a stream of bile-coloured liquid across his usually pristine white deck.

TWO

Monday 4th September, 8.15 a.m.

'Welcome back, Alana. Had a good holiday?'

Detective Alana Mack held out a hand to take the pile of post offered, her bright smile causing the skin around her eyes to crinkle. 'Wonderful. I can certainly recommend it, Mary. Much happen while I was away?'

'No, nothing. Quiet as the grave.'

Not the best of analogies but Alana wasn't going to comment apart from flashing her another smile before making for the lift. Once inside she lost the smile as she started to shift through her mail with a careful hand.

The last few weeks had passed in a whirlwind of paperwork and bureaucracy, ever since the Garda Síochána Ombudsman Commission (GSOC) had decided to take a very real interest in their last case. Catching a serial killer was one thing, having to explain links to members of her team when no one could have known or even guessed as to those links, had her thinking of handing in her notice.

She hadn't only thought about it, she remembered, settling

the letters and packages on her lap to propel her wheelchair out of the lift. The document was written and filed away in a folder marked *not urgent*, the same folder she kept an assortment of other non-essential documents. She knew where to find it if she needed to. That was comfort enough.

'You're a sight for sore eyes, Alana. Remind me to disappear off to Malaga just when the summer weather goes tits up for the rest of us.'

'That bad, eh, Paddy?'

'Rain, rain and with a side order of more rain for good measure.'

'In fact, your typical Irish summer then,' she said, taking a moment to reacclimatise to being back in the incident room after a fortnight away. The first holiday she'd taken since the end of her marriage, and the end of her life as she'd known it up to that point.

'That's a bit harsh.' Paddy perched on the corner of her desk, all set on a good gossip. 'True but harsh,' he added on a laugh. 'So, what did you get up to then?'

'Just the usual, you know. Sat round the pool and vegetated with a good book. Nothing exciting.'

As lead detective of the Clonabee branch of the National Bureau of Criminal Investigation, she had more excitement than she could manage. Oh, she managed simply because there was no choice not to, but it was at the expense of any kind of a social life. The last case had seen fit to escalate into a storm of media interest, propelling her into the spotlight in a way she'd never seen before and never wanted to see again.

Her new boss, Detective Superintendent Leo Barry, was in his element and instrumental in offers for her to appear on the likes of *The Late Late Show* and *Morning Ireland*, needless to say with him at her side in a supporting role. That she'd refused was a contentious topic and one which had led to her choosing to leave the country instead of the kind of staycation she favoured. There was nothing more stressful than trying to navigate a holiday on wheels. Once she'd arrived, she'd loved every minute. It was the getting there and returning home that had her in need of another break.

'So, not much happening then?' she said, glancing around the empty office in relief. If there was something on the books then the desks would be heaving, with no thought to the time of day, or night.

'I wouldn't go so far as to say that.' His reply was carefully worded but then everything about Paddy Quigg, her trusted second-in-command, was careful from his conservative suit and plain tie to his regulation shoes.

'Really?' She watched as he checked his phone. Something was up, and more serious than he'd first assumed, she thought, reading his mind. Alana wasn't into mystic shit but, after working with the man for two and a half years, he was like an open book to her.

Her hands tightened around the arms of her chair. It was either work or something to do with Irene. Dr Irene Burden, their go-to forensic psychologist, and Paddy's pregnant fiancée. No. She closed her eyes. Anything but that.

'Flynn messaged me an hour ago. He had a call from his dad about one of his mates over in Howth,' Paddy finally said, jumping off the desk, not that it was far to jump, and heading to his usual spot by the window. 'It sounded all a bit garbled. Bones in the bottom of a crab pot. Said he was happy to check it out instead of wasting the guards' time.'

Flynn O'Hare was their go-to boaty person on the team. What he didn't know about boats and the sea in general wasn't worth mentioning. A necessary skill given Clonabee's prominent position on the coast, slotted between Blackrock and Booterstown. He was also the most cautious of the team. If he thought there was a problem then there was a very good chance he was right. Certainly, serious enough to involve the NBCI instead of the gardai.

Alana suppressed a groan. Her first day back. She'd planned on having the time to catch up on all the routine paperwork that she'd been adding to the non-urgent folder, keeping her resignation letter company. 'What does he think we've got?'

'A pile of bones picked clean. Flynn thinks legs and the like but he's not sure.'

'Let me guess. He thinks they're human.'

'That's right.'

'Why would someone do something like that?'

Paddy shrugged. 'Your guess is as good as mine. What do you want me to do?'

She threw him her keys. 'You can drive.'

THREE

Monday 4th September, 9.15 a.m.

There was nothing wrong with Howth. In fact, there was a lot right with it. The village, situated on the east of Dublin city was a delight, with the most picturesque harbour imaginable. Last time she'd visited she'd been lucky to see a colony of seals. This time, her luck had run out. Her gaze shifted from the line of assorted fishing boats in a rainbow of colours hugging the harbour wall to Dr Rusty Mulholland and where he was climbing out of his jeep.

'Had a good holiday, Alana?' he shouted, the wind whipping the words from his mouth.

'I can't remember! Sorry for having to drag you away from the office like this.' In Rusty's case the office meant the pathology department at Clonabee Hospital where he reigned supreme.

'I can imagine.' He stood looking down at her, a gentle giant of a man with carroty locks and an intellect to envy. 'You'll have to come round for tea and tell us all about it. It seems an age since you last visited.'

'I'd love to,' she replied, waving across at where Paddy was standing beside Flynn and a tall, burly stranger dressed in canary-yellow salopettes and matching wellies. 'Come on, I think we're wanted.'

The *Margaret M* was a bright blue twenty-seven-foot Aquastar with red gunwales and white wheelhouse. It was also the first fishing boat that Alana had had any dealings with, which wasn't a problem with Flynn on the team.

'Hello, Flynn. Mr Mulcahy? I'm Detective Alana Mack and this is the state pathologist, Dr Mulholland. I see you've already met Detective Paddy Quigg. Now, what do you have for us? From the beginning if you please.' Alana could see that Flynn was keen to intervene, but a sharp look and his mouth clamped shut. First impressions were important, never more so when they didn't know what they were dealing with.

'I run a few strings of pots.' Mr Mulcahy reached up a hand to scratch his scalp before dropping it back to his side. 'I went out this morning, same as I do every Monday to check on them, weather allowing, only to discover...' He paused a beat to take in a huge gasp of air, his ruddy features taking on a sudden greenish hue.

'Only to discover?' Rusty prompted.

'I'll show you, just there in the boat. I didn't do anything with it, or the rest of the pots.' He started to turn only to stop at the sound of Alana's voice.

'No, that's fine, Mr Mulcahy. We'll take it from here. There's nothing else you'd like to tell us?'

'I was a bit sick after... you know.'

To see such a strapping man diminished into an unhappy, shivering wreck was almost proof enough of his innocence. Not quite but it certainly didn't go unnoticed by anyone who watched the way he bowed his head, his hands clasped in front of him. They still had to take him back to the nick and interview him but that could wait until he'd settled his stomach on a gallon of tea, or whiskey. It was no odds to her as long as he didn't end up over the drink-driving limit. It wouldn't be the first time they'd been compassionate only to find their witness the worse for drink and impossible to interview until they'd sobered up.

'Hardly surprising. If you can give Detective O'Hare the keys. We'll be sure to lock it up after.'

'We'll also need the location of the pots,' Rusty interrupted, in the process of flinging his leg over the side of the boat. 'For the dive team.'

'I keep a note of all the strings' locations on my GPS. The numbers are jotted down on the black notebook in the wheelhouse. It was the first string, fourth pot.'

Rusty nodded before clambering aboard, as if he knew what the man was talking about, which was a good job because Alana didn't have a clue. No doubt her evening would include genning up on fishing boats. Great!

He was back within seconds, the notebook in his hand, his expression replaced by a stony mask, the flickering look all telling. They had a crime scene on their hands. An unusual one but a crime scene nevertheless.

'Before you head off, Mr Mulcahy. I see you have a basket full of brown crab. From the same string or...?'

'From the same string, doctor.'

'Good. Oh, I'll also need a water sample, Flynn.'

'I'll ensure you get one.'

A water sample? Alana hadn't a clue what Rusty was on about but that didn't worry her. The mind of the esteemed pathologist wasn't her problem.

'We'll also need your shoes and clothes and what have you as well as your prints for exclusion purposes, Mr Mulcahy.'

'You what?'

. . .

The pathology department at Clonabee Hospital was located down a dimly lit corridor with the autopsy suite on the left and Rusty's office situated next door. It was a place Alana and Paddy both knew well so they didn't waste any time in getting gowned and gloved up before joining Rusty.

Alana glanced from the bones set out on a bottle-green, clinical sheet and across to where Paddy was adjusting his mask, his eyes as confused as hers. It's not as if there was much to autopsy but then they were dealing with someone special in Dr Mulholland. A state pathologist was one thing, but the man also had a combined doctorate in osteology and forensic anthropology, which he'd achieved after a prolonged spell working and studying at a body farm in the USA early on in his career. Alana had made the mistake of googling body farm after she'd read his impressive list of credentials, a mistake she was yet to forget.

'So, what can you tell us then, doc?' Paddy said, obviously finding it easier to compartmentalise the reality in front of him from the horrors yet to be revealed.

'Apart from the obvious of someone chopping up the victim before ramming it inside the pot?'

'If you like, although I would have worded it slightly differently myself.'

Alana watched as Rusty picked up the bones in turn, swivelling them through his gloved hands before passing them on to Dean, one of the pathology porters, for weighing and measuring.

'Baiting up a pot is quite a skilled task,' Rusty carried on, heaving the crab pot onto the trolley. 'The bait must be placed just so inside. If it's not secure or it's too near the surface the crab and lobster will pull it out.' Rusty placed his hand in the top of the pot for emphasis. 'The idea being to funnel them through the hole at the top and into the body of the pot, thus trapping them in the centre until the fisherman pulls the string.'

'So, you're saying that the murderer must have had some knowledge of fishing?' Paddy said. 'Surely not that difficult to come by what with YouTube and the fact a lot of fathers round here take their kids fishing at some point, even mine.'

'And mine.' Rusty grimaced.

They both looked across at Alana, who was shaking her head but then they'd probably forgotten it had been her mum who'd brought her up, something she wasn't about to remind them of, and as for her ex... Colm wouldn't be seen dead anywhere near a rod and line. The nearest he got to the sea was when he was blatting across the harbour on his rib.

'This is the actual pot?'

'The very same and as useless as a tap in the desert. I'll obviously see what I can do with it before popping it across to the boffins over in the Technical Bureau but the effects of a week in saltwater will have done more damage than a bucketful of bleach and a scrubbing brush.'

'And anything about the bones themselves?' Paddy asked, lifting his head from where he'd been scribbling some notes, using his bended knee as an impromptu table.

'Definitely human. Two femurs, or thigh bones if you like, and two humeri, from the upper arm. Also bones from the shoulder and pelvis. We should be able to gauge an approximate height from the length of the femur. Ageing is going to be more complex without the presence of any epiphysial cartilage but from the degree of degenerative changes I'll put my neck out by guessing you're looking at someone older. Probably mid to late fifties,' he added, his eyes squinting behind his black-framed glasses.

'And what about matching it with a missing person?' Alana said, shifting nearer to the trolley.

Rusty threw her a look over the top of the pot, where he was now using forceps to extract something from the frame. 'It's possible, although, of course, I'll need to have a sample to match it with.'

'Of course,' she parroted. 'And what's your guesstimate as to how long he or she has been in the water?'

'That's more difficult. We know Mulcahy baited up seven days ago.' Rusty shrugged. 'Could a gang of greedy crabs have stripped a carcass that quickly from its flesh? Oxygen levels, water temperature and ocean depth are all determining factors. There's also research on this exact issue although with pigs instead of humans. All I can say is there's a strong possibility that's what we're seeing here.'

'We'll have to find the victim and the date of their last known sighting to narrow it down.'

'Oh, I think I can be of a little more help to you than that, Alana,' he replied, gesturing for them to follow him across to the other side of the room and the basket, which she'd only just noticed. 'I'm not sure if you know anything about the digestive processes of a brown crab?'

'Not a scooby.'

He laughed. 'Why am I not surprised! Basically, with the help of a marine biologist I intend to harvest a sample from this little chap's digestive glands for analysis. If the bones were inserted with the flesh still attached, a theory that's supported by the amount of brown crab clinging to the sides, then we might be able to analyse the contents. Having the bones submerged in saltwater isn't good. Flesh encased in a crab's digestive system is a completely different problem.' He rotated his shoulders briefly. 'I'm no expert but I'm more positive that we'll be able to ID the victim than if we only had the bones. Shame the head's missing, probably too much to ask.'

FOUR

Monday 4th September, 12.05 p.m.

Barney Mulcahy and, presumably his wife, were waiting for them by the time they returned to the station. A very different Barney to the whey-faced fisherman decked out in head to toe yellow. His clothes, which had been placed in a bag before being carted off for analysis, had been replaced with faded jeans, baggy round the knees and the bum, and a striped shirt, the sleeves bunched at the elbows.

Alana was undecided whether to interview him on his own. He hadn't done anything wrong. Being in the wrong place at the wrong time wasn't a crime and the presence of his wife might in some way deflect any sense that he was to blame for finding the remains of a body in one of his pots.

Mrs Mulcahy was a scrawny woman with thinning hair pulled off her face in a French pleat and a liking for electric-blue eye shadow and cherry-red lipstick, an interesting choice given her inelegant leggings and Lycra T-shirt. It was her sharp gaze and even sharper mouth that led to Alana reconsidering her plans.

'About bloody time too if you ask me. We've been waiting ages.'

'Mrs Mulcahy?' Alana waited a moment for the slight almost regal tilt of her head in acknowledgement before continuing. 'I'm Detective Alana Mack and this is Detective Patrick Quigg. We just need to take a statement off your husband. You can wait here.'

'I'm coming with.' She bundled up her bag under her arm, pushing to standing as they started to lead Mr Mulcahy to the nearest interview room.

'No, I'm afraid that's not possible. There's a drinks machine and what have you.' Alana glanced towards reception, spotting someone she knew. 'Garda Shorrt, if you wouldn't mind...'

'But...'

Alana didn't wait to hear the rest of her buts. She could still hear the woman's complaints when Paddy shut the door behind them, her tongue whiplashing the guard about her rudeness and the state of the Irish police force in general.

Change the bloody record for once. I'm only doing my job.

'Sorry about the missus. She gets a little intense at times. Hormones, you know.'

Alana nodded, taking her time in arranging her notepad and pen before pushing a glass of water in his direction.

'Your full name and address for the record,' she started, keen to get the business of his statement over and done with.

'Barnabas Michael Mulcahy, Three, The Rise, St Finian's Road, Sutton, Dublin 13, D13FD30.'

Alana paused, the tip of her pen pressing into the paper on the i of St Finian's. 'A nice place to live and only a stone's throw from Howth.' She settled the pen on the side of the pad and propped her elbows on the table. It was time to get down to business.

'Before we start is there anything you'd like to ask, bearing in mind we now have an active investigation on our hands so there's little enough that I can tell you.'

'Only when I'll be getting my boat back?'

Alana smiled, having predicted the question as soon as she'd met his wife. 'Well, that depends on what the team find, if anything, Mr Mulcahy. If the preliminary results come back a negative, there's every chance that you'll have it back in a couple of days.'

'It's a her.'

'Excuse me?'

'My boat. All boats are women. Equally contrary and expensive, so it figures.'

Alana saw Paddy's shoulders heave out the corner of her eye and sent him a filthy look. If she could withhold the guffaw climbing up her neck, then so could he. It was all very well being witty but not at the expense of the entire female population.

'Moving on. We'll need to take a buccal swab from you for elimination purposes but that's something we can sort out easily enough after we've taken down your witness statement.' She tapped the side of her cheek to emphasise where they'd be taking the swab from before continuing. 'Right, now that's out the way. If you can tell us your recent movements and whether anything untoward has happened over the last few days, let's say from when you last dealt with the pots. Anything odd that doesn't fit in with your normal week. For example, anyone follow you or any strange phone calls?'

'Anyone follow me?' He laughed, a large bellow rippling across his stomach before spitting out of his mouth, his eyes watering in amusement. It took him a good thirty seconds to control himself, seconds that had Alana floundering as to the cause.

'Sorry. It's just. Me! Who the heck do you think I am anyway?' He rubbed his eyes with the tissues she'd pushed in his direction, concentrating on the corners of his eyes before blowing his nose. 'No one's interested in me and what I get up to and, before you ask, I don't get up to anything, alright. Howth Yacht Club on a Friday and maybe a Saturday with the missus. The rest of the time I'm either in the house, the shed or on the boat.'

It would be a shame to break it to him that set-in-their-ways, routine-driven individuals, one of which he was declaring himself to be, got murdered too. Statistically, they were probably at a higher risk than those people who didn't know what they were up to from one minute to the next simply because they were impossible to track with any level of accuracy.

'So, to clarify, since the last time you tended your pots, you were either at home, at the Yacht Club or on your boat?'

He smiled as he nodded, revealing a mouthful of crooked teeth.

'Okay.' She made a quick note. 'What about your movements for today?'

'What do you think?'

'Apart from that he was lucky you didn't reach over the table and lump him one for his comment on why he named his boat after a woman, not a lot.'

'As if I'd do something as silly, with you as witness,' Alana said, exiting the lift and making her way to the incident room, Paddy trailing in her wake. 'If we get a move on, there might be time to pop back to check on the dive team while the light is still good.' She pulled up short at the sight of Detective Superintendent Leo Barry standing beside her desk, his hands idly flicking through her inbox tray.

Alana had suspected for quite a while that someone had been rummaging through her desk. That it was only her boss instead of one of her colleagues was a huge relief. It didn't mean that she wasn't annoyed, not that it showed apart from a slight curling of her fingers. Leo was someone she could manage. A disloyal member of her taskforce less so. She didn't know everything about her team, she didn't need to. The fact she would trust them with her life was about the sum total. With Leo, the stakes were far less important, if no less irritating.

'Looking for anything in particular, DS Barry?'

The room closed in around them. Paddy somewhere off to one side, while Tatty, Lorrie and William were heads down pounding away on their computers with a force that told her she'd be signing off on a requisition for three new keyboards before the year was out.

'Your August report is still due,' he said, his hands now in his pockets, a bland smile pressed into his mouth as he turned to face her.

And you won't be finding it in my fecking in-tray, now will you, because I always email it.

She thought about what he was searching for but it was almost as impossible a task as setting those poor divers to find the rest of the missing bones. Her in-tray currently held her milk bill and a pile of research articles she'd finished but had yet to file. Nothing of interest. That didn't make her happy. It wouldn't until she could work out what he was up to.

'It's not due until the 10th or have the rules changed?' Alana stayed put, her brakes engaged, refusing to manoeuvre around him.

'No, the 10th is fine. I thought you might have sorted it before your holiday. How was it, by the way?'

'Fine, perfectly fine.' *What little I can remember of it*, she added for her own benefit. Yesterday morning she'd squeezed in a final breakfast and a last look at the shops before the taxi had arrived to take her to the airport. She'd have liked a day to acclimatise. Time to reminisce while she scrolled through the photos on her phone, deciding on which, if any, to print off. She should have known better.

'Gather round, everyone. I'm not sure if the DS is staying for a catch-up but, as time is racing away from us, we do need to get on.' She spoke from her current position and not the usual one fronting the room. Leo would have to move for that, which he finally did, sauntering over to the window to take up Paddy's usual spot. That was for him to deal with.

'As you all know we have a situation on our hands,' she said, her tablet now lying on her palm as she busily updated the whiteboard with the new case. 'Fifty-six-year-old Barney Mulcahy, who runs crab pots just outside Howth Harbour, got more than he bargained for when he found a dead body in the bottom of one. To be exact, eight bones from an as yet unidentified victim. We've mobilised the Technical Bureau and the forensic diving team, both of which are currently all over the boat and the seabed, which luckily Barney had the foresight to mark on his GPS. Any news on that front?' Alana turned to Paddy and where he was lounging at the far end of the window. The space between him and Leo was interesting, as she had thought they were friends of sorts, having graduated from Templemore Garda College at the same time.

'Just checked. A couple of additional bones from the divers. Nothing of any note from the boat but it's too early for any forensics. All they can say is that, if the crime was committed there then there's no evidence apart from the bones.'

'Like a suicide note or a pile of discarded clothes?' Alana replied, her voice dry. 'I think the bones are pretty definitive on their own account.' Tablet ignored, she picked up her mobile as a message pinged through. 'Lorrie and William, what about any missing persons we should be interested in?'

'That's difficult, isn't it, due to the time frame?' Leo interrupted from his corner. 'The bones could be anything from hundreds of years ago to yesterday.'

'In this case irrelevant as we know how old the bones are, or we will do shortly.' Alana replaced her phone on her lap, starting to enjoy the conversation.

'Impossible. Any fool knows that radiocarbon dating of bones is only accurate up to a point – that point being a year for soft tissues, of which you have none or are you going to tell me there's hair, nails and teeth among your findings?'

Ooh, someone's been burning the candle wax late into the night. At least he's finally realised what we do is evidence based as opposed to hearsay and speculation. Also, was that fool crack aimed at me or...?

'No. In this case we're lucky enough not to have to rely on carbon dating. What we have is far more powerful and makes dating the bones irrelevant. It also confirms what we suspected. Someone pulled Barney's pots probably within hours of laying them, baiting them up with the victim instead of the fish frames he usually uses.' Alana wrote as she spoke, her thoughts transferring onto the board in her lazy scrawl. 'I've often thought Dr Mulholland a genius and, again, he's proved me right by deciding to dissect the crabs found in the pot. I'm still not that au fait with the digestive system of the brown crab but, from what he tells me, I don't need to be. Tissue doesn't lie although he did have to consider the effect cold saltwater had on the body's decomposition.' Alana lifted her phone and waved it in the air. 'He's been able to isolate adipose, connective and epithelial tissues with the help of one of his colleagues and is working on trying to get a DNA profile. He always has the bones if he fails. Apparently, DNA degradation in submerged victims is a huge problem.'

'And what next?'

And what next?

Alana was tempted to repeat his words out loud, rolling the vowels and syllables over her tongue, savouring the moment along with the stupidity of the question. There were set processes to follow as with any murder investigation. Just because the place of discovery was a little different didn't change a thing.

'You mean after we've ID'd the remains and matched them to any misper reports we might have? That's enough to be going on with for now.' She turned back to Lorrie and William. 'So, what have you got for me, if anything?'

Their look of disillusionment said it all.

FIVE

Monday 4th September, 4.15 p.m.

The sea had moderated to a glassy stillness, the mirror-like quality only interrupted by the occasional ripple caused by boats shifting on their moorings. Alana took a moment to look out across at the idyllic view of the harbour in amazement and disbelief at the difference a few hours could make to the view, the colour of the sea merging with the cloudless sky in a blended palate of blues instead of stormy blacks and greys. It was as if the storm had disappeared without a trace. But there was a trace, she remembered, turning her gaze to the blue emblazoned van of the police dive team before switching to Flynn and where he was chatting to one of the SOCO officers. A trace that would be impossible to erase from memory. The loss of a life.

She started to make her way over to Flynn when the officer headed back into the tent, keen to give him the space he needed without her peering over his shoulder. The garda on watch let her into the cordoned-off area by lifting the yellow tape high enough for her to slip under. The guard was an important part of the investigation now the media had turned up to snoop.

'Alright. Anything happening?'

'Not a lot. A few bits and pieces of interest. They have about three and a half hours' daylight left before they quit for the night.' Flynn placed his hands in his pockets. 'The seabed is murky at that depth. It's almost impossible to see anything even with the large LEDs they've managed to get hold of.'

'What about the boat?' she said, joining him in watching the white-suited team scrabbling round the hull and the deck, now the *Margaret M* had been craned out of the water.

'They've removed all the bait knives for analysis, bearing in mind that it's a boat and Barney does a bit of lining for mackerel and the like so there's going to be a lot of blood. The bilges and scuppers have been swabbed and sprayed with luminol, but blood is blood.'

'So, pretty much a nightmare all round then?' she said, eyeing the SOCO who was carrying a pile of full plastic boxes out of the wheelhouse before handing them to another similarly polypropylene-suited individual standing on the ladder leaning against the hull.

'Exactly.' He walked beside her as she made her way along the quay. 'The problem is there's no way of distinguishing between fish and human blood using any of the usual presumptive tests such as luminal, a huge problem when the boat appears to be covered in the stuff. They won't be able to tell if it's false-positive fishy, or human, until they look at it under the microscope, all of it. They've already run through one batch of swabs and have had to send back to the lab for another.'

'Rogene is going to be spitting, isn't she?' Alana said, having yet to see the short, feisty lead SOCO. It was a rhetorical question, which didn't warrant an answer.

'She's in the tent if you would like to...?'

'I wouldn't but I'd better.'

'Hey, Alana, had a good holiday?'

'Can't remember. Think I'm in need of another one.' Alana hovered near the entrance, not wanting to distract from the activity, her gaze landing on the pile of drawings in Rogene's hands.

'Anything of interest?'

'Here, take a look.' Rogene passed the sheets across, her hands clasped in front of her, her expression one of anticipation.

She's waiting for me to spot it. The question is what!

The Technical Bureau staff, more commonly known as SOCOs or CSIs, each had their own roles within the very busy team. The boat would have been photographed from every angle, including video footage and, if they were lucky, captured by the skills of a forensic artist. A drawing might not seem to be of as much value as either a photo or a video, but nothing could be further from the truth, she thought, flipping through the four illustrations. The detailed pictures were sketches of the boat's interior from the different angles available, including areas of blood splatter, possible weapons and any other peculiarities like footprints clearly labelled. Alana squinted down to read the labels in the artificial light inside the tent. The bait knives. The blood. The clothing hanging up in the wheelhouse. The footprints.

'More than one type of footprint?'

'Bingo. Well done.' Rogene took the drawings back, arranging them in a neat pile. 'As we know, footprints are the next best giveaway after blood and DNA. Perps seem to have conquered the humble fingerprint, but they rarely remember what they're wearing on their feet or think about the wealth of information we can elicit about their footwear, from their size and weight to the type of shoe they're wearing. I'll rush through making a 3D model and checking it against the footwear database.' She settled the drawings back into a buff-coloured envelope, securing the flap. 'There are also a few bones from the first two trips. We're lucky to have them if I'm honest,' she added, pointing to the nearest bench and what looked like mud-covered lumps. 'Hopefully from the same victim, but nothing is guaranteed until the doc does his stuff.'

Alana wasn't convinced as to what she was seeing but, as Dr Mulholland had reiterated, the netting on the crab pot was narrow enough to keep all the large bones inside but small enough to let the rest through. It begged the question about the skull but that wasn't a place Alana wanted to go. The hope was they'd find it lying on the bottom of the seabed, a hope that was fast evaporating. Extracting DNA was only the first step in the process of ID'ing the victim. If they couldn't find any DNA matches on the database or match it to known missing persons on their system, then facial reconstruction was the next step in putting a face and hopefully a name to their bag of bones. No head meant no chance of ever finding out who had been used as an alternative to fish food but also no hope of catching their killer.

She was about to head back to the car, only to rapidly revise the plan at the sight of the dive boat speeding towards them. It slowed down to the regulated four-knot limit when they rounded the harbour wall, the 'A' diver-down flag dangling from the pole. Alana watched as they pulled along the wall, the three divers still wearing their suits and flippers, their tanks secured in the special racks attached to the side of the hull.

She shifted back a little to allow Rogene access to the ladder and the officer waiting at the bottom to assist her clamber onboard. Under normal circumstances she'd have joined her but there was nothing normal about trying to access a boat, and a professional diving one at that, in a wheelchair. Alana had recognised long ago that if she was to continue in the same role after her accident then acceptance of what she couldn't do was far more important than appreciation of what she could. It didn't make it any easier though.

Her hands gripped onto the side of her chair as she watched Rogene being led into the wheelhouse and out of sight of the TV and newspaper crew lining up against the limit of the crime scene tape. A second passed then ten before her phone pinged through a message. Four words. A game changer for the investigation.

We have a head.

'A second time in one day. I'm honoured.' Rusty stood back from his desk and stretched. His red hair, hence the nickname, was tousled from too much dragging his hands through it, his gaze fixed on the plastic box between Flynn's hands.

'Sorry. I hate keeping you like this,' Alana said, genuinely meaning it. Rusty was married with two children, a blended family made up of his son from his previous marriage and his wife's adopted daughter. A situation that was about to change now Gaby was eight months pregnant.

'No bother. Gaby has her brother over until tomorrow so there's more than enough to keep her occupied. What have you got for me? Something important like a head?'

'Yet again spoiling the surprise. You must be a nightmare to buy for at Christmas!' Their usual banter started up, pushing aside any thoughts of the grisly nature of the discovery.

'Let's have a look then.' He crossed to the door on the left, the one with direct access into the pathology suite, already pulling on a pair of surgical gloves from the dispensing unit on the wall. 'Place it on the bench over there, if you please, Flynn, and if you wouldn't mind opening the clasps. They're a devil when wearing these things.'

'Sure thing, doc.'

The box was an oblong of nondescript white with secure fastenings. The kind of box used for transporting all sorts of things from tools to pizzas.

Alana blinked when he lifted the head out, the features difficult to determine wrapped as it was in clear plastic.

'This is much better than a bag of bones but it does throw up a multitude of questions about her,' he said, using a pair of forceps to peel away the bag.

Alana pounced on the one part of his sentence that had her narrow her eyes in surprise. She knew he never made mistakes but how on earth did he know the sex from what little he'd been given.

'A her?'

'Yes. I was pretty sure by the bits of the pelvis, but the head confirms it. It will be easy enough to check now we have flesh to bones, or at least most of the flesh,' he continued, turning the head upside down and examining the inside. 'The plastic bag might be the cause of death, but strangulation is also on the cards. I'll check her hyoid bone, if it's there. The tight seal will have minimised crustation damage to the face. With a bit of luck, I might be able to harvest some of the eye for—'

'That's enough, Rusty. We get the picture. What about the science behind sexing the skull again?' Alana asked, starting to feel queasy, as was Flynn, if the colour of his skin was anything to go by. It was easy to forget that he was only a youngster. Twenty-five now but still nine years younger than her in age, far more of a gap in experience.

'Ah, yes. The skull is composed of twenty-two bones, excluding those of the ear but it's all in the larger orbital ridge here.' He pointed to the curve of the forehead along the brow line. 'And the size of the mastoid processes, the bone projections behind each ear. We will, of course, confirm it with DNA.'

Alana watched as he manipulated the jaw to look into the mouth before switching her gaze to concentrate on his hair and the way it was starting to sweep his collar instead of his usual short back and sides. She hoped that Flynn was choosing to do the same. There were no heroes in this room.

'Good. Good. We have what appears to be a comprehensive set of teeth, which will make DNA extraction from the pulp chamber a piece of cake if saline has managed to denature the DNA found in the tissues. It also tells me by the state of her dentition that we're looking for someone older than my initial estimate.' He placed the skull back in the box, closed the lid and started peeling back his gloves. 'There are clear signs of molar flattening due to wear and tear but an odontologist will be able to tell us more. It also means there's a strong possibility we'll be able to match our victim with her dental records. If we have no luck with the DNA, then I'll ship off her teeth to our dental forensic expert over in Tralee.'

'So, just how old do you reckon then?' Flynn said, the clear outline of his balled-up fists visible through the fabric of his grey trousers.

'That's an interesting question and one which raises a whole new set of issues, Flynn,' Rusty said over his shoulder as he washed his hands in the sink. 'I reckon we're looking at someone well into her seventies.'

Alana paused in the act of removing her gloves, her attention flickering between Rusty and back to the pile of bones. She was sure there were many reasons to murder a pensioner but, at that precise moment, she couldn't come up with a single one.

SIX

Monday 4th September, 8.10 p.m.

Alana pulled into her parking place outside her apartment block at ten past eight and turned off the engine. But, instead of starting to reassemble her wheelchair from where she'd flung the pieces earlier, a task she'd honed down to ninety seconds, she sat and stared at the red brick wall in front of her, trying to drag up a smidgeon of a memory from her recent holiday. An exercise in futility as too much had happened over the last twelve hours for her to think straight, let alone magic up the taste and feel of Malaga.

She didn't know how long she sat there, certainly long enough to attract the wrong kind of attention, she realised at the sight of movement out of the corner of her eye. Kilmacud was safe enough, she'd certainly never had any problems in the years she'd lived there, but that didn't mean she could let her guard down. She never let it down, not these days. The apartment was her sanctuary, her escape from the harsh realities of the job but she never truly felt safe, and the reason she'd fitted a top of the range burglar alarm and security door and windows before moving in. Billy called it Fort Knox. He wasn't far wrong. She already had her mobile in her hand, her finger reaching for the nine when she saw a green Chinese food bag being waved in front of her.

'What are you doing here, Billy? You nearly gave me heart failure!' She opened the door, only to watch on as he set about assembling her chair, placing it just so before reclaiming the food from where he'd left it on top of the bonnet. Only then did he reply.

'The same as you, I imagine. Starving for my tea after the day from hell back at the office.' The office being the headquarters of the *Clonabee Globe*, Ireland's answer to the *Irish Mail*, the *Sun* and the *Star* rolled into one, and all for the price of fifty cents a day. 'When are they going to fix the security lights in this damn place?' He finally stopped what he was doing to look at her. 'They've been out for weeks.'

'Waiting for a part. There was an email about it this morning.'

'Bloody ridiculous. It's okay at the moment but not when the clocks go back,' he said, closing the car door after her and waiting, his arms folded across his chest. Belligerent was his middle name. It was a shame for him that stubborn was hers. 'I take it that you're involved with the happenings over in Howth and, before you say anything, it's already been on the Six One News and no doubt will feature on the front of every newspaper across the land by the morning?'

Unlike almost everyone Alana had met over the course of the day, Billy hadn't opened the conversation by questioning her about her holidays. There was no point as he'd accompanied her on the trip. She'd been in two minds whether to accept when he'd produced the tickets. That the trip was part work – Malaga was hosting a huge, international journalism convention – and came with his reiteration that he was happy to accept her wish to only be friends were why she'd caved under the pressure. If he thought he could wear her down like water on a stone then he clearly didn't know her very well.

'Yes, and no I can't tell you anything. You probably know most of it already anyway. If you promise not to harangue me on the subject, I'll be very happy to share your food. Without the meal bribe, you'd have had no chance of the pleasure of my company this evening.' By his chuckle, he obviously thought she was joking. She wasn't. 'What's left of it,' she amended, glancing at her watch.

Her one-bedroomed flat was situated on the ground floor of a smart apartment block in the centre of Kilmacud. An impulse purchased following her divorce but one she was yet to regret. It had everything she needed, including glass doors leading to a small, enclosed patio area with only room for a couple of chairs and a few planters. A godsend now she was the proud owner of a stray ginger cat called Goose.

'You go sort yourself out while I feed the cat,' Billy said, making his way into the kitchen area of the lounge, Goose winding between his feet. 'Come on, boy. Dinnertime.'

Thirty minutes later found Alana leaning back in her chair, a wine glass cradled between her fingers, her attention on where Billy was finishing off the last of the king prawns, the troubles of her day pushed aside by the tide of good food and good company. Billy was in full raconteur mode, a skilled after dinner speaker, which was reflected in his weekly editorial column. In truth, the only section of the *Clonabee Globe* that she read on a regular basis.

'That was delicious, thank you. I didn't know I was hungry until you dished up,' she said, grinning at the sight of her empty plate. 'Coffee? Tea? I won't offer you a nightcap as you're driving.'

'You coppers are all the same. Spoilsports the lot of you. Coffee if you're making it. I'll bring this lot through.'

'So, what's happening in the world of international journalism? Anything juicy while we've been away?' she said over her shoulder, the kettle on and mugs waiting on the tray.

What she actually meant was what's been happening in the rest of Ireland while they'd been lazing about under the Spanish sun. As lead detective of the Clonabee branch, she tended to focus on the crimes on their books. The good, the bad and the truly horrible outside of Dublin held no interest unless it was in some way related to her own patch. It wasn't a perspective she was proud of but all she could manage without it taking its toll on her mental health. Her bathroom cupboard still held a packet of antidepressants. She wouldn't take them now but there was comfort in their lingering presence. A reminder of how fragile she'd been following the breakdown of her marriage and her accident. Accident was a generous term for how she'd managed to find herself unconscious at the bottom of the central staircase in her former home. The person responsible was under permanent lock and key, a fact that provided little comfort for her own life sentence in a wheelchair.

'The breaking news about Mason Clare's disappearance is the hot topic outside of Dublin.'

'Really?' Alana handed him the tray and followed him back to the table. Talking shop was always her go-to default topic of conversation but rarely in his presence. It would be good to discuss a case she had no say in and no influence over. 'When and where?'

'Last seen yesterday morning in Kerry as he left for his daily swim. Reported by a concerned neighbour yesterday teatime who heard his dog barking in the back garden.'

'That's not long in the scheme of things,' she said, concentrating on her drink.

'Unless they happen to be a retired New York police officer.'

'Ah. I knew there must be something for you to sit up and take note.' She smiled, her interest sparked.

'They're now thinking his car might have gone off the road somewhere along Slea Head even though there's no sign of any debris. It was his morning routine to drive from Dingle to Ventry Beach for his daily swim. That road looping the peninsula has had more than its fair share of accidents over the years. Ever been that way?' He picked up his mug and took a small sip.

'I don't think so. Possibly when I was a kid but not that I can remember. We used to go camping all over,' she replied, half to herself, a flickering, fading memory of her and her mam struggling with a tent that leaked as they tried to make the best of the summer on a limited budget that didn't include foreign holidays. The memory quickly got overtaken by a far more compelling thought.

'No debris on the side of the cliff is a little unusual. Even if it's only excoriation to the wall or damage to the shrubs lining the drop. Any wife, partner or significant other in the frame?'

'A retired bachelor through and through. He's a bit of a mystery man by all accounts. Returned to Ireland last year after thirty years living in the States and, if you believe the gossip, has lived like a recluse ever since.'

'Strange indeed. When you say retired, how old exactly?' she asked, her mind leaping the short distance to the pile of bones currently residing somewhere in Rusty's department. She'd never known the man to make a mistake, but the age might be a fit if not the sex.

'Only fifty-four if my memory serves. You sound interested?'

'That's young to be retiring but not if you're a copper, and I'm always interested in anything work related. You should know that by now. While we're talking about work, I have a day of it planned for tomorrow so I'm going to boot you out but with my heartfelt thanks for a lovely meal.' She shifted back from the table, her meaning clear. 'Next time I'm paying.'

'You're on.' Billy picked up his jacket from where he'd draped it on the back of the sofa and dropped the briefest of pecks on her cheek before making for the door.

Alana barely registered he'd left. She started on her usual night-time routine of checking the windows and doors. She was in the bathroom in front of the sink squeezing toothpaste onto her brush when the thing that had been worrying her about the case over in Kerry pinged into her consciousness from where it had been poking at her brain with a pointy stick of curiosity ever since Billy had mentioned it.

Why did Mason Clare leave his dog at home if he was seen heading for the beach?

SEVEN

Tuesday 5th September, 8.20 a.m.

'Morning, everyone.'

Alana's greeting was met with a variety of responses. A brief salute from Paddy. A grunt from William, a wave from Lorrie and a 'hi there' from Flynn. Of Tatty there was no sign, which as family liaison officer was nothing unusual. There was no need to ask what the team was up to or if there was any news. There was an unwritten rule that Alana was alerted to all meaningful developments by text, day or night. A system that worked.

Instead of stopping at the coffee machine – she'd had her fill of hot drinks in the small hours – she slid behind her desk, booted up her laptop and started sifting through her emails, her finger hovering over the delete button. There were 203 new messages since yesterday and only a handful that interested her. Nothing new from Dr Mulholland or Rogene but it was still early yet. What there was, much to her annoyance was a royal summons to the boss's office for half-nine. That's all she needed!

There was also a message from Billy, a surprise especially as he'd only left at ten but for him to use her work address was the most perplexing. The reason was clear as soon as she opened it.

Hi Alana

Thanks again for last night. I have attached all the news articles I could find on Mason Clare. The lead detective is a Ruan O'Hagan. I've included his contact details below. Off to London on business. Back tomorrow.

Billy

Exactly what she didn't need right now was to get involved with another case. There was a mystery with the disappearance. She'd sensed it straight off from the briefest of descriptions and it was presumably why Billy had pounced on sending her the articles. Alana stemmed a laugh. He was getting to know her too well. However, he should know that it wasn't her responsibility, not yet anyway. As part of the NBCI, her remit included the investigation of organised and serious crime across Southern Ireland, along with her counterparts who worked out of Harcourt Street. That didn't mean they had the time to go looking for crimes to solve. That's not how it worked. They had enough problems from local garda teams thinking they were glory hunters looking to cream off the best cases, without going out of their way to add to their workload.

Alana clicked print. While she might not have the time to deal with it now, that didn't mean she couldn't take a look at it when she did. There was also no harm in finding out a little of what she might be letting herself in for if she did decide to act on her suspicions.

'Anyone know anything about a Ruan O'Hagan?'

She wasn't particularly looking at Paddy but if anyone was going to remember the man it was going to be him simply because Paddy was a walking encyclopaedia of people's names. He astounded her and the team over and over again at his recall when she couldn't remember the name of someone she'd met yesterday let alone the day before. No, faces were her thing but as for putting a name to them...

'Over in Dingle, or Daingean Uí Chúis as it's more commonly known,' Paddy replied, his pronunciation of the Gaelic, pitch perfect.

'Known by whom, Pad?' Alana lifted her head from where she'd delegated three-quarters of her current inbox to the delete folder, her hand pressed against her brow like a silent movie starlet. 'Don't tell me fluency in Gaelic is another one of your talents? No, don't answer that. Of course it is. You with your love of foreign language movies and all that. Never stop surprising me. Go on then, surprise me some more about this Ruan lad.'

Paddy laughed. 'Hardly a lad. Sixty if he's a day. Kerry born and bred. Sat beside him at a conference on cyber security about seven years ago. I read somewhere that he'd been promoted to superintendent over in Dingle. It's bound to be the same man. Nice enough as coppers go. Very committed to reducing crime rates in *Kerry*.'

And someone who wouldn't take kindly to any interference from outsiders like me, Alana thought, reading between the lines.

She made a quick note on the top of her notebook before glancing at her watch and slipping her phone from her pocket, her fingers swiping at the screen. She'd ring Rogene. After, there'd be time enough to decide what she intended to do about the little problem over in Kerry after she'd read through what Billy had sent her. Now she had a murderer to find and a body to ID.

'Morning, Rog. It's Alana.'

'As if it would be anyone else at this time!'

'Sorry, you know how it is. Got anything for me?'

Alana heard her tut-tutting her disapproval over the line, Rogene's standard response when she was under stress.

'The dive team started again at a quarter to seven. A tad early with sunrise only at 6.41 but they know best. I'm waiting to hear back but I think it's unlikely we'll find much more. They've been taking it in turns to conduct a circular search, radiating from the fixed known point of where the crab pot was located from the GPS coordinates. As for the shoe print, we've taken a plaster cast of the tread and sent it off to the footprint database.'

'What about fingerprints?'

'Only the owner's. Either the perp wore gloves, Mulcahy is guilty, or the *Margaret M* wasn't the boat used to dump the body.'

'And the blood found in the vessel and on the knives?'

'One hundred per cent fish.'

Alana frowned as she ended the call. She didn't need to ask if she was sure. Rogene didn't make mistakes no matter how much stress she was under. No human blood at the scene didn't rule Barney Mulcahy out of the picture but it did topple him off the top of the suspects list. Either he wasn't the killer, he'd come up with a foolproof way of chopping up a body without leaving a shred of forensic evidence or he'd used someone else's boat to transport the victim to her final resting place. Either way, Alana was out of ideas until Rusty came back to her with the results of the DNA.

'Everything okay, Al?'

She glanced up and caught Paddy's eye. 'I'm not sure. Let's have a quick update to see where we are, eh?' She raised her voice to draw the attention of the room, her mobile exchanged for her tablet. 'Gather round, everyone. I have news of sorts. Not sure what to make of it though.'

The next thirty or so seconds was punctuated by the sound

of chairs being moved and conversations cut short. Alana only started to speak when the room fell silent.

'I've had an update from Rogene, which basically confuses matters. What we've got is a dead body in one of Barney Mulcahy's pots and no means of getting it there that we know of unless another boat was used.' She turned to Flynn. 'What do you think?'

'It's not unheard of for a fisherman to lift someone else's gear,' Flynn replied after a second. 'Totally illegal. Stealing is stealing whether it's in the middle of the ocean or in a shop but there's no one to stop you, is there. I've known of whole strings being nicked and not just the contents, or another trick is to cut the ropes and set them adrift. At upwards of seventy euro a piece it's an expensive game losing your pots, which is what they're aiming for, and that isn't even including the cost of the rope used to tie them all together. Less gear means more fish in the pots that are still fishing.'

'I had no idea. Surely they report them?'

Flynn shrugged. 'No point. How are you going to prove what's happened either way? Boats get scuppered for less.'

'Scuppered?'

'Opening the scuppers to let the water in and sink the boat.'

'It's a whole new language!' Alana added a couple of entries under the heading of *Margaret M* to the board. 'So, what you're saying is it would be easy enough for someone to lift Barney's pots, even to know they're his and where he's fishing?'

'Absolutely. They'd recognise the type of bobber he uses to mark the string for a start, especially if he's written the boat number on, which is common practice in these parts. Nothing is secret on the sea. It's not as if you can hide a fishing boat under a cloak.'

'If Mulcahy isn't involved then we have to consider that someone had a grudge against him,' William piped up from his desk near the door. 'Another fisherman if what Flynn says is true and, obviously there's no reason to doubt him.' He darted a quick glance across at Flynn before continuing. 'Or someone else. Someone we have no knowledge of.'

'You mean someone happy to put him in the frame for the woman's murder? Sounds all a bit *Black Mirror* for my liking,' Lorrie said, joining in the conversation, her blood-red fingernails on display round the side of her mug.

The suppositions were flying but it was always the same at the start of an investigation. Alana checked her watch a second time. 'Right, I'm heading upstairs in a sec to meet with his lordship. In the meantime, I'd like you to ask around your mates in Howth about the gen on Mulcahy, Flynn. Lorrie and William, I'd like you to do the same but electronically. All the records you can find on the man, from his birth to present day. If he has been framed, we need to find the reason and quickly. As we all know, in this game one body frequently ends up as two, or more.'

EIGHT

Tuesday 5th September, 9.20 a.m.

Tatty Kearney fished out her phone to check her messages, the sudden movement causing a wave of nausea. Why on earth had she thought it would be okay to open that bottle of wine to celebrate Paddy and Irene's five-month scan. Especially as he didn't really drink, and Irene couldn't.

'Another tea would be lovely, as long as it's not too much trouble, Mrs Mulcahy.'

'You might as well call me Deirdre.'

Tatty replaced her phone in her pocket, watching on as Deirdre piled mugs on the tray, her hands reddened, the skin on the back wrinkled and dry. Worker's hands. 'Here, let me get the door for you.' She jumped to her feet and rushed across the room, aware of Barney in the chair opposite, absorbed in staring down at the thick grey carpet under his feet.

He'd barely moved since she'd arrived. If it wasn't for the sight of his chest rising and falling underneath his bottle-green V-neck jumper and the occasional cough, Tatty would have felt forced to check on him. The role of family liaison officer was a make-it-up-as-you-go-along sort of role, all based on research but even so. Having a good instinct was far more important than excelling in the many courses she had to attend. In this instance, she'd decided on mostly staying quiet and playing along with the verbal cues thrown at her. If that meant supplementing the poor conversation flow with copious cups of tea, then so be it.

The Mulcahys lived in a small semi-detached red-brick house halfway along St Finian's Road. A little cluttered and with a liking for Swedish flatpack but nice enough if you were into cool blues and greys with a dado border to brighten the walls instead of the artwork she'd come to expect from her many visits to other people's homes during the course of her job.

'Your husband seems to have taken it hard,' Tatty said, the silence in the kitchen oppressive while they waited for the kettle to boil.

'Fishing is his life. If he's not out on the boat, then he's doing something to it. The best looked after boat in the whole of Ireland.' Deirdre took her time in picking teabags from the open box beside the kettle, her movements slow.

'I think you said something about not having children?'

'Weren't able to, more's the pity. Barney's boat is his substitute family. The kids he couldn't have.' Deirdre poured water into the mugs and reached for a teaspoon, her attention on the task, her face turned away.

'That must have been pretty hard on you?' Tatty said, filling the sudden silence.

'Too old to worry about it now. I feel sorrier for his dad than I do myself. Two boys and not a single grandchild between them.'

'He'll be a good age now,' she said, wanting to shift the conversation in a different direction. Difficult questions like infertility were best left until they knew what they were dealing with, and then only if it was relevant to the case.

'Eighty-nine.'

'And still living alone?'

'In an old people's home over in Donnybrook. He's not that well at the moment.'

'I'm sorry to hear that.' Tatty picked up her mug. She didn't bother taking notes. She always felt that notetaking wasn't a good look for a FLO. Instead, she made a promise to check on Barney's birth certificate when she went back to the station and take it from there. The likelihood was that William would have beaten her to it. He was a smart one and no mistake.

She propped against the edge of the work surface. 'No problems with the other fishermen? I hear some of them can be a bit of a nightmare especially when they have a few beers inside them. There's no reasoning with some of the oiks around here. Think they rule the ocean bed along with everything in it.'

'Hah. There's a certain amount of that but they wouldn't dare.' Deirdre picked up her tea and sipped at the hot liquid. 'Barney has friends in all the wrong places like his da before him, if you know what I mean?'

Tatty knew exactly what she meant and, as a line of questioning, it was something she'd make sure to tell the boss about. They'd already checked Barney out on PULSE, their computer system. It was one of their first priorities after he'd contacted them, which might sound counterintuitive, but it wouldn't be the first time a criminal had alerted them to their crimes as a way of declaring their innocence. Barney's name hadn't appeared, even for a traffic violation. On paper he seemed a fine, upstanding pillar of the community. His wife's words disputed that notion somewhat.

The ringing phone was a nuisance but one Tatty took full advantage of, tipping her tea down the sink before following Deirdre out into the hall to eavesdrop on the conversation she was having on the landline. That their landline was located in the hall was nearly as much of a shock as the unfolding conversation was proving to be.

'Yes, you were right to call us. Terrible news, so it is. They weren't close but still. He'll be devastated.'

NINE

Tuesday 5th September, 9.30 a.m.

'You wanted to see me, Leo.'

Instead of replying he perched on the edge of his desk, hitching his trousers up to reveal the predictable regulation black socks, his attention on his fingers instead of the woman studying him. A beat. Two beats before he lifted his head. Two beats where Alana had no idea what might be coming next.

'The office was quiet without you.'

Alana blinked, her mouth firming back against her teeth to prevent words spewing forth. Words like *what the hell is going on here* and *let's get back to why you dragged me away from what I'm being paid for*. He'd asked her about her holiday back in the office. She'd answered. That was the end of the conversation as far as she was concerned.

'I didn't think I was that noisy but—'

'I didn't mean—'

'I'm sure you didn't. Is that all or...?'

'Oh, no, that's not all, far from it.' He skirted the desk before taking his chair. Alana couldn't understand the reason for the immediate change and neither did she want to. His hands were again his main focus, but his manner professional with a capital P. 'I've decided to shake up the team somewhat. It's about time, don't you think?' he continued, looking up suddenly.

No, I don't. What? What on earth are you up to, Leo Barry?

'I'm not sure I get your meaning, sir,' she said, lifting her proverbial jaw up from the floor. 'I thought we were doing well.' With the best arrest rates in the country, she knew it, as did he.

'I wouldn't have expected anything less from you, Alana. No one likes change, but as a progressive station it's up to me to ensure we stay that way.' He shuffled through the papers in front of him, papers that looked suspiciously like their staff records, their passport photos pinned to the top. 'You're a young team. No one over fifty, or forty for that matter and that counts.'

Counts for what. For us or against? They were doing a good job so that stuff shouldn't matter.

'It's not as if we had much choice at the time – they hadn't been given one – and Flynn, Lorrie and William have all proved their worth.'

'I know they have. I'm not going to redeploy any of them, if that's your worry. And as for Detective Quigg, it would be unfair to move him until he makes the decision for promotion on his own accord.'

She watched as he lifted a staff folder before dropping it back down on the desk. 'I see he's completed all the relevant exams needed. It's only a matter of time before the right job comes along.'

Lose Paddy. Alana's expression remained impassive, or she hoped it did. Had he been to see Leo? Was that what this was all about? Surely, he'd have spoken to her first. How would she cope? No, scratch that. She'd cope. One of life's copers. Sometimes it was a label she despised.

He leant forward, his elbows now on the desk, the papers ignored, his hands clasped in front of him. 'I'm not taking Paddy from you, so no need to worry on that score. Instead, I'm trying to help take some of that crazy workload off your shoulders. I interviewed for a new detective in your absence and she has accepted the transfer. She'll be starting with you first thing tomorrow. Today she's on induction.'

Alana didn't know what to think apart from feeling surprised that he'd been able to read her fears about Paddy when she hadn't said a thing.

'That's fine,' she said, when it really wasn't. 'If you'll give me her name, I'll make sure to have an information pack ready for her.'

'Sure. It's—'

The sound of her ringing phone drowned out further conversation. 'Sorry, I need to...' She hoped her look was apologetic. She didn't care either way, but it was better to go through the motions. Her team only ever phoned her with the important stuff.

'Hello, Mack speaking.'

'It's Tatty. I'm over at the Mulcahys'. We have a situation on our hands that you need to know about.'

'Yes?'

'They had a call while I was there. Barney's brother is missing and, reading between the lines, foul play is suspected.'

'Crap. That's all we need. Anything else?'

'Not a lot apart from his name.'

'Hold on. I'll make a note.' She plucked off a Post-it from Leo's desk along with his posh pen without a flicker in his direction. 'Right. Fire ahead.'

'It's a Mason Clare over in Kerry.'

TEN

Tuesday 5th September, 1.40 p.m.

'Detective Alana Mack? Where have I heard that name before.'

Alana didn't reply for a second, hoping that it was a rhetorical question. There was no way she was going to remind him of any of her headline cases.

'I'm not sure.' She pitched her voice to busy woman at work, who didn't give a fig about what he might have heard, good, bad or indifferent. 'And do call me Alana, Ruan,' she added, cutting through any ideas that the detective might have had of her addressing him formally because of his seniority. 'We seem to have something in common, although I'm not sure the how's or the why's currently. You, or one of your detectives, got in touch with the lads over at Howth about your missing man, Mason Clare. His brother, Barney Mulcahy is a person of interest in one of our cases over here. You might have heard about it already. A fisherman who found far more than he bargained for when he pulled his pots yesterday in the nature of a dead woman layering the bottom, or what was left of her. We're still trying to get an ID.'

'Ah. Mason is his adopted brother, if it's relevant?'

She cradled the phone under her chin and, reaching for her pad and pen turned to a new page. 'Thank you. I was wondering over the different surnames.'

'Why don't I give you access to everything we've got, and you do the same? That way we can put our heads together and see if the cases are linked or simply coincidental.'

'How'd it go?' As Alana hung up the phone, Paddy placed a coffee on her desk along with the cheese and tomato roll she'd commissioned him to get when he'd gone to meet Irene for lunch.

'Seems prepared to cooperate,' she said, peeling back the wrapping on her roll and opening the bread to inspect the filling before taking a bite. 'Thank you for this. How much do I owe you?'

'Seven euros. Don't leave the county.'

'Hah. What are you, psychic?'

'What do you mean?' Paddy had started to turn back to his desk, only to pause at her words.

'It means, Pad, me ole mucker, that I'm thinking it might be best for one of us to take a trip out west.' She wiped her fingers across her lips, scattering stray crumbs on her shirt, which she brushed onto the floor with her hand. 'I'm considering sending you and one of the young ones to Kerry but do say if that's a problem with Irene and all. I don't want to cause you any difficulties. The thing is, there's not much happening here until we can get a fix on who the victim is and Barney's missing brother could be vital to that, bearing in mind he was once part of the NYPD. What do you think?'

Alana left out that she would have suggested going herself if it would have been in any way possible, but they'd had that conversation too often in the past for him not to know about the fears and difficulties she faced. Repeating them was unnecessary.

'No, I'm good, thanks. I can't think of anything nicer than a trip to Kerry. Shame I'll have to be working while I'm there. Which one do you want me to take?'

'What about William? I'll need Flynn here so it's either him or Lorrie,' she said, starting to read the pile of newspaper articles Billy had sent her. 'Oh, I almost forgot. We have a new member of the team starting tomorrow. A woman. She's on induction today.'

'What's her name?'

Alana stopped reading, instead lifting her head to find Paddy staring at her with an expression she couldn't read. Horror? Worry? Anxiety? All three?

'Why? What do you know?'

'I'm not sure. Probably nothing.'

'Paddy, tell me or I'm riding into the sunset with your seven euros and cancelling your wedding into the bargain.'

'You can't cancel my wedding. It's paid for.' He sounded astonished.

'But I can cancel your annual leave,' she said, a Mona Lisa smile in evidence. 'You can marry on the Saturday and be back behind your desk on the Monday for all I care. Come on now, tell me.' Her voice was now the wheedling one.

Paddy chortled. 'What are you like. Pretty sure I can report you for speaking to me like that.'

'You can try! Come on, spill.'

'Oh alright. It might be nothing, I hope it's nothing but I'm pretty sure I saw "the nun" being given the grand tour by that woman from HR earlier.'

'Why on earth is she called the nun? No, don't answer that. I'll be finding out tomorrow but the least you can do is tell me her name so I can prepare myself.'

'Eve Rohan.'

Alana made a note before glancing at the file of people strolling through the door now their lunchbreak was over. They usually returned in dribs and drabs, which meant they'd decided to lunch together, a cheery thought that brought a smile to her face, which faded rapidly when she remembered the new team member being foisted on them. Team dynamics was like walking a tightrope in a force ten gale. She had no way of knowing what impact this new person would have, and when they appeared to be getting on better than they'd ever before. There was no sign of Detective Superintendent Barry but then she hadn't been expecting him to attend.

With her tablet on her lap, she updated the board as she spoke. 'The case of the woman in the pot is getting weirder and weirder.' She paused, disliking the moniker the media had coined for their headlines. 'We can't keep on calling it that. Anyone got any good ideas? Last time it was Operation Octopus, but I don't think we should stick with the fishy theme and, before anyone mentions it, I know brown crab aren't fish, alright. I'm not sure what they are but certainly not fish.'

'Cephalopods,' Flynn muttered from his desk almost opposite her.

'I'll take your word for it! Right then. What's it to be?'

Every station had its own way of choosing what to call their current case, from flowers, fruit, animals to using a random generator. Alana had a more universal approach, leaving it to the team to decide with the proviso that it shouldn't be related in any way to what they were actually dealing with.

'What about Operation Enigma. It's certainly a puzzle,' Lorrie said, twiddling her fingers in the air.

'Great stuff. Operation Enigma it is.' Alana added a header to the first of the boards before abandoning her tablet in favour of eye contact. 'I think we're in for a bumpy road with this one. A currently unidentified elderly woman found in the bottom of a crab pot, the presumption being that she was murdered instead of dying of natural causes, but there's no proof of that currently until the good Dr Mulholland has completed his report.'

'I think it's unlikely she placed herself in the pot, Al,' Paddy said.

Alana took a breath but not before sending him a look laced with disgust. 'As I was saying before being so rudely interrupted, as the cause of death is currently unknown, we have no way of knowing whether Jane Doe died of natural causes or was murdered *before* being placed inside the pot. We also have no guarantees from Rusty whether he'll be able to narrow down her cause of death from what little we've given him. Now, this is where it gets strange. Remember I asked earlier about anyone knowing Ruan O'Hagan over in Dingle?'

She shifted forwards and backwards on her wheels, her hands barely registering their position on the rims as she sifted through what to tell them.

'Ruan is looking into the disappearance of Mason Clare. A fifty-four-year-old retiree from the NYPD, no less, who just so happens to be our very own Barney Mulcahy's adopted brother.'

'Were they close?' Paddy asked from his position over by the window.

Tatty had just arrived back and was in the process of unwrapping her scarf. Alana had messaged her to return to the office for the briefing if she was able, on the proviso that she'd be able to return to the Mulcahys' if she felt she was needed.

'Not especially,' Tatty replied, tucking her scarf in her jacket pocket. 'They were when they were younger but that's probably to be expected given their start in life.' With her bag on the desk, she removed a sandwich before closing the top. 'They were both adopted within weeks of each other but they're not biological brothers.'

'And what about their different names?'

'Deirdre, Barney's wife, told me that when Mason hit eighteen, he went completely off the rails trying to navigate finding his birth parents and when he couldn't he walked out, leaving them desperate to find him. They didn't hear from him for years and when he did finally get in touch via Facebook, they learnt he'd changed his name before emigrating to the States.'

'It's like something from the movies. All we're missing is a bag of popcorn,' Lorrie said, leaning forward in her chair, her chin propped in her hand. 'You can understand why they might not have been the best of mates, him living the life of a New York cop to Barney's fisherman. Nothing in common.'

'That we know of.' Alana glanced from her to the board and back again, trying to work out how Barney's wayward brother could be linked to their Jane Doe. 'If the cases are linked,' she carried on, 'then it's up to us to discover how and as quickly as possible. Flynn's obviously the right person to lead on the Howth side of things, which leaves William and Paddy free to head over to Dingle and see what's going on with Clare's disappearance.' Alana broke off and turned to William. 'That okay with you?'

William threw off a shrug, which was probably as much of a response as he was going to make. 'Good. Arrange the finer details with Pad. I'll forward you both everything I have on the man's disappearance.' It would also include everything Billy had given her but only after she'd stripped away any mention of who'd sent it. 'In the meantime, you and I are going to be stuck here, Lorrie, I'm afraid. A day trawling through Barney's life. Fact checking everything he's already told us and delving into all the murky corners he wouldn't share with the guards or even his missus. What do we have that's still outstanding apart from a name for the victim?'

Alana scrolled through the densely packed information presented on the boards, looking for the boxes still without ticks, the simple but visually impactful way she used to organise their workload.

'Ah yes. Start with Rogene and where she is on that footprint from the boat while I nag Dr Mulholland...' She dropped her gaze to her ringing mobile and the name flashing up on the screen. 'Speak of the devil. That's him now. I'll put him on loudspeaker. Afternoon, Rusty. What you got for us?'

'Afternoon, Alana. Good news and bad. I've managed to extract usable DNA from one of the crabs as well as from what we think is the victim's head. I'm in the process of harvesting from the bones too in case of any courtroom queries later...'

Alana smiled at that. Rusty was the kind of pathologist who always conducted himself with the thought of the trial running concurrently in the background. It was far too early to tell if they'd manage to arrest someone for the crime, but he was already envisaging the line of cross examination he'd be on the receiving end of with regards to data reliability.

And how can you be assured, doctor, that the crabs hadn't feasted on a different corpse before arriving in the pot? I see you can't. Milord, I strike to have the case dismissed due to lack of reliable evidence. Not on Rusty's watch!

'So, what's the bad news then? I'm guessing no DNA matches on the database?'

'Perhaps we should swap jobs,' he said, his tone laced with irony.

And why would there be with only a small fraction of the population appearing on the database, Alana thought, losing what little hope she had of finding out the woman's identity.

The taking of DNA by the guards was governed by a strict set of criteria, which excluded the majority of the public, who went about their lives as law-abiding citizens. There were other options open to them now that they had the head but, with no reports of any missing people remotely fitting the woman's age, they had little to go on. Jane might not even be Irish. She could be a visitor or even someone living below grid. There was also the chance she was American, a new link forged with Mason's disappearance.

Alana made a mental note to request a Black Notice with Interpol, an international alert system to help name unidentified dead bodies. It was something she should have done straight away but with little to go on she'd been hoping the woman's DNA would have negated the need. Fat chance of that now.

'And any further thoughts as to her cause of death?'

'Still waiting for the tox results to come back and you know how long that can take. Same goes for news from my dentist friend but I am chasing.'

'Thank you.' She signed off, placing the mobile back on her lap, her fingers curled around the black plastic as she considered where the news left them.

'What about Forensic Investigative Genetic Genealogy testing or FIGG as it's called, or is that not something we're allowed to look at yet?' William said, interrupting her thoughts.

'As in tapping into the DNA data held by ancestry sites?' She lifted her head from her phone.

'Absolutely. It's certainly something we should be thinking of if Forensic Science Ireland feel we can get it past the Ethics Committee,' Paddy said, a glimmer of excitement overtaking his usually composed features.

'I don't think it's as easy as that, Pad,' she replied, switching her attention between them. 'If only it was. Up to now, uploading a DNA profile to a commercial site, such as GED Match, and comparing it against their many millions of users has only been done on cold cases, a last-ditch attempt to catch the killer if you like and only with limited success, if the journals are to be believed.' Alana twisted her pen between her fingers, dragging up the information from a recent article she'd read on the subject and the complexities involved. 'While I agree that it sounds a great idea, Europe is way behind the USA in regulating and controlling this type of data use. It's a very good suggestion but currently a non-starter, although that doesn't mean I won't look into it. Don't worry though. There are other things we can try instead. There's still Interpol while we wait for the dentals and let's not forget the footprint from Barney's boat or indeed facial reconstruction. Advances in digital reconstruction using AI are mind-blowing.' She placed her pen back on the table, adjusting it just so.

There was also Mason Clare to find. A coincidence or a link in the chain that was Jane Doe's life?

ELEVEN

Tuesday 5th September, 4 p.m.

What did a twenty-three-year-old and a thirty-four-year-old have in common?

Absolutely nothing, as far as William was concerned, which made the thought of the four-hour trip to Kerry cooped up in the confines of Paddy's car almost unbearable.

'Cheese and onion or ready salted?' he finally said, fed up with his own thoughts.

'Either is fine. I'll have to remember to bring you on more of these ad hoc trips we get,' Paddy said, throwing him a smile while he adjusted his speed now they were approaching Naas. William had arrived with a large carrier bag, in addition to his holdall, which rustled every time he shifted position. He viewed the ten-minute detour on the way back to the station to fuel up on snacks and fizzy drinks at SuperValu as an essential part of the trip and Paddy was obviously of a similar opinion.

He popped open the crisp bag and balanced it in the drinks holder before flipping through a string of attachments on his laptop. The initial misper report and witness statements from

Clare's friends and neighbours. The article on the front page of the local newspaper appealing for information. There was even a photograph of the big grey dog, which elicited a rare smile. William was a dog person. He certainly had little time for humans.

'In your professional opinion would you say that Clare was a low, medium or high risk with regards to disappearing then?' He needed to lead the conversation in the direction he wanted it to go. That started with understanding the initial risk assessment and priority classification and what someone with Paddy's immense experience would have done. William might have trust issues relating to his haphazard upbringing by tug-of-war parents who'd hated each other within days of sperm hitting egg but Paddy had never let him down. The reverse was true, he remembered, staving off a blush at the memory of how the man had saved his life during the case of The Puppet Maker, Ireland's worst serial killer to date.

'Oh, definitely low in spite of his age. The old and young are usually classified as high automatically but fifty-four isn't old,' he qualified, indicating to overtake a peloton of cyclists. 'There are no triggers. Nothing to make us think of him as a vulnerable adult, or to think that he'd ever disappear into the distance and why all the stops are being pulled out. His GP was one of the first people the guards questioned. There'll be a report somewhere in that lot. The initial report is always the best place to start when backtracking through someone else's case.' He waved a hand in the direction of the laptop balanced on William's knees before reclaiming the steering wheel. 'Clare had no history of mental health problems, no suicide ideation. No issues with drugs or alcohol that we know of. The man wasn't on antidepressants. No previous episodes of disappearing outside of what Deirdre had told Tatty. No financial concerns or family ones. He wasn't married, was he, and no kids?'

'That's right.' William grabbed a handful of crisps and picked through to find the ones he wanted to eat first, not that he was thinking about what he was doing. 'You see, I don't think I'd have sent out the hounds if it had been me on the receiving end of the neighbour's report, and that worries me. A low-risk male of an age which falls outside the expected for disappearing – only five per cent are over the age of fifty-five – and without any of the side orders of disability or dementia to make it seem more likely.'

'You're forgetting three things, William. Clare's previous profession, his routine and his dog. Those things combined, rightly or wrongly, shove our Mason Clare right into the danger zone. I'm tending to think we can ignore the previous copper bit simply because of the difficulty in arranging a hit in another country. It would have to be some kind of serious vendetta for someone to track him down all the way across the Atlantic Ocean, but stranger things have been known to happen. And as for the other two facts...' Paddy slowed down before coming to a stop at the traffic lights ahead, taking the opportunity to dip into the crisp bag and half turn in his seat. 'We know that Clare was an all-year-round sea swimmer. A strong swimmer who would travel the twelve-minute drive daily to give the dog a run before stripping down to his bathers and going for a dip. Have you found the initial report Alana sent us earlier?'

'I'm pulling it up now.'

'Have a read and tell me the very first thing that strikes you.'

The gardai, like every other police authority, used a standardised A4 online form to document a missing person. The front sheet contained the absentee's personal details including their name, estimated height, weight, eye and hair colour, teeth, glasses, hearing, ethnicity, identifying scars, moles, tattoos and piercings to a list of possible clothing worn, but it wasn't the front sheet that William was interested in. It was the space at the back where the interview was recorded. In other words, the statement provided by the person making the report. In this case a Miss Roberta Longstaff, Mason's sixty-two-year-old neighbour. He gave the front cover a cursory look before scrolling down to the back one.

Q: Tell me why you're concerned about the whereabouts of your neighbour?

A: Mason leaves the house like clockwork every day to take his dog, Wally, for a run on the beach. I see him leave the house from my front window, which looks out onto his drive and he always gives me a little wave.

Q: And what was Mr Clare wearing, Miss Longstaff?

A: His usual garb of dry robe, crocs and a woolly hat. The stick he's had about wearing crocs and now they're coming back into fashion too.

Q: And was he carrying anything?

A: Just his holdall for his towel and bathers, same as every day.

Q: He doesn't mind you watching him?

A: No, we're firm friends and he knows it helps me pass the time. I'm housebound since my stroke. Spend my time sitting in the chair by the window watching the world go by until my carers come and shift me for meals and the like before assisting me into bed. If it's not him it's the neighbours on the other side.

Q: And you're watching from what time?

A: Differs depending on the time the carer gets to me but I'm usually up and about for eight or shortly after. This morning it was five past.

Q: And you say he waved as normal but that you didn't see the dog?

A: Wally. No. Unusual. In fact, it's never happened before. It was only when my teatime carer told me about the barking coming from next door that I decided to give you a ring. There is no way Mason would leave his dog like that. Maybe for a short while at a push in an emergency but even then. Where Mason went Wally went too.

William ran over the main points of the document before returning to that last sentence, his stomach clenching under his smart work shirt.

'She's speaking about him in the past tense as if he's already dead.'

'She suspects he's dead, or at least that something terrible has happened to him,' Paddy amended. 'I tend to agree with her, as does Alana, which is why she twisted the superintendent's arm in allowing us to drop everything on a wild goose chase the other side of Ireland when we have Operation Enigma on the go.'

'But they're linked?'

'I know that, and you know that, but trying to convince our esteemed DS Barry is something else entirely.'

William glanced out the window and the sign up ahead for Whitewater Shopping Centre now they were approaching Newbridge. He knew that the super and Paddy had trained together at Tullamore College. The rumour was that they were firm friends outside the station, a rumour he tended to disbelieve for no other reason than it seemed an unlikely friendship.

'I'm still not sure splitting the team like this is the right thing to do.'

'And no one's arguing with you on that, William. But look at it this way. There's not a lot more that we can do until we have a name for the woman. Your idea on Forensic Investigative Genetic Genealogy was inspired but Alana is right about the barriers to that currently, barriers you can appreciate. Imagine if it was your DNA, which you'd uploaded onto one of these genealogy sites in order to trace your second granny twice removed, only to find the guards at your door trying to pin a murder on you.'

'It doesn't work like that.'

'I know that, and you know that, but try convincing the public that they're not going to be arrested for a crime they didn't commit. It's not as if they're genned up on the supporting role DNA plays in crime fighting. All they'd be concerned about is the possibility of a miscarriage of justice or, God forbid, being framed.'

'How does she know all this stuff anyway?' William said, thinking back to earlier and Alana's seamless reply. The only part of the conversation she'd had to check was whether he was asking about FIGG or something else before slamming the door on his idea. 'It's only something I found out about by accident yesterday.'

'Hah, it's amazing what that woman knows. I haven't an answer to all of it but having been married to a forensic child psychiatrist is the reason behind her interest in all things with a scientific bent. She told me once that her ex used to have a mountain of medical journals piled up beside his chair and one day she started reading them. When they split, she set up her own subscription and here we are. Lucky for us, eh?'

William wasn't completely satisfied but, if he was honest, he was rarely satisfied with anything. No, that wasn't quite true. He was coming around to the thought that he was exactly where he wanted to be, in his work life at least. When he got back to the hotel room later, he intended to do some more investigating into the role of FIGG and DNA searches.

'What do you think Jane died of?'

'Ah, now you're talking. There's not much to go on, is there but there are things we can probably rule out due to the evidence we do have. If I had to choose though I'd go with poison.'

William started, nearly spilling the rest of his crisps over his lap.

'How do you come to think that?'

'Simple, my boy. Those dead crab crammed inside the pot. Something killed them and, as it wasn't either the murderer or the victim, poisoning is the most obvious solution. Humans are by far the most dangerous species that inhabit the planet but not usually after they've died!'

TWELVE

Tuesday 5th September, 8.10 p.m.

Alana left the office after a fruitless exercise in updating the information on the whiteboards. It all felt a waste of time. There was nothing useful to add. Still no lead on who Jane was. No matches after hours spent trawling through acres of missing person reports, both at home and abroad. All the major agencies had been alerted, which was one good thing but not if they couldn't get a match. She didn't know what to think. Surely someone somewhere must have noticed that she was missing. How had she lived? Where had she lived and where had she shopped? Who collected her bins? Who cleaned her windows or cut her grass? All the little day-to-day facets that made up a life. There were those tragic cases to consider where people had been found dead after many months, even years and not one person had come forward to report them missing. Someone knew something. The murderer for one.

It was half-eight by the time she pulled into her designated car-parking space outside her apartment block and switched off the engine, ready to start the usual routine of assembling her wheelchair before grabbing her bag and slipping her laptop case from where she always hid it under the passenger seat. Sometimes she forgot the case and had to head all the way back outside to fetch it, but Dublin, in the way of every other capital city, wasn't as safe as it once was and there were numerous documents she couldn't afford to fall into the wrong hands. Twisting, she reached across the back seat only to twist back at the sound of her mobile jumping round to the sound of Michael Jackson's 'Smooth Criminal' – a joke from her best friend, Kari, one boozy night more years ago than she cared to remember and one she'd never got around to changing.

It was either going to be Billy, Paddy, Rusty or Colm, all of whom were used to a delay in her picking up, depending on what she was doing.

It was Rusty.

'Hi, Rusty, you're late again. Another burnt tea or will it be in the cat like the last time?'

'Hah, you know my wife so well. Actually, it's our wedding anniversary so no harm done. We're just heading out to Johnnie Fox's to celebrate.'

Alana thought about the lacklustre pile of vegetables in the bottom of the fridge with derision before remembering her recent holiday and blushing at the thought. She'd had her time in the sun, literally, and she wouldn't be jealous of Rusty. The number of meals that man had missed was legion. It was a good job he was married to an ex-cop. In Gaby he'd found the ideal partner. If a little part of Alana remained envious, it was the part she squished flat with the voice of reason. She'd tried marriage once and look where that had got her. Divorced and with her life, and body, in tatters.

'I won't keep you then,' she said, her code for him to *get on with it before taking that gorgeous missus of yours out while I eat my sad plate of vegetables and overcooked rice.*

'Right. I've decided to put my neck on the line by saying I think Jane was poisoned.'

'What?' Alana nearly asked him to repeat the sentence. After working with the man for well over two years she'd never known him to make a guess at anything. 'I thought you said the tox screen would be ages yet?'

'I know but I've just spoken with an eminent carcinologist so I'm happy enough to provide this insight.'

Alana frowned down at the phone, trying to place the relevance of cancer in the conversation and failing completely.

'You're saying that she had cancer, and that she was poisoned?'

'No, sorry.' Alana heard the makings of a laugh, quickly disguised by a cough. She was obviously missing something. 'Carcinologist as in someone who specialises in crustaceans, not cancer.'

'Well, that's as clear as mud then, isn't it?'

'Crustaceans as in crabs and lobsters. Cancer pagurus, the other name for brown crab?'

'Ah, I get you.' Alana felt a fool but how was she meant to know that. It was a long time since she'd been in school, and she'd never gone in for eating shellfish. Peeling a prawn was as far as it went, and she didn't even like doing that. 'And this specialist told you that...?'

'We had to consider the number of crabs found dead in the pot. All or just some, and as the water sample we took came back clear of toxins and excessive amounts of algae bloom, then the next thing to consider was poisoning. Crabs, as we know, are scavengers. That's why they're so easy to catch. Bait the pot up with something smelly and they'll consider it Christmas and their birthday rolled into one.'

'That's gross.'

'Totally. And on that note... Night, Alana, sleep well.'

'You too.'

Alana placed her mobile on the dash and started the laborious job of reassembling her chair. She worked on autopilot, relying on muscle memory to grab the wheelchair base and push it out the door before reaching for the back and slotting it into place, her mind on the case and not on the way the darkness had invaded every corner now the time was approaching nine and the nights were starting to draw in at an alarming rate. The lack of light was a nuisance in the same way her legs were, but she'd been living in the apartment block long enough to be well versed in negotiating the short distance between the car park and the main entrance.

With the wheelchair assembled, she grabbed her phone from the passenger seat, ready to slide across the small distance when a movement out of the corner of her eye had her pause.

The man came out of nowhere or that's what it seemed. Dressed in head to toe black and with the hoodie obscuring his face – the only details she could make out before he wrenched her from the car and onto the tarmac, her right hand snapping back under the weight of her body landing on top. The pain was as sudden as it was excruciating, whipping away any thought of trying to fight back even if her useless legs would have let her. He didn't say anything, he didn't need to. His intentions were clear in the way he reached for her phone and her handbag. She stretched out her left hand in the vain effort of grabbing his leg – she had to do something – only to get a kick in the stomach for her efforts.

Alana gave up then as she tried to navigate the pain in her wrist along with the stabbing agony that was her belly. In the old days he wouldn't have had a chance; a combination of fit-boxing and Jiu-Jitsu along with a daily jog had kept her in peak physical fitness. Now she felt like a useless blob of a woman unable to defend herself from the lowlife scumbags that would beat up a defenceless woman and all for the price of a fix. She rested her head on her arm, the sound of his shoes slapping against the pavement fading into the distance, unable to stop the tears.

Minutes passed, vague uncountable minutes where she tried to regulate her breathing while she waited for the pain in her belly to dim. Steel-capped boots probably. Bruising was the best she could hope for. Her wrist was another issue entirely. Definitely fractured – her worst fear of all, far worse than a broken leg considering she relied on both her hands to mobilise.

Sitting was a slow process, involving using her left hand to manoeuvre her legs into place, her right arm clutched to her stomach in a protective movement, the hand dangling like a puppet with its strings cut. It was only by pure stubbornness and determination that she managed to negotiate it back into the wheelchair, a herculean effort that left her almost biting through her bottom lip at the pain.

She sat there, not quite believing the alternative evening to the one planned and no further forward as to how to get from the car park to her flat without the two hands needed to move her in anything other than round in circles.

You stupid fuck!

It was all very well purchasing a top-of-the-range manual wheelchair, as light as air instead of the power one she'd been recommended. She knew they thought her mulish in not taking the easier option but for her it was tied up with her crazy need to be as independent as possible. Powered chairs were all very well but not if she was determined to push her body to preserve the muscles she had available to her, which included negotiating the many hills found around Dublin, without assistance, mechanical or otherwise.

Alana glanced at her hand, the tissue already starting to swell around the damaged bone, barely believing what she was thinking of doing but it was that or the possibility of spending the night in her chair. If there'd been anyone in screaming distance she'd have used her lungs to their fullest – she felt like doing it anyway, but the car park was situated off to the side so there was little hope of her being heard over the roar of the traffic.

There was nothing to strap her arm with apart from her blouse. Getting that over her swollen hand was an exercise in discipline, it was also a chance to feel her stomach with her good hand, the tender ridge of flesh already engorged with blood. She didn't care about that, only the threat of underlying damage, which made her next movements non-negotiable. With the fabric wrapped as tightly as she could tolerate around her hand and arm, she gritted her teeth and started the slow, arduous journey to the front door, the feel of the edges of bone grating against each other bringing on a strange combination of nausea and dizziness that she never wanted to experience again.

The outside keypad entry system was a godsend as was the fact she always kept her bunch of keys in her pocket, one less thing to worry about losing during the day. Getting them out of her pocket was something else entirely, her hand a throbbing mess of hot, raging agony by the time she shut the door behind her, Goose coming out to meet her with a plaintive meow of a greeting.

Where's my dinner?

'In a minute, puss.' It would be more than a minute. She even considered making it a priority but the thought of muddling through to the kitchen area not to mention tearing open a packet of cat food with her teeth was one thought too far. She needed help and urgently, but the question was from whom. With the hours she kept she didn't mix with her neighbours apart from the odd greeting in the corridors but who else was there?

Like everyone she knew, Alana stored all her phone numbers in her mobile. Long gone were the days when she could remember her best friend's or even Paddy's. Another stitch in her shirt of shame, the shirt currently laced around her hand leaving her sitting there in her bra and ripped trousers. She didn't care about that. Nudity, and she was perfectly decently covered, had never been an issue. If it had she'd never have coped with the months spent in hospital and then rehabilitation over in Maynooth Rehabilitation Centre. What she did worry about was that she needed urgent medical attention and there wasn't a single person she could think of to call on apart from dialling 911, something she was loath to do.

She stared at her landline in consternation, hemming and hawing as to who to call, weighing up the pros and cons of alerting the control room and, by association, Clonabee Police Station as to her predicament. All emergency calls were rooted through the same operators and telling them she was a guard was part of the system they had to adhere to. There was no way she'd be able to keep it under wraps.

Alana grimaced. There was one number she'd never have envisaged calling again but the only one she knew by heart.

THIRTEEN

Tuesday 5th September, 8.30 p.m.

'Where did you say we were staying again?'

'The Seaview. It's facing the marina, apparently.'

'I've got it. Take the first left and then the next right,' William said, peering down at his phone, the brightness muted now they were driving in darkness, the orange glow of sunset only a memory.

'What do you want to do first?'

'What I want and the reality are two very different things, Will. A beer followed by supper and a hot shower before sinking into a comfy bed with a good book are what I'd like, but I've arranged for Ruan to meet us in the bar. At least we'll get a beer.'

It was another twenty minutes by the time they made their way down the red carpeted stairs and into the bar. Only long enough for him to dump his bag on the middle of the bed and make a quick trip to the bathroom.

Ruan was easy to spot. The only man sitting at a table by himself, an untouched pint of Guinness in front of him along with a thick manilla folder. Either that or he'd decided to bring his wife, William thought as he scanned the bar, surprisingly full of couples now the summer season was over and the schools back. But this was Kerry, he remembered, following Paddy across the room where Ruan had stood to greet them. Half the world was related to a Kerry man, the other a Galway one, which meant it always had its doors wide open to tourists.

Ruan was a big man, a bruiser as his ma would say. All bunched forearms and polished scalp with a peculiar scar splitting his forehead from eyebrow to crown. The handshake was unexpectedly soft, all that power hidden behind a wide grin and gleaming eyes.

'Good to see you again, Paddy. What will you and the young fella be having? A couple of Guinness? Great. Men after me own heart. Shea, another two when you've got a minute. Take a seat, lads. A good drive down?'

The talk was nonstop, the soft burr of the Kerry accent present in the rounded off vowels and consonants. William sank into the red plush seat and stayed quiet while the two men reacquainted through a string of pleasantries. This wasn't his show. The Guinness had just the right amount of head. In truth he'd have preferred a Bud, but he hadn't felt comfortable enough to ask. The story of his life.

'You've certainly got a strange one up in Dublin, and you think it might be linked to our missing man here?' Ruan lifted his glass and took a long sip.

'It's looking that way. For them not to be related seems too much of a coincidence. Thanks for sending all the stuff through and agreeing to work with us on this, by the way.'

'Not a problem. So, how are you thinking the two cases are linked?'

'Not a clue.' Paddy spread his hands. 'That's where you come in,' he said, nodding in the direction of the folder.

'Don't get too excited. It's only the report from the team of techies I sent out to Slea Head and, whichever way you look at it, it's not good news. There's nothing, either in the sea or along the cliff face. As far as we can make out the man has disappeared into thin air.'

But he hasn't. That's not how it goes.

William touched the icy cold glass, his attention on the thick creamy white head, his finger scooping up a drop of condensation and wondering what they were doing here. Mason was clearly missing, but missing of his own accord. There was no evidence to suggest otherwise apart from the neighbour's statement. If it wasn't for the dog no one would think anything of it.

'Tell me about the dog?' Paddy asked, clearly on the same wavelength.

Ruan plucked his glasses from his shirt pocket and took a moment to settle them on his nose before slipping the band on the folder.

'A two-year-old Weimaraner called Wally, a rescue from a local charity. He got him within weeks of moving back from the States. The neighbour says she's never seen him without Wally, they go everywhere together.'

A companion or a guard dog? William had never heard of the breed so it was difficult to gauge.

'Her view or one supported by other testimonies?' he finally said, deciding to join the conversation. If the woman was housebound, surely she wouldn't be the right person to ask about his movements.

'Definitely supported by the other neighbours, both on the cul-de-sac and in the neighbourhood. Dingle is a small community. The sort where everyone knows everyone else and nobody's business is their own, if you get my meaning. Clare is a private man by all accounts but also very distinctive.'

'Distinctive? In what way?' Paddy asked.

'In the way of flamboyant men who go round with white

bushy beards and wearing wide-brimmed hats distinctive, even before teeming them with a selection of brightly coloured glasses chosen to match their Dicky bow. I don't know the man and, to my knowledge, I've never met him, but I recognise him as someone I've seen out and about from that description alone.'

'And yet he decided to head out Sunday morning, purportedly for his daily swim, and leave the dog cooped up inside? Sunday was warm, wasn't it? It was certainly in the mid-twenties in Dublin,' William said, finally attacking his beer. A brief sip for appearances' sake before placing the glass back on the table and pushing it towards the middle. He had a feeling he'd need his wits about him. Not surprisingly Paddy had only taken the top off his before doing the same.

Ruan nodded. 'Here too but he wasn't inside. Enclosed in the back garden. The rampaging lunatic made a fair attempt at trying to get out by the scrapes and scratches to the fence panels. Ripped his claws to shreds in the process. If the neighbour hadn't intervened, he'd have escaped.'

'And where is he now?'

Ruan smoothed his hand over his head, his attention suddenly on his beer and the rapidly decreasing volume. 'With the rescue centres chocka I decided to take him home with me. Not ideal but there was no one else and I couldn't very well leave him to spend the night in the cells, not after the damage he made of his back garden. Docile thing too now he has company. I'll have to see about a centre further afield. The wife's allergic, more's the pity. You can meet him if you like?'

Docile thing or rampaging lunatic? William didn't know the first thing about dogs, but it almost felt as if the detective was talking about two different animals.

'We can meet him?' Paddy asked.

'Yeah. He's here. Well, when I say he's here, I mean in the back of the car.'

'You wouldn't have the keys of Clare's house on you, would you?' William said. 'I'd like to try something.'

FOURTEEN

Tuesday 5th September, 9.10 p.m.

With no streetlights the cul-de-sac was almost pitch black, the only thing lighting their way the dim glow from behind closed blinds and curtains and the sheen from Ruan's headlamps, which he dipped as soon as he pulled into the residential area.

They'd decided to travel in Ruan's car, at his suggestion. He knew the area and hadn't spent four hours cooped up in the same vehicle. It was also a way for them to meet Wally, not that the dog showed any interest apart from an initial sniff before turning his back and curling into a tight ball. William thought he looked unhappy. Could dogs feel sad? He didn't have a clue but that's what his gut was telling him and the reason he opted to sit in the back. He spent the short journey stroking the dog's head.

The house was in darkness, which wasn't surprising. It wasn't a crime scene so there was no need to leave an officer outside or indeed have a SOCO team inside searching, swabbing and generally scrubbing about for evidence after their initial visit to eliminate any trace of foul play, or indeed a body.

It wasn't a crime scene yet.

Paddy and William were in agreement on that one point and the difference between a provincial team working their home patch and the excesses the NBCI were used to seeing in Dublin. Just like Alana yesterday, the dog worried them. Without the dog, they wouldn't have given the man's disappearance a second thought. They certainly wouldn't be in Kerry, with or without the links to 'the woman in the pot' unless they'd had more to go on.

'Let's leave the dog here while I give you the grand tour. It will only take a couple of minutes.' William would have preferred not to leave Wally, but it wasn't his show.

The inside of the house wasn't anything special. Nice enough but bare of the usual personal effects he was used to seeing. Wooded flooring throughout and white walls with only the odd painting to offset the monotony. A mahogany coat stand in the corner of the hall. One of those old-fashioned free-standing ones used for an eclectic display of hats of all things.

He quickened his pace, following Ruan and Paddy into the lounge. Tidy enough and with wall-to-wall bookshelves. Nowhere to hide a body. The kitchen was the same, the cupboards open, the SOCOs having spent most of the day on the place. The bathroom cabinet with a stock of toothbrush heads, a tube of toothpaste and a bottle of Zopiclone, a well known night sedation. A nearly empty bottle of Dior Sauvage standing on the shelf underneath. Both bedrooms were bleak, the smell of aftershave and the stack of books by the bed table in the first the only indication that this was Clare's room, the bed made, the top pillow with a slight head-shaped indent. The man had lived alone, which probably accounted for the spartan air, where books again took preference to the knickknacks William had come to expect from other people's homes. He liked the lack of clutter, it suited the way he lived his own life, and it made him feel a sense of affinity with the man, the issue of his choice of headgear notwithstanding. But as for the house… there was nothing to see. No dead body and no clues as to what might have happened to him.

'Let's see what Wally thinks,' he said, following on behind as they made their way across the enclosed back garden and over to the shed. The tools tidy. The workbench clear.

'You're sure you want the dog in on this? Intelligent beast. He obviously knows something's up.' Ruan headed for the car with them trailing behind, the sight of Wally with his head pressed up against the window clear to see.

'It can't harm. Come on, Wally.' William opened the back door and coaxed the dog out, his hand on his collar, his voice crooning soft. 'There's a good boy. Nothing bad is going to happen to you.'

They were only words but lies, all of them. William had a pretty good idea what they'd find, just not where they'd find it. Mason's body. It didn't ring true that an animal could be so distressed at being left, not unless he knew something or, God forbid, smelt something. His nose wrinkled up at the lingering aftershave scent, which was powerful enough to seep into his mind. William still hadn't worked out what was going on yet. He'd need to meet with the neighbour for that and as she was a disabled woman living on her own and dependent on carers, that wasn't going to be tonight.

Despite Wally's size, William picked him up in his arms and cradled him to his chest, the dog surprisingly thin under his thick coat, the thump of his heart confirming his anxiety if his squirming body wasn't enough. Once in the hall, he placed Wally on the floor, his hands circling his trembling, squirming body to hold him in place while he whispered in the dog's ear.

'Take me to your daddy.'

He felt stupid saying it but not so stupid when the dog stilled before giving a little yelp, pulling out his arms and racing up the stairs, his paws scrabbling against the sheen of the floor in his hurry to find purchase, William, Paddy and Ruan following on behind. They found the dog at the top of the stairs standing in front of the first of the bedrooms, his liquid brown eyes intent on the white of the wood, a tiny yelp the only sound.

'I don't know what he's about. It's the bedroom. Nothing to see.' Ruan reached out a hand and pushed the door wide open. 'The SOCOs have been all over and not a trace of anything. No blood splatter or stains. No fingerprints apart from the owner's and his cleaner's and we've eliminated her from our enquires,' he said, standing back and waiting as Paddy and William walked into the bedroom. The dog whimpered before lying down, his head in-between his outstretched paws.

'What about under the bed?' Paddy said.

'We're not gobshites down here, Pad. The techies are as highly qualified as yours up in the city.'

'I didn't mean to...'

William ignored them.

He walked into the centre and did a three-sixty, his attention on the room and not on the placatory conversation between the two men. The open suitcases and open wardrobe doors, the clothes pushed back to reveal dust mites and little else. The heavy curtains flush to the wall. The chest of drawers with the drawers pulled out. The spartan bed. No hiding place in sight.

If it was me, where would I hide a body? And why the overbearing smell of aftershave? The man had been missing for two days, two and a half. How long did it take for a body to smell?

He took a deep sniff, expanding his lungs to the max and almost gagging as the overwhelming smell of something with vanilla undertones. He'd read somewhere that the odour from a decomposing body was one of the main reasons for storing the dead in mortuaries. Up to now, he'd been lucky enough never to have experienced it. Something had him thinking that was all about to change.

The bed was last. The high wooden bed where there was

room to hide a body underneath. He dropped to his knees to double check, ignoring both Paddy's sharp intake of breath and Ruan's heavy sigh.

With his nose nearly touching, it was here the stench was overpowering enough for him to hold his breath and, before he knew it, he'd flung the pillows to the floor and stripped back the duvet to reveal the yellow sheet below.

'I don't think he's hiding between the sheets,' Ruan said, a bemused expression on his face, which William ignored.

'Pad, give me a hand?'

'I'm not sure what you're up to but...'

Paddy walked round the bed to the opposite side and, following William's example, hooked his hands around the handles. 'Okay. On three. One, two, three and flip. What the hell!'

FIFTEEN

Tuesday 5th September, 10.25 p.m.

Instead of returning to the hotel for a meal before bed, they were in Dingle Garda Station being treated to sandwiches from the staff canteen. Cheese and pickle. William didn't like pickle as a rule but that didn't stop him from bolting down the packet before wrapping his shaking hands around the mug of strong tea placed in front of him, a stream of guards filing in and taking up the seats provided. His stomach felt like he'd been down Niagara Falls on a life raft but the sandwich, at Paddy's insistence, had him feeling better already.

'Eat and drink something, eh. It will make it better in the long run.'

How Paddy knew the state of his stomach was beyond him, but then William wasn't aware of his ghastly green face to accompany his trembling fingers. He closed his eyes, but it was no good. The picture of Mason Clare, waxy grey in death, laid on top of the bed base remained, the scooped-out mattress discarded against the wall.

Genius and horrific in equal measures.

'I still don't know how you did it, William. If you're ever thinking of relocating to Kerry we'd love to hear from you.'

'No, you don't, Ruan. You keep your grubby mitts off my staff,' Paddy said, scrunching up his sandwich wrapper and aiming it at the bin before leaning against the wall, his arms folded across his chest. 'William isn't going anywhere and certainly not until he explains how he knew to check the underside of the mattress.'

'Blame Wally. After that it was a process of elimination.' William dropped his hand to the dog's head, rubbing gently. Wally hadn't left his side since, which was going to cause a problem as dogs weren't allowed in the hotel.

'Nope, try again. You were standing in the middle of the room with a strange expression on your face, nothing at all to do with the bleedin' dog,' Ruan said, refusing to be deterred.

William blinked, thinking back when all he wanted to do was head to the hotel and stand under a hot shower in the hope he could get the smell of death and Dior out of his nostrils.

'It was the aftershave,' he said finally, aware that the team weren't prepared to loosen their chokehold.

'As in the bottle in the bathroom. I don't get you?' Ruan said.

'Clare kept his aftershave in the bathroom so why did his bedroom reek of the stuff, or something. It almost felt as if he'd spilt it but if that was the case then...'

'We'd have found the bottle on top of his chest of drawers along with his cufflinks and what have you,' Ruan completed, turning back to the room and leaving William to concentrate on his tea, aware of the wall of eyes from the detectives and SOCO team buried into the back of his head. It wasn't his fault that his mind was wired differently. It suddenly didn't feel like an asset.

'Which none of us spotted. Well done, lad. So, our perp

strangles Clare and places him on the bottom of the bed before covering him with a carved out, body-shaped hole cut into the underside of the mattress,' Ruan said, updating the whiteboard. 'They remake the bed with sheets and no one is any the wiser, which in no way explains the neighbour's testimony.' He zeroed in on a petite blonde with a wide mouth sitting at the front. 'It also doesn't explain what he did with the mattress stuffing, but we'll get to that after. You interviewed the neighbour, didn't you, Jean?"

'Went round to see her yesterday to take her statement. She can't very well come to the station,' she replied, tucking her hair behind her ear. 'Adamant she saw Clare leave for his regular daily swim Sunday morning, down to his sports bag flung over his shoulder and the daily wave she's come to expect.'

'How's her eyesight?'

'Not something I asked but I'll check first thing,' she said, tapping a quick note on her phone. 'I wouldn't like to disturb her at this time of night.'

'Okay. Anything from the New York side of things, Dave?' he said, speaking to someone at the back of the room.

'He lived in a brownstone in East Village. I managed to get hold of the chief of patrol; Mason was a patrol officer. There was nothing of note on his file and nothing to suggest he would have been involved in any of the sorts of crimes that would lead to an international hit but his boss is going to do a bit more sniffing around before reporting back ASAP.'

William tugged his mobile from his pocket, where he'd taken a screenshot of Roberta Longstaff's testimony, not that he needed it. He had a perfect recall of what the man was wearing. A dry robe and crocs, the same garb he wore every morning before presumably getting changed into one of his natty suits and pretentious hats on his return. The question was, did Roberta see Mason Clare? Or did she see someone dressed to resemble the man? An imposter who knew to imitate Clare's usual wave to his housebound neighbour. William thought he knew the answer, but it was a question of proving it. What he didn't know was why, or indeed how, to share it with a room full of intimidating senior detectives. The only way was to blurt it out.

'Jean.' He smiled briefly. 'Can I ask if any of the people you interviewed in the cul-de-sac reported unusual cars or strangers over the last few days? If so, is it possible to check them against the handheld ANPR systems deployed in your garda vehicles?' He felt all eyes on the room pointed in his direction, including Paddy's, but in his case with a raised eyebrow and an encouraging smile, which made him add, 'Oh, would it be an idea to get in touch with Dr Rusty Mulholland over in Clonabee before and not after the PM is performed if, as we suspect, our two cases are linked, and we have a double murder on our hands? Also, we need a copy of the list of items found at Mr Clare's home. You know. The contents of his black sacs, that sort of thing,' he finally said, his face now beetroot red instead of cabbage green.

'Reckon it's too late to phone the boss?'

Why are you asking me?

William placed his glass back on the table, allowing the refreshing taste of his first sip of Bud to hover over his tongue before pushing it to the back of his mouth and swallowing. The first sip was always the best, he wasn't going to allow Paddy talking through it to change that.

'Depends,' he finally said, his eyes travelling down the long list of human detritus found in Mason's home from empty dog food tins, the packaging from a chicken along with a pile of chicken bones, some spent matches and a scrunched-up piece of plastic wrap.

'On what?' Paddy leant forward, a deep frown perched on his forehead, his lager shandy already half empty.

'On whether she's the type to ball you out over either interrupting her evening or waking her. Makes no difference.'

'Knowing Alana, it's more likely she'll ball me out if I don't phone,' Paddy replied, reaching for his mobile and pressing a few keys, his frown deepening as he concentrated on his screen. 'That's strange.'

'What is?' William tried to stem a yawn then changed his mind. It was eleven o'clock after one of his busiest days on record, he was allowed to do what he wanted. Clocking-off time was meant to be five and it was long past that hour, he remembered, covering his mouth just in time to capture the yawn.

'It's saying that her number isn't in service.'

'Ah.' William picked up his lager and started sipping it at speed. There was a very good chance the comfortable night's sleep he'd been planning was about to be whisked out from under him. At least he was going to enjoy his drink.

'What does "ah" mean?'

William placed his empty glass down on the table. 'It means that either you've phoned the wrong number or...' He raised his hand at the sight of Paddy opening his mouth to argue. 'Someone's nicked her phone. What about her landline?'

'I'm not sure I have it.' He started searching through his contacts. 'Oh, yes I do.' He lifted his head, his finger on the call button. Then after a few seconds. 'No answer. Shit.'

'What about round at my dad's?'

'You know about their... er... friendship?' Paddy looked flummoxed, which wasn't a surprise as William had never given any indication that he knew what was going on between the pair of them.

He shrugged. He liked Alana, far more than he liked or trusted his old man. Part of him wanted to warn her about him but the other part was happy enough to let it be. She'd find out the hard way that Billy didn't know the meaning of the word faithful. If they were only friends, well and good, but he had an inkling there was more to it. 'I can always ask my mum. She keeps abreast of what he's up to as a form of self-flagellation.'

'That's bananas.'

'As I've pointed out many a time but she's friends with someone on the *Globe* so it's easy enough for her to keep tabs. What's even more peculiar is the fact she'd have him back if he asked her. No accounting for taste.'

'S'pose not. She won't be in bed?'

'Not until the small hours, or when she's reached the bottom of the bottle, whichever comes first.' William leant back in his chair, his ankle balanced on his right knee, his phone in his hand, unaware of the piercing glance sent his way. The call didn't last long.

'Ma says he's in London for the night. Some posh party or other. So, where would she go if she was in trouble? Who would she contact?'

'Hell. I don't know. You're sure about her phone?'

'As sure as I can be. Hang on a minute. I have an idea.' William lifted his mobile again and within seconds was speaking to the telephonist over at Clonabee Hospital. It was either that or the station and he had a good idea that Alana was the kind of person who liked to keep her private business private. He didn't even know about how she came to be in a wheelchair, no one did. An attitude he respected. 'She was in earlier. They wouldn't tell me anything apart from advising me to contact her next-of-kin.'

'Bloody GDPR. How are we meant to—' Paddy stopped abruptly as if he'd been shot, or shocked – not much difference if the change in his colour was anything to go by or the way his hand tremored as he reached for his lager, his head tilting towards William. 'Alana doesn't have any next-of-kin, not really. No blood ones anyway apart from a pile of cousins over in Killarney, and one very ex-husband.'

'Who wouldn't count, surely?' William said, thinking of his own parents.

'You wouldn't think, eh.'

SIXTEEN

Tuesday 5th September, 9.30 p.m.

'A break in the distal end of your right radius. The medical term is a Colles fracture.'

'You what?'

Alana had arrived in Clonabee Hospital's Emergency Department within forty minutes of her call to her ex-husband and was seen within five, thanks to Colm working there. There were many strings she'd never agree to pulling, queue jumping included, but she was barely holding herself together. Before she knew it, she'd been whisked through triage, bypassing the crowd of people lining the corridors.

She stared up at the doctor from her position on the hard trolley, trying not to notice the way his breath stank of garlic. How could she be nauseas and ravenous at the same time was a question she didn't know the answer to. The overpowering smell of garlic didn't help but as she'd interrupted his evening meal it was probably to be expected.

'One of the long bones in your forearm, a bit has broken at the wrist end.' He turned the screen around and pointed to the

X-ray image with his fingertip, the white/grey/black image of no help whatsoever to her understanding. 'We'll get it plastered up for you and send you home with a prescription for some strong painkillers.'

God. Really. Shit. No chance I can stay the night. But what she said was, 'How long?'

'About four weeks give or take. We'll call you in for an X-ray and decide then.' He lifted her notes and scan read the covering page, the one with her personal details. 'Shouldn't be too much of a problem. I see you were brought in by your husband?'

'My ex-husband,' she corrected, unprepared to explain that her old phone number was the only one she'd been able to remember. The one good thing about all of this was that Colm had made himself scarce as soon as she'd been whisked into the department, muttering something about going to get a coffee while she was being seen to. For a doctor to be squeamish at the grittier aspects of society as found in an emergency department at night was laughable and one of the many reasons why Colm had decided to specialise in the head instead of the body.

'Ah.' The doctor pulled over a stool and sat beside her, his face showing only concern and no sign of any irritation caused by his abandoned garlic whatnot left to grow cold in some staff room or other – did they even have a staff room? She didn't know why the thought suddenly troubled her as much as it did or why her eyes decided to let her down in such a spectacular fashion by filling with tears.

'There now, it's not the end of the world.' He grabbed a pile of tissues from the box conveniently situated under the trolley and stuffed them into her good hand. 'You are happy to be released into your ex-husband's care or is there something you're not telling me?'

She almost laughed at that. There were many things her ex was, but a wife beater wasn't one of them. 'It's fine, really. A plain ole mugging, which wouldn't have happened if I'd been more prepared.'

'Who's ever prepared for something like that?'

'I'm a copper, doctor, so someone like me.' She lowered her voice to a whisper. 'I keep a can of pepper spray in the pocket of my car door, but the bastard took me unawares.'

He sat back, dropping her hand. 'Isn't that illegal?'

'Only if it's discharged by a member of the public. As a guard, I'm sanctioned to use it and I wish I had.'

'Oh, well, that's alright then,' was what he said. His face told a different story entirely. She was sure the first thing he'd do when he discharged her was to check that she was who she said she was. It's something she'd have done. 'So, to confirm, you're happy for me to send you home with your ex or is there someone else you'd like me to contact?'

Like whom? She wouldn't interrupt Rusty on his wedding anniversary and Billy was off in London for the night. The only other people were Paddy, who was in Dingle or her best friend, Kari, who had three-year-old twins in toe. With no mother, a father she'd never met and no siblings, there was no one she could call on except the last person in the world she'd ever ask a favour of. Not because he'd take advantage of the situation – as a doctor, an esteemed forensic psychiatrist with a string of letters after his name, he was as honourable as his title suggested. That he still loved her and would use every avenue open to him to make her change her mind about him wasn't the problem. The problem was that he might be successful.

She took a second, just one where she pressed the tissues against her eyes, heaving in a breath at the same time before lowering her hand and offering him a watery smile. It wasn't his fault that she had such a messy life. 'No, it's fine really. Thank you and sorry again for interrupting your supper, doctor. If you're ever in need of some pepper spray, the answer is no!'

He grinned, the smile lightening up his tired face and pushing down her estimation of his age by ten years.

'Actually, that was my breakfast. It's toast and marmalade for supper in about...' He tilted his head to the clock on the wall. 'Ten hours, give or take. I'll send in the plaster technician and get someone to chase up your... er... ex.'

Alana blinked and her watch had jumped an hour, at least that's what it felt like. The reality was it was a quarter to eleven and she could barely keep her eyes open. Strong painkillers on an empty stomach probably, not that she'd told anyone about the hunger part. With some soothing gel on her stomach and her arm resplendent in a pink dynacast and cradled inside a sling, she was back in the lounge of her former home being treated like a guest and hating every minute. She missed her apartment, the whole of which would fit inside Colm's lounge. She also missed Goose even if she was comfortable in the knowledge that the cat, with free access to her bedroom and the bowl full of food which Colm had left out, wouldn't be missing her.

'Cheese on toast. Eat up while it's hot. I'll be back in a sec. Just going to sort out the guest bedroom.'

She picked up a triangle and started to chew, trying not to cry – crying wasn't the mask she wore in her role, and it certainly wasn't part of her private life – but she couldn't seem to stop. Colm had mopped her up from the hospital before decamping to the canteen with the excuse of getting a drink. It was an excuse. What he'd really been doing was sorting out her bank to ensure that her cards were stopped, and new ones ordered. He'd even reported it to the guards even though there was little hope that they'd capture the assailant. It was something she wasn't that happy about until her emotions caught up with her brain and common sense kicked in. It hadn't been a straightforward snatch and grab, far from it. She'd been too surprised to respond to the initial attack so why the need to pull her out of the chair? There'd been no need. The person who attacked her was violent and maybe next time they'd do more than break a bone.

Her gaze wandered around the room like a greedy child in search of treats. Nothing had changed, from the polished wooden flooring to the large squidgy sofas, and his chair. The pile of medical journals stacked beside looked larger if anything. And yet everything had changed. It wasn't her home anymore but then it had never been hers not really. She'd always felt like a guest, unable or unwilling to stamp her mark on the place. It was difficult to remember now, the past blurred and hazy, overtaken as it had been by the events that had followed.

'Ready?' He stood there, still dressed in his work trousers and shirt, the tie loose at the neck, his hair ruffled, the grey starting to impinge on the dark brown. A tall, handsome man with everything going for him apart from her. She was suddenly reminded of his persistent phone calls, most of which she'd left to ring out. A history impossible to ignore and the reason she felt incredibly uncomfortable in his presence.

'If you could help me into the bathroom. I should be able to manage from there.' It would be difficult but there was no way she was going to ask him to assist her.

'Of course, I found one of your old T-shirts, which I've left along with a towel, toothbrush and paste.' He stood back as she slid into her wheelchair, managing to withhold a grimace from the sudden sharp pain in her stomach. That git of a thief had done a real number on her. She intended to chase up on the report first thing. He deserved to have a very hard book thrown at him.

'I'll wait outside, shall I?'

'There's no need, Colm. As long as you're in hollering distance.' Alana looked up at him. 'Thank you once again. I'm not sure what I would have done without your help.'

'You'd have managed. You always manage,' he said, turning away and pulling the door closed behind him, his head bent, his shoulders starting to stoop.

Alana sat where he'd left her, looking at the closed wood-panelled door which had cost him 500 euros a piece. Coming here had been the worst of mistakes. The memories from the past were starting to swamp her mind and make her doubt herself but more importantly, make her doubt her reasons for leaving. The only thing that was real, that could ground her in the truth of having made the right decision, was the dramatic staircase set in the middle of the hall, only a few steps from where she was sitting. She felt her mind drift back to that fateful day...

'Hurry up, Alana. You're going to be late. It's blueberry pancakes.'

Blueberry pancakes were the very last thing she could face so she spent the few seconds it took to slip on her slippers and tie the belt of her robe to think up an acceptable excuse. Colm wouldn't object. He'd be delighted to stuff his face full of the epicurean delight instead of the healthy bowl of porridge oats he usually allowed himself.

She stood poised on the small landing, her fingers gathering the fabric of her dressing gown, which was a tad too long on her five-two frame.

With her hand on the banister, she caught the skirt up with one hand and started skipping down the stairs, her mood as exuberant as her feet. She had a full day ahead of her and that's where her thoughts led her. A quick catch-up with Paddy and the team before assigning the work out for the day.

Her foot slipped, causing her heart to leap in her throat as her hand snagged around the handrail, painted white to match the décor. A slight pause as the world stilled. Her fingers dug into the wood. A fingernail bent back, then another, the keratin snapping and breaking under the pressure – the very least of her current concerns.

She hovered a second, a cry wrenched from her lips. A scream ringing out and echoing through the high-ceilinged room as her body bent back in comic-book fashion before pitching forward, headfirst towards the floor below.

Alana reached for the new toothbrush and tube of paste that Colm had laid at the edge of the sink, determined to free her mind of the painful memory. Losing the use of her legs was the price she'd had to pay for her life. She still didn't know if it was worth it.

Half an hour later and she was resting against a pile of fluffed up pillows, the pain excruciating after her exertions. Colm didn't say much, but his silence was proof enough that he'd been on tenterhooks over having to help her into bed.

'Got everything you need? I've left you some of my journals in case you have difficulty getting off to sleep.'

'Thank you.'

He stood in the doorway. The awkward silence was shattered by the shrill ring of the phone.

'It's for you.' He looked surprised but then so was she until she remembered there was a reason she loved working at the station. She wondered which one of her sharp-minded colleagues had tracked her down and how they'd gone about it.

Paddy's voice filled her ear. 'Alana, you alright?'

'Fine. just a bit of an issue with a git nicking my phone,' she replied, her tone deliberately set to neutral. There was no point in worrying him any more than necessary. That he'd found her was proof enough he'd worked out something was amiss. 'What you got for me?'

'A very dead Mason Clare, I'm sorry to say. We've arranged for Rusty to be in on the PM tomorrow but it's definitely murder. You're sure you're...?'

'I'm fine,' she repeated, determined to move the conversation in a different direction. 'William okay?'

'A veritable genius. That boy will go far.'

Alana smiled at that. 'I won't keep you. Well past both our bedtimes. Catch up tomorrow.'

She ended the call abruptly, her lips settling into the well-trodden lines and grooves of a frown. Mason Clare's death hadn't been totally unexpected but it still came as a shock to have their worst fears realised. With a bit of luck tomorrow's post-mortem would shed some light on the situation.

SEVENTEEN

Wednesday 6th September, 11 a.m.

'Ruan, this is Dr Mulholland but call him Rusty. We all do,' Paddy said, stepping back to let the two men shake hands. 'Rusty, Detective Ruan O'Hagan.'

'Hello, Ruan. Thank you for letting me assist with the post-mortem. It's with Dr Gabby Quinn, isn't it? Not a name I'm going to forget seeing as I'm married to a Gabriella.'

'That's right. She's just arrived. Gone to gown up. Should be out in a minute.'

'I'd better join her so. This way?' Rusty nodded in the direction of the changing rooms attached to the pathology suite at the University Hospital of Kerry.

'Do we need to follow?' William said, unsure of protocol now he was in someone else's jurisdiction and not his own.

'Nah, you're not back in hicky clicky Clonabee now, son.' Ruan slapped him hard on the back, jarring his bones and bouncing his breakfast against his ribs. 'This is Tralee, with all the fancy facilities that go with a top of the range hospital. We even have hot and cold running water in the autopsy suite, to go with the piped air con, Bluetooth headphones and seating for 300 medical students.'

William smiled, there was little else he could do with Paddy flicking him a tiny wink. If he had a bruise he'd put in a complaint, he thought, knowing full well that was all hot air and wind. Ruan meant well but he'd be glad that, after today, he'd never have to see the man again.

'This way and all will be revealed,' Ruan said, gesturing for them to precede him through an open door before escorting them into what looked like a circular movie theatre with the stage in the middle, the devil in the detail of the draped trolley, row of sinks, and rolled up hose in the corner. The room was packed full of student types in an array of hoodies, T-shirts and jeans. The usual garb he remembered from his days at garda college before regulation haircuts and dress codes had turned him into the wuss he was today.

'Over there, William,' Ruan pointed to a few spare seats right at the front. They'd barely settled and secured the headphones over their ears before Rusty entered the room flanked by Gabby Quinn.

Dr Quinn was tall and skeletally thin, the only two things William could make out from her green scrubs and matching paper hat. No, that wasn't quite right. The woman also had a sense of humour if the sight of her daisy-emblazoned pink wellies was anything to go by. He watched as she headed for a table of tools while Rusty peeled back the green surgical sheet, folding the fabric back on itself to reveal the man below. The man who had once been the living, breathing Mason Clare.

William swallowed then swallowed again, his mouth uncomfortably dry, needing no reminder that this was his first autopsy. He knew the rudiments, there were enough videos on YouTube for him to appreciate the difference between the cop shows that his mother seemed to watch on repeat.

'Hello and welcome. I'd like to introduce you to Dr Mulholland, a colleague up from Dublin who's here to see how we do things in Tralee.' The titter from the crowd stopped almost as quickly as it started, failing to gain any momentum at Dr Quinn's next words, which had the students reaching for a variety of screens and, in a few cases, notebooks and pens.

'Mr Clare was discovered yesterday in a body-shaped hole carved out of the underside of his mattress.' She snapped on her gloves, adjusting the fit around her fingers as she spoke. 'I don't think it's necessary to explain why we're treating his death as suspicious or the reason we have Dr Mulholland up from Dublin to assist with the autopsy. As a rule of thumb, it is advisable to look on every unwitnessed death with a suspicious eye remembering that, as the physician you are the one who will be making decisions as to whether to request an autopsy. That Mr Clare was also discovered in unusual circumstances is a no-brainer. Today we are going to concentrate on the external inspection of Mr Clare, looking at his body for any signs of injury, disease or trauma. After, we'll be focusing on his overall condition, including rigor mortis, post-mortem lividity and decomposition. Good documentation is essential to this process especially as we suspect that Mr Clare did not die from natural causes – he certainly didn't place himself under the mattress – and that's the part I will be picking up on when we meet later to discuss this. If you can get the documentation bit right, then the rest will follow. Let's crack on, Dr Mulholland.'

'Sorry about this.' Ruan leant forward, his voice a whisper. 'It won't take long to get the teaching part out the way.'

William didn't mind. It gave him something to think about other than the way they were measuring the man. His height and his girth before starting on a full skin inspection and, for some reason, spending a long time on the eyes before shifting to any distinguishing marks like moles or tattoos, all relayed through his headphones while he concentrated on the soles of the man's feet, bluish grey in death. The hardest part came next, the Y-shaped incision that started at the top of each shoulder and extended down to the breastbone before continuing vertically, Dr Quinn's voice rumbling in the background.

'This incision allows us to access and examine the chest and abdominal cavities, thus providing us with a clear view of the organs within. While Mr Clare might be no longer with us, that's no reason to be sloppy. Too light a cut and we won't be able to get through the fascia below but too deep a one and there's a risk of damaging the organs.'

William allowed his concentration to wander, his eyes flickering left then right, watching the students diligently recording every word. It wasn't that he wasn't interested in the proceedings, the outcome of which would be vital to the investigation, it was more he was scared he'd disgrace himself by having to run outside to throw up. As a diversion, he tried to focus on why the killer had chosen to place the body in such an odd place. Mason would have been discovered earlier if the aftershave hadn't been man enough to mask the smell of decomposing flesh. It had given his killer a few hours' grace at best. But grace to do what and why? William blinked at the sight of the procession of organs being removed and inspected before being handed over to the porter for weighing, measuring and photographing. There was also the stuffing from the mattress to consider and what had happened to it until he remembered the large swimming bag that Mason was well known to take with him for his morning dip. William wasn't up to date on the different materials used in the construction of a mattress but presumably whatever it was could be squashed into a relatively small space before being zipped up and carried out to the car.

The cavity was empty, the discussion between the two doctors now a silent one as they walked over to the sinks to clean up. Someone had seen fit to switch off their microphones now the procedure was finished, and the med students were starting to file out. All that was left was for the body to be sewn up, a job that was being left to the pathology assistant by the look of things.

'Wake up, lad. No dawdling. Time for lunch or this crowd will beat us to the best grub. I've arranged to meet both doctors in the hospital canteen for a debrief. It's always liver and bacon on a Wednesday.' Ruan prodded him in the back with the tip of his finger before standing to his feet and stretching. 'Or the sausages are excellent if you don't like offal. I might see if I can snaffle a couple for Wally.'

William swallowed back a groan, his attention fixed on the two backs in front of him and not on the tray of organs awaiting the next step in the autopsy process: the removal of thin slices for study under the microscope. Either the man was impervious to the state of William's belly or getting his own back for yesterday. By the sound of his chuckle, he suspected that it was a combination of both. The sooner he got back to Dublin the better.

Ruan hadn't been lying about either the liver or the sausages, but William chose neither, instead settling for a bowl of soup and a slab of soda bread, which he concentrated on while the conversation ebbed and flowed round him.

'What's the rigor mortis time frame again?' Ruan asked, starting on his sausages.

'As in what time do we think Mr Clare died? Full muscle stiffening is usually around twelve hours and lasts up to twenty-four,' Rusty explained, placing his spoon on the edge of his bowl. 'Its presence or lack of can't be used as a reliable approximation of the time of death though but we're agreed on the small hours of Sunday morning, aren't we, Gabby?'

'Indeed yes. Poor Mr Clare most likely was asleep when he was attacked, and the hope is that he wouldn't have known much about it.'

'You know what happened then?'

'Not until we get the toxicology report back, but we did find a bluish cyanosis to the nail beds, mouth, lips, gums and fingers and petechial haemorrhages on the inside of both eyelids along with the sclera of the eye.'

'Then it's suffocation?'

'Not necessarily.' Gabby picked up her wrap and inspected the contents before taking a bite. It was a moment before she continued, the wrap back on the plate, cheese and tomato spilling out from the end. 'There was none of the discoid bruising we'd expect if hands were used to obstruct the neck.' She clarified what she meant by placing the pads of her fingers round her neck before using them to pick up her wrap. 'And no ligature marks if something else was used like a tie or a piece of string. Nothing in the windpipe to obstruct airflow to the lungs either and with the hyoid bone intact we're short of evidence to pin a cause of death to.'

'What about a pillow or a plastic bag?' Paddy said.

'Probably no to either. A pillow would need quite a lot of force and usually leaves bruising to the tissues, both skin and underlying, while a bag has to be secured in order to stop air from seeping in. We found no signs of trauma to any part of Mr Clare's head or neck.'

William had finished his lunch. He placed his spoon back in the bowl and turned to Gabby. 'In effect what you're saying is that Mr Clare was suffocated but by something that hasn't left any evidence on the body.'

Gabby glanced at Rusty briefly before replying. 'That's about right, William. A bit of a mystery.'

'What kind of thing are we looking for?'

'Anything really that cuts off the air supply. You agree, Rusty?'

'Not anything, Gabby. Something either small enough to be portable, bearing in mind the killer already had a bag full of mattress stuffing to negotiate, or something innocuous, a household item easily glossed over as unsuspicious.'

William stared at Rusty briefly, taking a moment to run through a mental catalogue of Mason Clare's house, made easy because of the man's spartan lifestyle, but quickly running out of ideas. There was nothing pliable enough, apart from a pillow or a plastic bag, which they'd already ruled out. No, that wasn't quite right, he remembered, thinking back to the contents of Mason's bin and what he'd found discarded on top.

'What about plastic wrap?'

EIGHTEEN

Wednesday 6th September, 12 p.m.

By the time Alana surfaced, Colm had laid the table for a late breakfast, and arranged for a selection of powered wheelchairs to be brought to the house for her to try.

'I'm afraid this is the only one we have in stock currently that will fit your frame, but the upside is that it's easy enough to use. An on and off button, a joystick controller, an emergency stop button and three speeds.'

Alana glanced over the fluorescent-pink powered wheelchair with a jaundiced eye before giving a sharp little nod. If she wanted to be mobile, then she had little choice but to accept. It was this contraption, going off sick or relying on the charity of others, and as the last two weren't an option she was stuck with the Barbie look. Oh joy. The only positive was that, with the wheelchair taxi pulling into the drive, she had no time to dwell on how her pink plaster coordinated with her mode of transport.

That came later when she manoeuvred up the ramp outside

work, coming to a shaky stop inside the automatic doors, the clock behind stretching towards one.

'Mother of God, whatever's happened?' It would have to be Mary staffing the front desk, again, Alana thought, managing to push out a smile. She didn't have a bad word to say about the woman, but she wasn't in the mood for her mothering.

'A little run-in with one of the oiks who have nothing better to do with their time. That reminds me. If you get a minute, can you give the guards over in Dundrum a bell to see if anyone has handed in a grey bag?'

'Of course. Is there anything you need? Your poor arm.' Mary blinked, her eyes popping out of her head at the colour of her cast and her chair. While Alana liked pink, she was usually a little more conservative in her choice of workwear. It was black, grey or navy, which made a mockery of the large sloppy blue top she'd borrowed from Colm – one of the few things she could drag her arm through. At least it wasn't pink. 'How are you going to push—?'

'Has the DS been looking for me?' Alana stopped her mid-sentence. A night spent mostly awake simply because she was too scared to close her eyes had left her polite gene in desperate need of a reboot.

'Asked you to go straight up once you'd finally arrived. His words not mine,' Mary qualified, looking embarrassed, which made Alana realise she might have been a little too abrupt.

'I haven't arrived, though. In fact, I've phoned to let you know I've been indefinitely delayed,' she said. 'Any post?' Mary joined her in a little smile, as they both remembered the far from funny incident with the suspected letter bomb during her last case. It was all that was needed to deflect the conversation away from her and back onto their normal footing. Alana couldn't cope with anything more than superficial currently.

The office was quiet until she caught the side of the door

with her wheel and sent it crashing back against the wall, causing Lorrie to jump out of her chair, her hand to her mouth at the curse which had slipped out. There was no sign of either Flynn or Tatty, which Alana considered a bonus. The jungle drums would hopefully be loud and powerful enough to negate the need for her to explain to all and sundry about her misfortune. However, there was a stranger in the spare desk by the window busily tapping away on her laptop with barely a glance in her direction. No, not a stranger. The new detective she'd been lumbered with. What was it that Paddy had called her again, apart from the nun. Eve Rohan. That was it.

'What happened?' Lorrie's question had her skimming through an abbreviated version of events while she watched her scoop up a spare mug and pour her a coffee, adding two sugars, giving it a stir and placing it on her desk.

So that was the way of things to come for the next four or so weeks, was it? People automatically going to her assistance without a word or a glance. She'd have to get used to it. No, she'd never be able to do that.

Ideally, she'd have liked a moment or two to adjust to this new normal but not with the sight of their new recruit pushing away from her desk and heaving to her feet. There wasn't time to do anything except to set her face to neutral at the sight of the high-neck cream blouse, dung-brown cardigan, skirt and shoes ensemble. *The nun* as a nickname was cruel but strangely apt.

'Hello, I'm Alana Mack, good to meet you. Eve, isn't it?' She held out her left hand. 'Excuse the state of me,' she suddenly felt compelled to add. There was something about the quiet, middle-aged woman that made her feel uncomfortable, as if she was being judged and found wanting. Paddy had told her that Eve was a miserable piece of work with a downer on both sexes following a nasty divorce, which was all she needed on the team. However, Alana was the type of person who liked to make her own mind up about her colleagues. While she'd listen to the gossip, she discounted most of it.

'That's right.' Eve ignored the hand, instead placing her mug down on the counter with a little bang. 'I'll have one if you're making it, Lorrie. Tea, no sugar, hold the milk.'

'I'll make it.' Alana flicked the switch of the kettle and plonked a teabag in the centre before adding hot water and giving it a quick stir. 'Here you go. Sorry, I can't carry it to your desk for you.' She turned back to face Lorrie. 'Can you do me a fav please and let Tatty and Flynn know we'll have a full catch-up at four, when Pad and William should be back. Also, see where we are with the DNA for Jane. I think it's worth trying Interpol's new Bonaparte genealogy programme. It's something I only heard about myself last night.' That she'd read it in one of Colm's journals while she'd tried to get off to sleep was none of their business. 'We really do need to find out who she is.'

'I've already seen to that.'

You've already seen to that. Alana shifted her gaze from Lorrie's startled expression and over to Eve and where she was leaning back in her chair, her look smug with a touch of belligerence round the edges.

'Really?'

'I could see immediately from the notes that finding Jane Doe's identity was key to the investigation moving forward, therefore I did what I deemed necessary.'

Alana had already reached seven in her count to ten by the time the woman had finished her sentence, simply because she couldn't come up with a better alternative for stemming her sudden temper flare. She took the extra three seconds needed to complete the task before formulating a reply, not that it did any good to either her mood or her manner. She didn't need Paddy's warning for her to know that Eve was going to be trouble. A loose cannon in their tightly knit team but one she was quite happy to take on.

'It will be your turn to make the drinks next. We take it in turns in the office. I view all the staff of equal value and that includes in the coffee-making department.' She ignored Eve's scowl, instead approaching Lorrie. 'Pop up to see how Rogene and the team are doing and if she'll be free for the briefing, please.'

NINETEEN

Wednesday 6th September, 4.30 p.m.

Alana returned from her meeting with Leo to a room full of chatter, which dimmed as soon as everyone caught sight of her new contraption. No one had asked her about her injury when they'd traipsed back from lunch, and she hadn't referred to it. With Mary in the know the news would have spread throughout the station like wildfire. Paddy and William were also back, which meant they could get on with finding this maniac.

'Afternoon, everyone.' She caught Rusty's worried look and managed a brief smile before continuing. 'I'd like to introduce you to Detective Eve Rohan, who's just joined us from Roscommon.' She waited a beat for the mumbled welcomes to die down before continuing. The only concession she made to her fractured arm was in passing her tablet over to Paddy with a nod.

'Let's start with Mr Clare. Mr Clare's body was discovered in his bedroom late yesterday evening, hidden under the burrowed-out mattress. Luckily for us Dr Mulholland was able to be present at the PM. What have you got for us, Rusty?'

'A straightforward case of suffocation, although the method used is highly irregular. Based on our findings we believe that Mr Clare was killed sometime during the early hours of the 3rd of September. The team found a half-used bottle of Zopiclone, a well-known night sedation, in his bathroom cabinet, which suggests that he suffered from insomnia and usually took a sleeping tablet to help him drop off, something his doctor was happy to confirm. The SOCOs bagged and tagged his hands at the scene but we could find no evidence of the defence wounds we'd expect if he'd tried to fight off his attacker, the implication being that he wouldn't have known what was happening to him.'

'At least something to be thankful for. And the irregular method?' Alana said, gently massaging the tips of her fingers.

'That's down to the clever deducing powers of William.' Rusty smiled over at where William had dipped his chin to his notebook. 'He remembered a scrunched-up piece of plastic wrap disposed of in the kitchen waste, not unusual until we realised that there weren't any rolls of the stuff or indeed any empty cartons awaiting recycling.'

'So, the killer smothered him by wrapping...?' Alana didn't continue, there was no need. The image was more than enough to give her nightmares for the rest of the week.

''Fraid so. We were completely at sea as to how it had been done and with no fracture to the hyoid bone or suffocation marks on the face or neck. The scenario is the only one that fits the evidence available. It also comes with the added possibility of securing finger or palm prints from the wrap,' he continued.

'That's brilliant. I'm still puzzled by the neighbour though. Her testimony seems to be more than a little contrary or am I wrong in thinking that she was adamant she saw Mr Clare leaving for his morning swim?'

'Ruan has agreed to re-interview her,' Paddy said, looking up from the tablet before returning his attention back to updating the board. 'Mr Clare was such a distinctive gentleman, distinctive in his appearance with a long flowing white beard and in his form of dress, which usually included a hat and brightly coloured clothing. All it would have needed was for someone to have dressed up and behaved in a similar manner for the short spell of time it would have taken them to make their way from the house to the car, a large bag slung over their shoulders, which we think may have included the compacted stuffing from the mattress.'

'And there's no sign of the car?'

Paddy shook his head. 'They're revisiting the ANPR in the area as well as performing a house to house in the immediate vicinity. Mr Clare must have been watched and for some time for someone to model his actions almost exactly.'

Alana drummed her fingers against the side of her chair, her eyes on the board as she tried to work out if the team over in Kerry had ticked all the right boxes or if there was something else they could be doing. Finding the car was important but realistically it could be anywhere. Kerry was well known for its scenic, narrow winding roads where there was little point in installing the expensive camera systems that monitored number plates. The car was either out of the area or hidden away in someone's garage or lock-up, either way impossible to find with their current lack of manpower. There were more important things the guards could be doing other than looking for something impossible to find.

'What do we know about Clare's background both before he returned to Ireland and after?'

'Lived quietly in Kerry. Used to be seen out walking his dog but, apart from his morning swim, he was a bit of a recluse by all accounts. Ruan remembers seeing him. He apparently made for a flamboyant presence with his choice of dress and immaculate beard.'

'Which is a lesson to all of us although I'm not sure what in,' Alana replied, her voice dry. 'And New York, Pad?'

'According to Ruan, he worked for the NYPD for twenty-five years before taking retirement. He's been in contact with his chief of patrol and is now trying to catch up with his partner from the 76th Precinct, which is the station he worked from.' Paddy shrugged, clearly at as much of a loss as she was as to the inner workings of America's law enforcement.

'And what was his role?'

'Patrol cop, which, from what I can gather, relates to one of our uniformed guards.'

'Okay. Let me know when you have more. Oh, and can you put Barney's dad onto the interview list please. We'll also have to bring Barney back along with his wife to see what their alibis are for Mason's death.' She watched him add the names, leaving a blank next to that of the interviewer. There'd be time enough to assign staff at the end of the update. 'Right, let's move on to Jane.' She tilted her head at Rusty. 'That's you.' She smiled. 'Anything of interest from the tox reports?'

'You could say that. Not from the bone itself but you already know my thoughts on that. A negative result isn't indication that poison wasn't used, only that the type of toxin is one not routinely laid down in bony tissue.' Rusty leant back in his chair, the front legs leaving the ground in a manner that had terrified Alana ever since her accident. 'What I did find was glycyrrhizin acid in the stomach of the dead crab, and in a dose larger than would be expected from an occasional consumer of the product. In short, Jane was tipped into a condition known as pseudo-hyperaldosteronism through over-ingestion of the glycyrrhizin root, leading to a heart arrhythmia and subsequent cardiac arrest.'

Alana prevented herself from rolling her eyes, but it was touch and go for a second. The doc, as much as she liked him, did have a bad habit of reverting to medical speak at any given opportunity. 'In English if you please.'

'She ate too much liquorice, causing her heart to stop.'

Alana hadn't been expecting that and, by the collective sharp intakes of breath from round the room, neither had anyone else. 'She ate too much liquorice, as in the sweeties? But surely…?'

'It's rare I'll grant you, very rare indeed but there have been a handful of cases to support it. Basically, too much of the root, and we're talking a considerable amount rather than the odd sweet or even box of sweets, leads to a sharp lowering of blood potassium and a related rise in blood pressure.' He qualified his words with a wave of his hands. 'It would have taken days, weeks probably. If she'd been found at home with the associated empty boxes of the stuff in her recycling we wouldn't even be here, particularly if her heart had already been known to be compromised. Death would have been assumed to be from natural causes induced by over ingestion of the stuff. But we're not. The question now must be whether she died of natural causes, linked to her medical history, or whether someone force-fed her the stuff before placing her in the pot.'

'And to do that we need to speak to her doctor, which we can't do until we know her identity,' Alana said, completing his sentence for him.

'Actually, I've just had a reply back from Interpol.' Eve raised her voice from her desk over by the window. 'Because of the urgency of the case, they decided to upload the DNA to Bonaparte straight away and it came back with a hit, almost immediately.'

Alana was tempted to throw back a sarcastic response along the lines of *well hurry up then, what are you waiting for, a drum-roll or a pat on the back.* Totally unfair, of course, as the woman was only doing her job. It was the way she was doing it that was irritating. The self-satisfied smug smile that was bound to put the other detectives' noses out of joint. Instead, she raised her left eyebrow while she waited for Eve to elaborate with Jane's real name.

'They've been able to come up with a first-generation match.'

'A first-generation match as in?'

'As in they were able to match the profile to a Ciara Buckley, Jane Doe's daughter. I've looked her up. She was easy to find. A single psychotherapist living and working in Bandon.'

'Well, that seems easy enough, doesn't it? Let's pull up Ciara's birth certificate and take it from there.'

'I already have!' The sigh was as heartfelt as it was long. 'Ciara's mother is called Paula Buckley.'

'Okay, good thinking. Let's find this Paula Buckley and start a deep dive into her life to see if it throws up any clues as to why someone would want to kill her.'

Alana watched as Paddy added the relevant tasks to the board, frustration suddenly warring with anxiety. They had two adopted brothers, one dead while the other was at the centre of the most peculiar of crimes. DNA, the magic bullet of modern policing had only gone and thrown another layer into the mix.

'There's a slight problem,' Lorrie said, popping her head up from where she'd been tapping away at her laptop. 'I've just traced Paula Buckley on PULSE. She's dead and has been for the last forty-two years.'

TWENTY

Wednesday 6th September, 4.55 p.m.

'That's... unusual.' Alana was going to use the word impossible, but experience had taught her that nothing was impossible when it came to the vagaries of the human condition. It might not be something she'd come across before, however there was bound to be an explanation. She dismissed her first thought of Interpol having made a mistake. Interpol didn't make mistakes, and as for DNA, the possibility of two people sharing the same DNA profile was minute unless they were biological twins. It was certainly something they'd consider but she didn't think twins was the answer in this case.

She glanced at her watch, noting the time with a frown. It's not as if they were going to be able to do much about it now. Staying late in the office was a completely different ball game after last night's assault.

'Okay. We'll arrange for Ciara to come in for questioning tomorrow.' Alana eyed the map of Dublin on the other side of the room and the smaller one of Ireland as a whole. 'Bandon's outside Cork so let's make it for eleven o'clock, which should leave her plenty of time to get here. Lorrie, give her a bell for me and I'd like you to sit in on the interview.'

'Hey, wait a minute...' Alana turned towards Eve. 'I think I should be in on that. I'm far more experienced for a start and I was the one who—'

'Who what? Contacted Interpol, thirty seconds before I asked Lorrie to do it? Is that what you were about to say? I don't need to remind you that this is your first day on the team and the first on the case, a case we've been working since Monday. For the record, I've put together a team induction programme for you, Eve, to complement the station one you completed yesterday. It should only take the morning. Tomorrow afternoon will be time enough to assign you tasks on the case.'

Alana turned away, furious that she'd allowed her displeasure to show in both her words and her tone. Paddy had warned her Eve was trouble and, when she had a minute, she planned to weasel out all the background she could on their newest recruit. She blinked then blinked again, forcing herself to focus on the board and not the antics of the woman in the corner clattering and banging her way through closing up for the night. There was Mason and Barney's father left to interview as well as Barney to reinterview. She'd ask Paddy and William to do the first while she'd get Flynn involved with the latter.

It took ten minutes to update the board while the office emptied of all the essential staff apart from Paddy. She'd intimated with a tilt of her head that she wanted him to stay.

'What's going on, Pad?' were her first words, her left hand instinctively reaching for her right in a protective move as if to shield herself from what was coming.

Paddy rested against the nearest desk, his hands in his pockets, the sound of coins chinking filling the air. 'Eve is well known for being trouble but I'm not sure what her beef is with our department.'

'But you do think there is something going on?'

'It certainly seems that way. The last I heard, she was happy enough making one of my friends miserable over in Roscommon, so much so that he asked about the possibility of getting a job on our team. She's like that. Has a reputation as long as you like for upsetting people. It's almost as if she views it her life's aim to manage people out the door.'

'So, you've no idea why she left Roscommon and moved up to Dublin?'

'Not a scooby but there will be a reason. Eve Rohan is the kind of person who only suits herself.' He slipped off the desk and went to pick up his jacket from the back of his chair. 'Probably after my job, or yours, or even Barry's,' he qualified. 'Good enough at the work but quite happy to trample over anyone who gets in her way to the top, so be careful, eh. You staying much longer? I'm happy to give you a lift.'

'Thank you, but I have a taxi booked.'

The lie traipsed off her tongue but there was no way she was prepared to ruin Paddy's evening for any longer than she had to. She had the number of a taxi firm who'd assured her they were happy to take her home as and when she wanted them to.

'Okay. See you in the morning.'

'See you.'

An hour later and Alana decided to call it a day. The writing on the screen was now a hazy mass of blurs; the combination of tiredness, strong painkillers and the stress of the last twenty-four hours had resulted in a niggling migraine. There was work to do, important work on Ciara Buckley's life, but it would have to wait until tomorrow. She wasn't a quitter, Alana had never quit on anything, but realistically, if she wanted to make it into the office in the morning then she needed to go home. It was a bit of a surprise at how quickly Eve had packed up her things and left without a quibble. No thought of carrying on unlike the rest of them, who she'd had to practically throw out the office with an assortment of threats ranging from disciplinary to intense disappointment. It didn't need a chat with Paddy for her to realise that they were going to have a problem with the woman. Eve was obviously intelligent and well read if she'd heard about Bonaparte, but she also appeared to have a hidden agenda, which seemed to include Alana's head sticking out the end of a pole somewhere.

That's it. Time to go or I'll be here all night.

Alana went to pick up her phone to call the taxi firm only to stop, the case crushing between her fingers, her heart lurching towards her mouth at the scrabbling sound outside in the corridor – the corridor on the detective's floor which she knew to be empty apart from her.

The reality of the corridor being situated in a busy garda station or that it might be someone returning to collect something they'd forgotten, didn't filter through her sudden, irrational wall of panic. Her scaredy-cat switch appeared to be on permanent override since last night's attack.

She scanned the top of her desk for a weapon, hysteria warring with tears at the sight of her laptop, her mug and a box of pens. The station's empty desk policy was a serious one, failure to comply accompanied by a stern rollocking from the chief every time she left anything on top. There was nothing of use unless she was planning on poking the intruder in the eye with her biro.

She attacked the chair's controls with as much force as she dared. Facing the perp suddenly seemed as important as the pen, which she'd slipped up her sleeve with no thought of how she intended to use it.

With the controls engaged, she shifted the chair towards the door and the corridor beyond, her knuckles gleaming white under her clenched fist.

TWENTY-ONE

Wednesday 6th September, 6.15 p.m.

The corridor was empty of strangers. It was also empty of people, officers or otherwise. Instead, she found herself staring into the mournful eyes of the largest dog she'd ever seen.

Alana had been, up until recently, an animal ambivalent. Someone who'd never had a pet and therefore didn't see the point. All that had changed when Goose, her stray cat, had arrived on the scene. That didn't make her an animal lover, far from it. She'd never owned a dog and was of the opinion the less she had to do with the beasts the better for all concerned.

'Wally, where are you?' The sound of William's hushed tones underpinned by a sense of urgency didn't quite make her smile; it would take a few moments longer for her heart to settle back where it belonged and for her to try manoeuvring her lips into something so superficial.

'Wally. Come here, boy.'

Alana dropped her arm down, hoping against hope that the dog wouldn't decide to damage the only part of her still working outside of her brain and her gob. By the time William rounded the corner, Wally was sitting by her side, his head resting in her lap while she played with his ears.

'Ah, I can explain.'

The taxi driver pulled into Alana's apartment complex, with William following behind in his jeep. Within minutes she'd directed him to her ground-floor flat, a large bag of dog food and biscuits dangling from one of his hands, Wally's lead in the other.

'It's nice enough here, isn't it? I'd like to buy my own place when I can afford it,' he said, glancing around the airy lounge before making for the wall of shelves and browsing through the books.

Alana nodded but remained silent. She'd never envisioned that she'd be the part owner of a dog but there'd been no other choice when William's mother had flatly refused to take Wally.

'At least he seems to have made himself at home.' She watched Goose conducting a grand tour of all the best sniffy bits before jumping on the bed and regally waiting for Wally to join her.

'You're sure you don't mind?'

I don't have much choice about it.

But she didn't, not really. What she did mind was the sound of her intercom beeping because there was only one person who ever called round this late. It looked like father and son were about to be reunited, whether William liked it or not, unless he decided to hide under the bed or in the wardrobe. Alana would at least give him the option.

'That'll be your dad, William.'

'Thought it might. You know, it doesn't bother me that you're seeing him.'

That's good of you. Alana wasn't seeing Billy, she wasn't

seeing anyone, but that was none of his business. Instead of replying she maintained a dignified silence.

'I'll let him in on my way out, shall I?' he added, with a sudden look of uncertainty in the way his eyes couldn't quite meet hers. 'I'll also bring some more dog food into work, no point in you being out of pocket.'

'Why not drop it off on the way in tomorrow? We can interview Barney's dad straight after. I had intended for you to accompany Paddy, but it will be good to get that little box ticked as soon as.'

'You're happy enough me pushing you round? That yoke won't go anywhere near my car,' he said, nodding at the powered chair. They both ignored the impatient-sounding second ring.

A morning out of the contraption, as she was starting to term it, would be welcome. Her own chair had been made to measure and fit like a glove. This one made her ache in places she'd forgotten she owned. It would have the added advantage of delaying her start time and therefore any interactions with Eve.

'More than happy, thank you. Going round in circles isn't a good look.'

'Okay. Wally can come too. He's used to the car now.'

He pushed the door open with a force that had Billy reeling backwards, giving him the opportunity needed to squeeze past with only the briefest of greetings.

'Hi, Dad. Bye, Dad.'

'What the hell?' Billy stood in front of the door, his head swinging between the empty hall and where Alana was struggling not to laugh.

'Come and meet my new dog, Billy,' she said, pointing in the direction of the bedroom, where the two animals were curled up in a tight ball, forgetting for a second that she hadn't told him about her accident.

So much had happened since she'd last seen him that she was struggling to keep up.

'What the hell, Alana,' he repeated, the door closed, a takeaway pizza box abandoned on the table along with what smelled like a bag of her favourite garlic dough balls.

'Oh, this little thing?' Her nonchalance was only partly successful, her eyes glistening as the memory of last night's attack resurfaced in all its technicolour glory. 'Had a run-in with a thug and sadly this time I came off worse. Most remiss of me.' She swallowed the lump in her throat and added a shaky smile for good measure, her voice taking on all the characteristics of an X-rated night-time chatline. 'The good thing is that William has been kind enough to furnish me with his dog although I'm not so sure he'll be much good when the chips are down.' They both turned to look at where Wally was now lying on his back, a rumble of snores audible across the room.

'I didn't even know William had a dog.'

'I wouldn't let that worry you. Neither did he until earlier.' Alana managed to manoeuvre to the table and the enticing smells wafting across the room. 'Go grab the plates, there's a love. I probably should be sending you away for the sake of my waistline but that's not happening.'

'There's nothing to you.'

'Which won't last if I'm not able to come up with some kind of an exercise programme while I'm incapacitated.'

He arranged the plates on the table, before opening the box, not bothering with cutlery. 'You know I'm happy to arrange for—'

'A personal trainer? If that's what you were about to say, then forget it. I'll sort out my own programme, but thanks for offering,' Alana replied, holding a slice of pizza an inch from her mouth, aware that Wally had shifted from the bed in less time than it had taken for her to decide on which slice to start with, his inner food radar in no need of a service anytime soon. He was now staring at her tea with a gimlet eye. Were dogs allowed pizza? Probably not but that didn't stop a sliver of chicken finding its way from her plate to his mouth.

'Okay, I know when I'm beaten. So, how's the case going? Found out any more about your Jane Doe or Mason Clare for that matter?'

If he was trying to annoy her, he wasn't going to manage. She was used to his ways. Instead of replying she took a moment to choose a dough ball before taking a large bite. Her way of ignoring the question.

'The neighbour has agreed to be interviewed,' he continued, choosing another slice of pizza.

'The neighbour has what!' Alana rested the bread on the edge of her plate, her appetite disappearing as quickly as it had arrived, any thought of ignoring him forgotten.

'You heard. Her bath hoist has given up the ghost so...'

'So, you stepped in, and offered to replace it?'

Alana was furious at him, and furious with herself for becoming involved with such a slimy toad of a man. She'd thought they were on the same wavelength in Spain. She'd even considered whether her self-imposed singledom was selfish to both of them. When she next met with her physiotherapist, she'd ask whether it was possible to have a complete frequency reset.

Wally must have sensed the change in atmosphere. She'd read somewhere dogs were good at that. He turned round and walked back to the bedroom, his tail flagging to half-mast. She felt like joining him. In fact, there was nothing to stop her.

'Thank you for the pizza but I think you'd better go.'

'Nah, come on...'

'Come on nothing, Colm.'

She pulled a face at the slip, a slip that didn't go unnoticed if Billy's suddenly exaggerated movements, as he set down his barely touched slice of pizza, were anything to go by. After all, friendship or not, no man wanted to be reminded of the ex waiting in the wings.

Alana had never been one for sharing her innermost thoughts and feelings on the subject of Colm, especially with someone who she only thought of as a friend. She wasn't about to start now but she was suddenly feeling decidedly uncomfortable.

'I take it your ex was the one you called to come to your aid when you, er...?'

Alana lifted her phone, the old phone that Colm had lent her until she could find the time to sort out a replacement. 'It was Colm or the guards.'

'And you thought your ex was the better of the two evils? Skewed decision-making there, Alana.'

'I had no choice.'

'No, you had a choice. You had many choices in Malaga to shift our relationship onto the kind of footing you know I was hoping for. It's not as if I've made a secret of it.'

'Billy...'

'Not this time, Alana. I'm done.'

Alana was left staring at the closed door, and the feeling she'd lost something. She wasn't sure what.

TWENTY-TWO

Thursday 7th September, 9 a.m.

Waldo Mulcahy was thin, but not in the way of the naturally born skinny. There was nothing healthy in the pared back flesh clinging to fragile bone or the yellow hue to his hollowed-out cheeks. Waldo was ill, terminal even. Alana didn't have to witness the oxygen tubing piercing each of his nostrils to realise the man supping away at his mug of tea was managing on borrowed time. And here she was about to make it worse.

'He's deaf but don't shout, for God's sake. He can't abide being shouted at. I'll bring you some tea. It might encourage him to drink. He's not for drinking.' The nurse bustled out the room with a shake of her head, her red ponytail swinging behind her.

'What do the guards want with a poor ole man like me?'

The strength in his voice was a surprise as was the way he flicked his gaze to the corner of the room and the only other chair, which William was quick to settle on. 'Always rest your arse cheeks when you get the chance, eh, lad.' The cackle was accompanied by a wheezy cough, which went on and on, changing his lips from red to blue. William went to stand only to sink back at the sight of the man flapping his hand at him. 'Alright in a sec,' he managed to gasp. 'The asbestos hasn't won, yet.'

The nurse came back, her eyes flitting around the room, taking in the scene in the same way Alana would a crime one, and reading it exactly, her hand now on Waldo's wrist while the other adjusted the level of oxygen being delivered.

'Ah, Mr Mulcahy, don't be distressing yourself or I'll be sending them on their way,' she said, her voice stiffening along with her spine.

'Don't be like that, Dora.' He took a couple of deep, steadying breaths, his hands now held out in front of him, rock steady. 'There, you see. Nothing to get your knickers in a twist for.'

'Upset him and you're out of here quicker than you can blink, got it.' She plonked the tray down before turning with a swish of her hips, totally lost under the bagginess of her scrubs.

'And the worst of it is she means it. Heart of gold, not that any of us have been able to find it.'

'Right.' Alana frowned, using the microscopic time particle to rearrange her thoughts. She'd checked Waldo Mulcahy up on the system before she'd left the office and knew all about his past. A bit of petty thievery when he was barely out of his teens then the life of a perfect citizen, or one that covered his tracks. Either way it wasn't important. It wasn't as if he was in the frame for either death. That he recognised them for what they were was indication enough that he was on one or other side of the fence. Cop or criminal. It was only relevant that she knew which. 'This is Detective William Slattery and I'm Alana Mack from the Clonabee branch of the NBCI.'

'Here to tell me about Mason.' He wrapped his hands round his mug, the knuckles almost ready to break through the threadbare covering of skin, his attention now fixed on the hazy skim forming on the top of his drink.

She wondered who he'd heard it from, not that it mattered, not really. Probably Barney. The main thing was that the door had been pushed open on the conversation, something she was about to take full advantage of but not before offering her respects.

'We're very sorry for your loss, Mr Mulcahy.' A quick incline of his head was all she got in response. 'Had you seen your son recently?'

He looked at her then, his eyes rheumy and with a thin film of moisture trapped on the surface. 'Mason was never one for family – well, for our family when he found out he'd been adopted,' he amended, his speech slow and laborious. 'We rarely spoke after he left. Nothing in common, or some such twaddle.'

There was a running dialogue hidden between the words, a script she'd heard before many times. A New York cop like Mason Clare, albeit retired, with an ex-con for a dad and a fisherman for a brother. Alana always thought being ashamed of one's background was one of the worst sins imaginable. Barney was a decent enough bloke, the same as his dad appeared to be. There was a chance she was reading the situation incorrectly, but she didn't think so. This family disconnect required careful probing.

'So, when was the last time you spoke with him?'

Waldo spread his hands, answer enough that it was too long for him to recall with any degree of certainty. 'Years.'

The poor, poor man.

'What about Barney?'

'He popped in yesterday.' He raised his mug but not as far as his mouth. 'But then Barney's me mate. Always has been. They're not blood brothers. You know that, right?'

She nodded. 'You adopted them both?'

'They were inseparable. Take one and we had to take the other. Not that big an ask, at the time.'

She hesitated briefly. 'I don't mean to be intrusive but according to our records you adopted them both a year into your marriage. Was there a reason for that?' Alana had friends who'd adopted but it was usually after a period of trying to conceive. A year didn't seem long enough somehow to make such a big decision.

'I couldn't have children or that's what the doctors told me. Mumps when I was a kid.' He took a sip of his tea, his hands shaking, the liquid rippling across the surface. 'Dympna was a bit younger than me but already set on a family. It was something we agreed on before we walked down the aisle.'

'And yet, within a year of being a mum, she left, leaving you holding both babies, so to speak?'

'That's right.'

'Any ideas as to why?'

'No clue. She didn't take anything except her bag and her coat. I thought she'd be back in five minutes.'

'And the boys – they never heard from her after?' William asked, leaning forward, his elbows on his knees, his chin resting in his cupped hands.

'And why would you want to be knowing about that, young fella? It were years ago.'

'Just trying to get some background on Mason. You know about what happened to Barney and what he found in his pots?'

Waldo rummaged in his pocket before withdrawing a pile of tissues and taking a moment to dab his mouth before popping in a mint and chewing for a couple of seconds. 'And you think I know something about that?'

Alana glanced down at where her left arm was clasping her right before meeting his gaze. Did they think that? A possibility but an unlikely one. 'And do you?'

He laughed then, a rough chortle that ended in sharp, short coughs. 'Not a dickybird.'

'And what about your wife, Mr Mulcahy? Ever heard what happened to her?'

Waldo dabbed his mouth again before balling up the tissues and placing them in the bag stuck on the end of his bed table. 'Not a peep after she walked out on the pretext of having run out of bread. She strolled out the door in her second favourite dress, her handbag slung over her shoulder, asked me if there was anything I wanted and that she'd be back in five minutes.' He flicked her a brief glance, his expression unreadable. 'We'd known each other for three years, married for two of those and yet, I never knew her at all. Barney barely remembers her, Mason certainly didn't.'

'What did you do?' William asked gently.

'What could I do. I got on with my life after the initial commotion died down. With a job and two kids of four and two there wasn't time to breathe let alone think. The guards did their best for us, I can't say they didn't. Thought she'd been taken ill at first or taken a knock to the head. Then they played around with abduction for a while but with no clues and nothing to go on they soon gave up trying to find her. One of life's mysteries never to be solved.'

'What do you think happened to your wife, Mr Mulcahy? Was she depressed, or acting out of character in any way?' Alana pressed gently.

The case had a particular quality about it that made her query everything she knew. They were no further forward in identifying Mason's murderer and seemed to still have quite a distance to travel in unravelling the whys and wherefores of Jane Doe's death. The mystery of what had happened to Dympna Mulcahy, although unlikely to be relevant, was still a puzzle.

'Difficult to know or remember. I was working as a docker

for Sealink over in Dun Laoghaire in them days. Very early mornings then picking up extra, working as a bouncer in one of the local bars. With two kids to feed and a woman with expensive tastes it was my job to see there was food on the table and clothes on their backs.'

'It sounds like you wouldn't have had much time to see her, let alone the kids?'

'That's about right. Ships that passed in the night.' He started taking small sips as he was talking, his voice taking on a thin thready quality. 'All the woman ever wanted was a kid of her own, the one thing I couldn't give her. Once she knew that, all she went on about was adoption, until the reality sank in.'

'You think she upped and left when she realised being mum to two little 'uns was harder than it looked?'

'All I can think of. There wasn't another man. I'd have known if that were the case.' He settled the empty mug back on the bed table and pushed it into the middle before folding his arms across his chest, the skin on his arms hanging off the bones. 'Dympna was special, like one of those painted China dolls with never a hair out of place. Loved her the first time I saw her, and I love her still even though she was too good to be true.'

'In what way?'

'A man can't get by on looks alone, love. There has to be a spark, a passion if you like. Difficult when Dympna refused to get her hair and make-up mussed. I reckon she married me expecting the dream of the perfect husband and perfect little family only to find neither existed.'

'And you never heard from her again?'

'None of us did although I thought I saw her once. It were a few years back, mind. Maybe thirty or forty. Doubt I'd recognise her now. Doubt she'd recognise me,' he said, laughing at his own joke. 'I hollered across Powerscourt Shopping Centre. I'm still convinced it was her, but she ignored me. Didn't even turn her back. Just carried on her way, her nose in the air, her blonde hair as bright and perfect as a shiny new penny.'

There was something about the way he couldn't quite look at her that set off a small alarm in the back of Alana's head. There was a lie there, a lie hiding in plain sight. Something about seeing his wife or something else. Difficult to tell and impossible to question him for fear of being shown the door. She'd make a note to run the conversation over again later to see if she could tease out what was going on.

'You wouldn't have anything belonging to her here, would you?' William piped up, his mug empty and resting on the floor by his feet.

'What, after fifty years? Not a chance, mate. Got rid of all her paraphernalia as soon as I could, all that tatty junk. No place in a man-only house, or that's what I told the boys.'

Alana glanced across at William, pleased that he was working along the same channels as she was. With no blood relatives that they knew of, unless they went searching through Dympna's family tree, it was unlikely they'd be able to find out what happened to her. Most likely irrelevant after all this time but still an interesting puzzle, not that she had the time to ponder on it too much. They'd come to talk about Mason and that's the one person they'd barely mentioned in the ten minutes the nurse had allowed.

'I know you said you hadn't been in touch with Mason, but is there anything you can tell us that might help us find who did this?'

'He was such a lovely little boy, glorious twinkling blue eyes and rounded cheeks. It all changed when he found out that I wasn't his real da. He went off on an escapade to trace them and rarely bothered with us after.'

'And did he ever find them?'

'Doubt it. The records were all sealed until last year, weren't they?'

'And you couldn't tell him?'

'I told him he was adopted, I told them both when they reached sixteen because I thought it was the right thing to do. Barney wasn't worried but then Barney's a bit like me. Mason is... was different. Cut from a different cloth. Good at sports. Good at everything when his poor old pa and his brother still use their fingers to count on. His brain and his brawn took him across the other side of the world only for something to drag him back onto Irish soil.'

There was a bustling sound from the corridor and the slip slap of feet. Alana's time was nearly up.

'He was always searching for something, something he never found because it was never there in the first place. A mother's love.'

TWENTY-THREE

Thursday 7th September, 10 a.m.

Leo was waiting for them when they arrived back at the station, as was her pink wheelchair. A peculiar job for a taxi but Alana had decided she needed the independence the powered chair gave her along with the comfort of her usual one. If that meant she was cluttering up the incident room, then so be it.

'William, pop my chair upstairs for me, would you, please. It will be easier if I use the powered. It will save the DS from having to push me.' Alana slid across and snapped the seatbelt fastened before following Leo to the lift and his office on the second floor, her good hand wrapped round Wally's lead. She would have happily escaped into the incident room until a time convenient to her if the DS hadn't decided to hang about reception chatting to the guard on duty.

'Well, I'm waiting, or are you going to continue staring at me all doe-eyed as if you don't know what I'm talking about?' Leo said, as soon as the door closed behind them.

'I don't know what to say.'

'Detective Rohan in tears about the way you're bullying her

is not what I expected from you, Alana.' He sat behind his desk, pressing his hand to his jacket to prevent snagging the buttons. 'Eve has offered up her very considerable experience to you, only to have it shoved back in her face.' He shook his head, his fingers furling into fists. 'I thought better of you, I really did.'

Alana stared back at him. He was making her feel bad. No, that Eve woman was making her so angry she could throw a punch at the wall, if she had a hand she didn't mind damaging. Turning on the waterworks indeed. Only a man as foolish as Leo wouldn't be able to recognise crocodile tears when he saw them.

She didn't respond. Instead she ruffled the top of Wally's head where he'd set up guard beside her chair, his jaw jutting forward, his eyes set to glacial as he stared across at Leo.

'And that's another thing. We're not running a pooch parlour here so why have you brought a dog? Working dogs only, or did you miss that part of the memo?'

Was there a memo? She very much doubted it. More a case of Leo making it up as he went along.

'This is Wally.' Wally shifted his head, his tongue lolling out of his mouth at her words. 'And Wally is a working dog. I need him to help me now I'm more incapacitated than usual.'

He didn't say anything to that, he couldn't. She'd read the policy on disability and inclusion in the workplace, which specifically stated that specially trained dogs were to be welcomed. That Wally had no training and was as likely as not to roll on his back with all paws in the air if faced with an attacker was something she didn't want to think on. He made her feel safe, and he had nowhere else to go, so he stayed.

Alana noted the way Leo was fiddling with the edge of a folder, one of the red ones that contained staff-related documents. An outdated method with the station's shift to electronic recordkeeping but one that was to her advantage.

'I take it that's Detective Rohan's file?' She looped Wally's lead round the arm of her chair and held out her hand. 'It is usual for me to have access, especially with a possible complaint pending.' He seemed reluctant but Alana knew her rights and access to her staff's files was part of those.

'You're sure you're fit to be at work, Alana?' he finally said, the folder now tucked down the side of her chair. 'I know there's a lot on but with Paddy and now Rohan there's no need for you to be killing yourself if you need to take it easy, dog or not.'

Over my dead body.

'I'm perfectly fine but thank you for asking. Apologies but I have back-to-back interviews lined up for the morning and I don't want to be late.' Alana engaged the joystick and manoeuvred her way out the door, Wally walking loyally beside her.

TWENTY-FOUR

Thursday 7th September, 10.30 a.m.

Alana wasn't lying when she said she had back-to-back interviews lined up. She raced into the office, with barely time to lock Eve's folder in her top draw and grab her notebook before making her way back down in the lift to the interview room and where Flynn was working through the preliminaries with Barney. She winced as she jabbed the lift button, her hand was throbbing and the nearest painkillers upstairs in the bottom of her handbag.

'Sorry for keeping you, Mr Mulcahy. I see Detective O'Hare has started with the preliminaries.' She settled her notepad down, her pen on top. 'Right, apologies for having to bring you in again but obviously things have changed with the death of your brother. We're all very sorry for your loss.'

'I can't believe it.'

'No, I'm sure it must have been a huge shock.' She pushed her tea aside. It was only for show anyway. If they actually drank all the cups offered, they'd spend most of the time in the loo. 'Do you have any idea why somebody would target your crab pot and then your brother?'

'No. As I told you before, there's no one.'

'We've met with your dad and he's been updating us on your family history. You never felt the same need as your brother to trace your parents, or indeed your adoptive mother?'

'I'm not sure what that's got to do with anything but no. Parents who deserted me and a woman who walked out on her husband and young family. Not the type of people I wanted to find out about.' He stared down at his hands, the nails blunt cut and torn in places, the skin red and rough.

'But your brother was different?'

'The thing you have to remember about Mason was that he wasn't like me or my dad.' He glanced up before returning to his hands. 'We're not related but, I'm guessing you know that already. Mason was intelligent. Good at everything. He saw things. He wanted things that weren't of any interest to us. At school he flew through his exams and, when he finally left, he continued with his education before opting to work for the NYPD. I only stayed on at school until I was sixteen because Dad made me.'

'Any idea why he became a cop?'

He shrugged. 'Because he could. Mam leaving before he could even remember her messed with his head. I always put it down to that.'

'Okay. And how did you get on with him?'

'Well enough. We were best mates until we grew up, then it all changed, he changed. Dublin wasn't a big enough place to hold him.'

'In what way?' Alana asked.

'He was always arrogant but more so. Disparaging of both me and Da. Didn't want anything to do with us once he learnt we weren't blood relatives. It hurt at the time but...' By his tone it still hurt and always would.

'What about his life after he left Ireland?' Flynn asked, his tea also ignored in favour of his notepad.

'Not a lot to say really. We kept in touch, Email and the like, but the only common ground we had was our dad and Mason didn't want to know. There's only so much conversation you can get out of how many crabs and lobsters are in the pots and he didn't, or couldn't, tell me about the work he did in New York.'

'Why do you think he was like that?'

'He was ashamed of Da, and me too probably. Of having hard-working people as his nearest and dearest. Simple folk not bothered about the bright lights of the Big Apple.'

'And how did that make you feel?'

'As in would it have made me annoyed enough to kill him?' He lifted his head and stared across the short span of table, his eyes taking on a wary look, his hand reaching into his top pocket and pulling a cigarette from the squashed packet. It wasn't the first time Alana had seen the same scenario played out. The comfort in familiarity despite the large no smoking sign over his head. The cigarette was fine. She'd only have a problem if he decided to light it.

'If you like,' Flynn intervened.

'To be honest with you, it made me feel sad. Da is a lovely bloke. Okay, so a bit rough and ready, and not the sharpest of pencils but then neither am I, and remember he worked two jobs to keep us out of the orphanage when Mam went missing. They wanted to take us back when she disappeared. I bet he didn't tell you that, eh? He fought tooth and nail, and Mason wouldn't even get off his arse to go and see him in the home when the old boy is clearly dying.'

'And any idea about why your brother moved back to Ireland? I believe it was two years ago, right?'

'He didn't have much to say about that other than he'd decided that he had enough money to retire, and Ireland was his home.'

'What about relationships? He never married but...'

Barney shrugged. 'Always looking for something he could never have, my brother. The type of women he wanted were the type who wouldn't have been interested in the likes of him.'

'And what about the last time you saw him?' Alana said, making a mental note to text Ruan a brief update after the interview.

'I haven't. Not since we went out to see him in New York all of five years ago and that turned out to be a disaster. We should never have gone but the wife was keen to travel, and we decided to drop in on him.'

Alana was confused by the comment. 'But you said you were still in touch. When was the last time you spoke?'

Barney withdrew his phone and swiped it open. A top of the range iPhone so fishing was obviously paying well. Either that or he had an alternative source of income. She picked up her pen and made a brief note to follow up on his financials.

'About a month ago. I sent him an update about Dad. He never responded. Mason's way of telling me to piss off. I got the message, loud and clear.'

Alana felt sorry for him, a dangerous emotion to feel about a person of interest in a murder inquiry and the reason she made an additional note to check Barney's vehicle on the system alongside the one about his bank records.

The interview was over and with nothing useful to show. She might as well wrap it up and was in the process of doing just that when she remembered something from the chat she'd had with his father earlier.

'You wouldn't still have something in your possession from the early days, would you?'

'What do you mean?' The cigarette was now in his hand along with a lighter and a look of intent.

'You know, a christening robe or a pair of shoes from when

you were a kid. Anything from the days when your adoptive mother was still around.'

'Ha, he wouldn't keep anything of hers. Hated her for what she did to us.' He paused, the cigarette lying in the centre of his open palm as if the most precious thing in the world.

'And what about you or your brother?'

'No, nothing. Nothing at all. Now, is there anything else or can I go. I'm desperate for a fag.'

Alana glanced at Flynn briefly before sending Barney on his way.

He was lying.

TWENTY-FIVE

Thursday 7th September, 11.15 a.m.

With Flynn tasked with chasing Barney's financials and car registration Alana teamed up with Paddy for the next interview, the one she was most interested in. The mystery of how Ciara managed to have two mothers, both dead.

'Hello, Miss Buckley. I'm Detective Alana Mack and this is Detective Paddy Quigg. Thank you for coming to see us, and apologies for taking you out of your way,' she said, greeting the tall, denim-clad woman in reception and lifting her arm in explanation of why she wouldn't be shaking her hand. 'Interview room one is free. This way.' She stopped short of wrinkling her nose when she was introduced. Where Barney smelt of the sea and stale fags and his dad of mint humbugs, Ciara Buckley's scent was something heavy and expensive. It suited her.

'It's all a little confusing as to why you need to see me at all,' Ciara said as soon as they were settled, a puzzled frown settling on her smooth brow.

Her whole face seemed smooth. Smooth skin with hardly a wrinkle, which made her age barely believable, but Alana had seen her birth certificate and official documents didn't lie. Ciara Buckley was a youthful fifty-six with styled pale blonde hair and a taste in dress that suggested she was younger than she was. As an observation it was an irrelevant one but Alana made a brief note at the top of her notebook all the same, remembering to flip the page between interviews, a rookie mistake which she'd made many times in the past but not recently.

Alana slid a printout of the woman's birth certificate across the table along with copies of her parents' death certificates before jumping right into the centre of why they'd asked her to attend an interview all the way in Dublin. 'What do you know about DNA, Miss Buckley?'

'Excuse me?' She looked confused, or as confused as someone could look with what appeared to be immovable facial muscles. Botox, fillers or something else. Alana wasn't experienced enough in the world of cosmetic surgery to tell.

'Deoxyribonucleic acid or DNA for short. We seem to be having some difficulty with yours or, to be exact, the DNA of someone we believe to be a close relative.'

'I don't understand,' she said, glancing between them.

'It's not all that difficult really, Miss Buckley.' Paddy rested his elbows on the table, his jacket bunching up, revealing his watch. 'Somewhere along the way, you must have uploaded your DNA, maybe to one of those genealogy sites? Does that sound like something you might have done?'

'No, absolutely not. I don't believe in all that nonsense.'

Alana looked across at Paddy in surprise. There was no record that the woman had ever been arrested and swabbed, a process that sat alongside being photographed and fingerprinted as part of modern-day policing.

'Well...' Paddy appeared as flummoxed as she was. 'I'm not sure...'

'Hold on a minute.' Ciara held her hand up, emphasising that it was her turn to speak. 'I joined the bone marrow register a while back. We all did but I distinctly remember reading the disclaimer about how my personal information would be used and nowhere did it state that I would end up being interviewed for God only knows what crime. This is appalling.'

Alana could see the interview derailing before her eyes and couldn't think of a way to prevent it. Ciara had her arms folded tightly across her chest, her mouth a thin line of disapproval. They now had the grim task of sharing that *the woman in the pot* was Ciara's biological mother.

'I appreciate your concern and will make sure to make a note of it, Miss Buckley, but that doesn't change the information that we have received via Interpol. As an aside, exactly when did you decide to join the register?'

She eyed them, clearly coming to a decision as to what her next move would be. Alana hoped she wouldn't decide to walk out. Taking a hostile witness into custody was as distasteful as it sounded but it wouldn't be the first time.

'Last year.' She pulled her phone free from her jeans and swiped the screen. 'The 10th of October 2022.'

Alana didn't know what had made her change her mind and cooperate. She was only thankful that she had.

'Can you forward me a copy of the sign-up email, for our records please?' She passed over one of her business cards, leaving no opportunity for the woman to object. 'Thank you. I wasn't aware that bone marrow donations can be given by people outside of their twenties,' she added, conversationally, while she waited for the forwarded email to ping through on her phone.

'Neither was I until a friend's child was diagnosed with leukaemia.' Ciara shrugged. 'Most companies won't do it but I did manage to find one. There's nothing more important than the life of a child.'

'No.' Alana paused to make a brief note. 'I can appreciate

it's a surprise to learn about your DNA being involved in a search. I'd like to explain how that came about if you'll let me?'

There were few people who Alana had come across that weren't inquisitive, in fact, she couldn't think of any. She was banking on Ciara's innate curiosity allowing her to continue. The slight nod was indication enough that she'd succeeded, for now.

'We've been following up on the information received from the DNA match, to see how that relates to you and your family tree and trying to link that to the information already on record.' Alana tapped the certificates with her index finger. 'And that's where we've come up against a brick wall. I don't want to blind you with science, but DNA is measured in centimorgans, or percentages if you like. I know this may come as a bit of a shock but it looks like there's a direct match between you and our subject.'

'How much of a direct match.'

'Your mother.'

Ciara laughed, a rip-roaring head flung back laugh, revealing a mouthful of white teeth. 'And here was me worried for a second.' The laughter stopped almost as abruptly as it had started. 'That is impossible.'

'Why would that be impossible, Miss Buckley?' Paddy said, lifting his head from where he'd been taking notes down in his careful hand.

'Because both my parents are dead, as you already know.' She tapped their death certificates with her fingers.

'They died when you were fourteen?'

'In a house fire, yes.'

Alana only knew what she'd been able to find on the system, which didn't go back as far as 1981, the year of the fire, and she hadn't had the opportunity to send someone down to the basement to look through the paper files in the archive office.

'How about you tell us what happened. Where were you at the time?'

'How about I show you.'

Ciara pushed back from the table and pulled her shirt free from her jeans before turning round and dragging the fabric halfway up her back. The skin of her back didn't look like skin or not the type of skin Alana had ever seen outside of post-mortems and scene of crime photographs. Thick welts of raised red flesh crisscrossing from one side to the other.

'Two years in hospital and a shedload of plastic surgery later, detective,' Ciara spoke over her shoulder, in the act of tucking her top back inside her jeans. 'My hands were the worst,' she said, nodding to the shiny skin pulled taut from wrist to fingertip. 'Is that enough proof for you?'

Alana was rarely bereft of words, and neither was Paddy, but the small room felt suffocatingly small suddenly with all the emotions bouncing off the walls.

Surprise. Horror. Sympathy.

'I'm sorry.' Sorry wasn't enough but it was the only thing that came to mind. 'You...?'

'I tried to save them and all I managed to save was the dog.'

'I'm so sorry,' Alana repeated, noting the resumption of Paddy's notetaking after the brief hiatus. She felt like taking a pause too after having misjudged the woman, who was now settling back in the chair. Ciara Buckley had already been through a terrible trauma and buried one mother. Now she'd have to bury a second one.

TWENTY-SIX

Thursday 7th September, 1.45 p.m.

A morning spent interviewing, interspersed with the meeting with Leo and time spent trawling through the information she could find on Ciara, and Alana was fit to scream but instead she shook out a couple of pills from the packet in her bag and dry swallowed them. She didn't mind strong painkillers, just not the effect they had on her. It was going to be an extra scoop of coffee in her mug if she was going to have any chance of not being found with her head stuck to her desk in a pile of drool. It would be a full house with both Rusty and Rogene invited along with Irene, their profiler, and Ruan via Teams. Not the time to embarrass herself.

'Here, I'd have got you some water,' Lorrie said with a tut. 'What about a coffee to send it along its way?'

Alana felt like a naughty toddler. 'I'm good but a coffee if you have a moment would be lovely.' Wally nudged her hand, his eyes large in his narrow face. 'And a water for Wally while you're at it. It's okay, boy, we're not ignoring you. You're going to have to get as used to us as we are to you.' She fondled his ears until the bowl took up his full attention, water splashing everywhere.

Ten minutes later and the office was heaving with bodies in an assortment of workwear, including Eve who was back from her morning navigating the policy manual. Alana had managed to put her out of her mind during the interviews but there was still her file to muse over and no time in which to do it. At two sharp, she manoeuvred her chair into its usual spot in front of the run of whiteboards, Paddy beside her as he set up the laptop to connect to the Kerry office.

'You're on,' he whispered before making his way over to where Irene was sitting in his chair, looking pretty in a pink dress, her baby bump already starting to show. Alana smiled as his hand pressed into her shoulder, the smile lingering as she tilted the laptop towards her.

'Afternoon, Ruan. Pleased you could join us, and thanks for looking after the lads over the last couple of days.'

'Not a bother. Just sorry it was under such difficult circumstances.'

She set the laptop at a different angle so that he'd be able to see most of the room before doing a quick round of introductions. 'Right then. It doesn't need me to tell you what a complex case we have,' she started, deciding to run through what they knew already.

'The bones of an, as yet, unidentified elderly woman found in the bottom of fisherman Barney Mulcahy's crab pot closely followed by the discovery of Barney's adopted but estranged brother, Mason Clare, murdered in his bed. While we've yet to confirm the identity of *the woman in the pot*, we believe, thanks to Interpol technology, her to be the biological mother of one Ciara Buckley from Bandon. And that's where it all goes to hell in a handcart because Ciara thought she had a perfectly good set of parents already. Her parents, Paula and Joseph Buckley, both died in a house fire in 1981. We can add to that the fact

Barney and his brother, Mason, while adopted from the same orphanage, weren't blood relatives, and the little issue of their adoptive mother, Dympna, disappearing when Barney was four and Mason only two, which all means we have a huge tangle on our hands.'

Instead of the usual questions she'd expect at this stage in a briefing there was complete silence, both in the room and from the laptop, but it was that kind of case. Too much going on to peel back the layers and reveal the truth. 'Lorrie has been looking into Ciara's background. What have you got for us?'

'Nothing exciting, but the way the case is going I don't think we can cope with any more excitement. Ciara Buckley, age fifty-six. Has spent most of her life in Bandon where she works as a psychotherapist. Single and with no dependants. Spent two years in a specialist burns unit when she was fourteen following injuries sustained during the same fire that killed both her parents. After, she was taken in by one of the doctors at the burns unit and stayed there until she was eighteen. At eighteen she used her inheritance from her parents to purchase her house, the house where she currently resides as well as practises out of with a fellow psychotherapist.' She glanced at her screen briefly. 'A Mr Lucas Pounder.'

'A professional relationship or something more?'

'I still need to fill in those gaps but he's been divorced for the last five years, about the same length of time his place of work changed to that of Ciara's practice.'

'Okay. A great start, thank you.' Alana turned to William, who looked a little the worse for wear with a smear of dust across his cheek, but a spell in the archives tended to have that effect on people. He also looked happy, happier than she'd ever seen him but then Wally had deflected from her side to lie under his desk as soon as he'd finished splashing water all over the place. The fluffy blanket and dog chewy might have something to do with it. Her lips twitched, remembering Leo's dig about running a pooch parlour.

'I see you've been busy in the archives. What you got?'

'I've managed to collect newspaper reports from the time as well as the official documents. The guard investigating the blaze was very thorough so there was a lot to go through.' He lifted his head from where he was shuffling through a pile of printouts. 'Garda Jonah Quigg. Any relation, Paddy?'

'My father. Why, what's he done?' he replied, eliciting a laugh from the room.

'Not a lot but he sure knows how to run an investigation. Every box I could think of was ticked in triplicate and a few new ones too.'

'I'll be sure to tell him, he'll be delighted.'

'And?' Alana didn't want to interrupt the banter, but a gentle nudge was needed if they were going to manage to get home sometime tonight.

'The inquest agreed that the fire started from an electrical fault in the fridge in the kitchen. Ciara and her parents were in bed asleep at the time.'

'I wouldn't have thought a fridge could catch fire?'

'Apparently it was something to do with the compressor. Garda Quigg made a timeline, part guesswork and part statements from the first responders. Would you like me to read it?'

'Go ahead.'

'Eleven o'clock. Fire starts in the fridge, situated in the kitchen, which is towards the back of the house,' he said, lifting a sheet of paper before placing it back on the desk.

'Three minutes past eleven and the ceiling in the kitchen catches fire. Ciara's bedroom is situated right above.

'Five past eleven, something wakes her. A sound from below. She gets out of bed and goes to investigate.' He glanced up. 'They had a dog, her dog, which she was responsible for. There had been problems in the past with it getting into the lounge and scratching the sofa so she was worried her dad would put his foot down and drown it like he'd threatened in the past.

'Six minutes past and the hall is ablaze. She manages to open the lounge window to let the dog out. She doesn't remember any more until she wakes up in hospital two weeks later.

'A neighbour is walking home from the pub at seven minutes past and sees flames through the open window of the lounge. He races across the street to wake up the nearest neighbour. At eight minutes past eleven, next-door neighbour, Joyce Cooke, dials 999. At twelve minutes past, two fire engines arrive from Bandon fire station. At fourteen minutes past they pull out the unconscious Ciara, coinciding with the arrival of the first ambulance. By a quarter past the roof over Ciara's bedroom caves in.' He stopped a second to turn the page. 'The inquest into Joseph and Paula Buckley's deaths was inconclusive, the coroner unable to decide if they'd died from smoke inhalation or crush injuries.'

He stopped reading and lifted his head, the room now deadly quiet. 'Shall I go on or...?'

'I think we get the picture, William. Thank you.' Alana concentrated a second on where Paddy was updating the board with the relevant points before continuing. 'So, I'm guessing the inquest also showed that opening the window caused a backdraft and hence Miss Buckley's horrific injuries?'

'That was stated.' His reply was soft, barely audible.

'Right.' Alana knew the blink of time it took for a fire to devastate. Fifteen minutes sounded about right. These days with smoke detectors and fire-retardant materials, casualties were a rarity instead of the norm but things had been different back in the eighties. She couldn't remember having a smoke detector when she was growing up and as for fire retardant furniture... Laughable when she considered the hand-me-down tatt, which was all her mum could afford. She made a promise there and then to check her smoke detector as soon as she got home, or at least to get someone else to check it and, by the look of her colleagues, she wouldn't be the only one.

'What do the newspapers add?'

'Not a lot. Only one of interest. A follow-up about what happened to the daughter. Where she was being treated, and the kind of thing expected for burns victims. Poor kid. In pretty poor taste if you ask me.'

'Quite! Okay, we have what appears to be a tragic accident, which in no way explains why Ciara was brought up by the woman listed on her birth certificate as her biological mother when we know that wasn't the case.' Alana shifted her right hand slightly, taking the opportunity to wriggle her fingers. 'I've just been trawling through the adoption records and surprise, surprise, the Buckleys don't appear so we're looking at either an illegal adoption or a child abduction. Any details on the Buckleys' financials among that lot, William?'

'Borrowed to the hilt. Something about an additional ten thousand euro loan too. Garda Quigg made a footnote about the bank threatening to foreclose if they couldn't continue paying their mortgage.'

'Which I take was finally covered by the insurance payout?'

'Exactly that.'

'Thank you. If you can carry on ferreting through Paddy's dad's records as well as taking a deep dive into the Buckleys' finances while Lorrie works the interview side of things,' she said, nodding at Lorrie. 'Start with Joyce Cooke, the neighbour, if she's still around. There's also Ciara Buckley's extended family to question, if she has any.'

Alana glanced over the sea of faces. It was a lot of work for one person, and the kind of work where a sensitive touch was needed, a sensitive but experienced touch. Leo had as good as told her to make use of Eve's skills. The problem was she wasn't quite sure what the woman's skillset was. But William and Paddy were only back from Kerry and Flynn and Lorrie working together was asking for trouble. For some unknown reason sparks flew between them whenever she paired them up. She'd been putting off dragging them into her office for a showdown, in the hope that, given time, they'd sort themselves out.

'Eve, I'd like you to work this angle with Lorrie, please. Any difficulties, you come to me, is that clear?'

'Yes, ma'am.' The ma'am was insolent, but Alana had more important things to worry about.

Irene had been watching proceedings with her usual enigmatic, Mona Lisa smile, her glasses pushed up against her forehead as she recorded the meeting, word for word. She wasn't the minute taker – that was a job Lorrie had made her own – but she had a sharp mind, outside of her role as clinical profiler and Alana always valued her input. She was already dreading the time when she'd be going on maternity leave.

'What's your take on things, Irene? Any thoughts on what we could be dealing with?'

'An interesting case, indeed. Certainly not the run-of-the-mill offering I'm usually brought in on.' She sat back, her laptop forgotten. 'Revenge is sweet, or so they say although the proof actually doesn't support that theory. In fact, the opposite is true.'

'So, we're looking at a revenge killing?'

'Probably vendetta would be a better word. Two brothers, one murdered, the other involved in a murder, has a *Hamlet* feel about it, don't you think? A family drama of the worst sort, with no happy ending waiting in the wings.'

'You sound as if you know what you're talking about?' Eve said, her tone at war with her choice of words.

Alana didn't like sarcasm, especially in the incident room where tensions were high. It would be interesting to see how

Irene coped. Paddy was already starting to bristle like a startled tomcat.

'Oh, I'm only a vector for the experts, Eve. It is Eve, isn't it?' Irene waited a beat for the reluctant nod. 'The caudate nucleus is the real giveaway. It's the area of the brain that makes up the cortico-basal ganglia-thalamic loop which, in simple language, allows for that dopamine hit, or reward if you like. Think about someone carrying out an act of revenge and how that would make them feel. The sense of justification. However, it's the same pleasure-pain principle as found in crackheads. The reward is never enough, which in drug addicts means an increase in the regularity and amount of the dose. In vendettas, it's a never-ending cycle of destruction with no positive outcome waiting in the wings. If you don't like *Hamlet*, then what about *Romeo and Juliet*? A classic example of Freudian's pleasure pain juxtaposition where the protagonists, in this case Messer's Montague and Capulet both end up losing because of their unwillingness to forgive and forget. The audience is exposed to all the pleasures of Romeo and Juliet's romance only for the emotional high to be whipped out from under them at their death.'

Eve was speechless as were most of the room. Alana however had a question, which had nothing to do with what she'd really like to say.

Well done for shutting that bloody woman up.

'Irene, what do you honestly think is going on here bearing in mind you could drive a ten-tonne truck through the gaps in our information.'

'You're asking me to guess?'

'If you like, although I'd prefer to term it an educated guess based on the information we do have.'

Alana watched as she removed her glasses before sweeping her inky-black hair away from her face, her fingernails immaculate, her pear-shaped engagement ring twinkling in the light. 'In short, you have a dead elderly woman and two missing elderly women – the Mulcahy lads' adoptive mother and Buckley's genetic one. I would be trying to prove if they're one and the same.'

Alana continued staring at her. It wasn't news, not really. It had been something she'd been considering ever since the question of multiple old ladies had arisen in the case. However, they still needed to find out about Ciara's mother, to confirm or disprove Irene's theory. There was also the discrepancy with Ciara's testimony to tease out, she remembered. It was only a minor detail, but cases had been solved on far less. Ciara had told them earlier that she'd tried to rescue her parents before heading downstairs. Why hadn't she mentioned that to Garda Quigg at the time?

TWENTY-SEVEN

Thursday 7th September, 3.35 p.m.

'Hello, can I speak to Mrs Joyce Cooke please?'

'Speaking.' The voice was cautious, which wasn't a surprise. Joyce Cooke was seventy-seven now and living alone following the death of her husband, if the local property tax information off the revenue was correct. It wouldn't be the first time that their information had been proved less than accurate but there was only so much personal data the guards had access to these days without having to justify their interest. At this point in the investigation the less people that knew what they were up to the better.

'Hi there, I'm Detective Lorrie Deery from the Clonabee branch of the National Bureau of Criminal Investigation.'

There was a pause. 'You're a bit off your patch, aren't you, love. Not sure what you'd be wanting with me. I know I was a bit late in paying that parking fine but it's me knees. Can't venture out without a bit of assistance these days.'

God love her!

Lorrie was thankful she'd made a brew before picking up

the phone. She had a feeling it was going to be a long conversation, not that she minded if it was going to be fruitful.

'It's not about your parking ticket, Mrs Cooke. You used to live next door to the Buckleys in the eighties.'

The next pause was lengthier. 'God, I've been trying to forget that all these years and here's you lot reminding me.'

'Did you know them well?'

'Well enough in the way you always know a bit about who's living next door but never the ins and outs. Paula was a bit standoffish, but the husband was okay. A cabbie so worked all hours.'

'And did you know them long?' Lorrie was trying a circuitous route to get to where she wanted, often the best way in a fact-finding expedition like this one.

'Let me see. Mmm, they moved in when our Jacinta was born and she's now fifty-six, so what's that. Fifteen years or so.'

Fourteen, but she didn't correct her. Instead, she made a note. 'So, your daughter's the same age as Ciara then?'

'Give or take. That poor child.'

'She moved away after?'

'Had to. With no next-of-kin living anywhere near there was no one to take her. Jacinta tried to stay in touch for a bit, but you know what kids are like and with Ciara in hospital. It was a very difficult time.'

'I can imagine. And I believe the fire was caused by an electrical fault?'

'I wouldn't know about that. Only what was in the papers.'

'And what happened to the property?'

'Rebuilt.' There was a pause on the other end of the line. 'Stood empty for ages. No one wanted to buy it. A couple from out of town eventually took it on but that was years after.'

'And what about the Buckleys? What were they like?'

'Didn't see much of him, always working to pay off the bills.

The wife didn't work but her sort never does. Used to mind her own business, her nose stuck up in the air.'

'She didn't fit in then?'

Joyce laughed. 'You could say that. Nice clothes and all and an immaculate house but fallen on hard times if you ask me.'

Lorrie's fingers flew over the keys, struggling to keep up. There was a lot to unpick. A snooty woman with no money in possession of a child who wasn't biologically hers. Unless it wasn't Paula who had died in the fire. As a thought, it was like something out of a thriller but that didn't stop Lorrie from adding a brief note to check on it.

'And where is your daughter now, Mrs Cooke? We'll need to arrange for a statement. Oh, and what happened to the dog?'

TWENTY-EIGHT

Thursday 7th September, 4.15 p.m.

'That was nice of the neighbour to take Ciara's dog.'

'Nice people do nice things, Paddy,' Lorrie said, strapping herself in. 'It's a shame we don't see much of it in our line of business.'

'Business, is it. You're making what we do sound awfully posh, there, Lor.' Paddy indicated left out the car park onto Poolbeg Way before turning into Torquay Road. 'So, what was your impression of the woman? Do we need to follow the conversation up with a visit?'

'I don't think so. I have the daughter's details, not that I think she'll be able to tell me much. The mother said they didn't hear from Ciara after she was discharged from hospital, but it would have been a difficult time for her being moved from pillar to post. Hospital from fourteen to sixteen when you've had everything on a plate before then.' Lorrie watched the succession of gated properties stream past her window, but Foxrock was a world away from deprived Clonabee with its run-down, red-bricked terraced houses and air of neglect. 'You'd think she'd have wanted to keep in touch if only for the sake of the dog but, according to Mrs Cooke, that wasn't the case.'

'Remember that things were very different in the eighties, or so I'm told,' he qualified, taking the first right at the roundabout and onto Glenamuck Road. 'No mobile phones and no email. It would have been letters or coins in a phone box depending on what the doctor that took her in was like.' He glanced at her. 'That's a job for us in the morning, checking up on the doctor.'

'Okay. It's easy to forget they managed fine without all this tech.'

'It's more that they managed in a different way. I wonder where we'd be if it all disappeared. At least not moaning about the speed of the Wi-Fi and always on our bleedin' phones. Can't remember the last time I saw someone actually reading a book.'

Lorrie loved reading almost as much as she loved gaming but now wasn't the time to pull out the paperback she'd added to her bag earlier that morning. She watched as he indicated right before pulling up in front of a three-barred metal gate and hopping out to open it.

'What we really need is a reliable source of DNA from the Buckleys, both of them,' she said when Paddy got back in. 'While Ciara might not have been biologically related to her mother that doesn't mean Joseph Buckley wasn't her father.'

'True enough. Let's hope Da can help with that. I hope you like baked goods, although there'll be more for me if you don't.'

'I'm as partial as the next person to baked goods,' she replied, scanning the small holding with an inquisitive eye now they were driving towards a single-story farmhouse surrounded by acres of green pasture, an upright man with a thick head of grey hair, sitting on top of a ride-alone lawnmower up ahead.

'Good.' Paddy stopped the engine and pushed the door wide, his hand raised in greeting as he walked the short distance to meet his dad. Lorrie took her time in following, pulling out her phone and checking for messages instead of being a silent observer as parent and son greeted each other, their exchange too far away for her to hear what they were saying.

There were no messages, no updates and nothing from Eve either. She'd been half expecting another diatribe from that direction, the concern being that she'd lose her temper with a senior officer and be shown the door. The spats she had with Flynn were child's play when compared with the antics Eve was getting up to. If she was this bad after a day, there was a good chance she'd be impossible after a week.

She dismissed the thought, placing her phone in her bag, rearranging the strap over her shoulder before letting it swing next to her hip as the pair approached.

'Hello, Mr Quigg, good to meet you and sorry for interrupting your day.'

'Not a bother, Lorrie, and call me Jonah. Mr Quigg was my father and his father before him. Can't remember the last time anyone called me that, eh, Paddy?' He slapped him across the back. 'Jonah until I joined the guards then Garda Quigg up to when I retired and back to being plain ole Jonah.'

There was nothing plain about the tall, burly, distinguished man gesturing for her to precede them into the house. He had the air of a copper in the way he both walked and talked, a laid-back authority that she'd witnessed over and over in the older members of the force she'd come across. He'd seen everything, done most of it, and had absolutely nothing to prove to either himself or anyone else. She liked that.

'I'll just pop the kettle on and grab some dishes.'

'Here, let me help.' She watched as Paddy started pulling open cupboard doors and drawers. 'What is it today?'

'Barmbrack with either butter or a slab of cheese.'

'It's not Halloween yet, is it, Da?'

'Brack isn't just for Halloween, Pad, and I'll have both cheese and butter, if it's on offer please.' Lorrie couldn't remember the last time she eaten the Irish fruitcake. Cakes and the like were few and far between when she was growing up and as for baking, her parents weren't the baking sort. They weren't the sort that should've had children either but that was a road she'd blocked off long ago.

'So, what brings you to sunny Glencullen then?'

They were sitting around the kitchen table, most of the cake and half of the cheese demolished and a large earthenware teapot already refilled once.

'I'm hoping you can put that big brain of yours to good use, and see if you can remember anything about the Buckleys' house fire in 1981? Your name has come up as being the lead officer on the case. If it helps any, it was the one where both parents died. Only the daughter survived but with horrific injuries.'

Jonah propped his elbows on the table and cupped his chin in his hands, his genial expression dimming as if someone had flicked a switch. 'Not likely a case I'm going to forget. Why do you want to know?'

Lorrie was interested in how Paddy would respond. Confidentiality was huge in the force, but would Paddy view it that way considering his father was a former copper.

'Ah, now, you know I can't really tell you that, Da. What I can say is, we're interested in anything you can remember about the relationship between the parents and the daughter, any gossip at the time. We've had information that they weren't the girl's birth parents.'

'Mmm. Paddy the Clam Quigg is it! She had a pretty name. Caro. Cora...'

'Ciara.'

'That's it, not that she looked pretty the times I went to see her in hospital, wrapped up in head-to-toe bandages.'

'You went to see her?'

'Poor kid wasn't allowed visitors and when she was there

was no one she'd agree to let in. Embarrassed about the way she looked or that's what the doctors said. I had an excuse because of the case but, by the end I was popping in almost daily just to say hello.'

'And what was she like?' Lorrie said, licking her finger before stabbing it at the crumbs on her plate and popping it in her mouth.

'Typical teenager. Sullen, morose. Uncommunicative and, it must be said, in a lot of pain so reason enough to be moody.'

'Can you remember if she said anything about her parents? I know it was a long time ago,' Paddy asked.

Jonah wiped his hands on his jeans before replying, his expression thoughtful as he stared into the middle distance. 'She didn't say much at all. These days it would be called post-traumatic-stress-disorder but back then the term would have been in its infancy. Completely locked in, she was. The hours I spent sitting by her bed with her staring at the ceiling not saying a word. Your ma must have thought all sorts about where I was, but I felt sorry for the kid.'

'We saw her back, but you say she was covered in head-to-foot bandages?'

'Plastic surgery after the wounds healed.' He lifted his hand to the side of his cheek and around his left ear. 'I take it she's okay now?'

'If you mean in looks, then yes. I really wouldn't have noticed there was a problem until she showed us her back. Alana commented afterwards about her smooth face and artfully arranged hairstyle, which was probably like that to conceal the scars. And you can't remember if there were any concerns about her and her parents or even anything about the cause of the blaze?'

'Started in the kitchen. The fridge and the only odd thing about the business.'

'In what way?' Lorrie asked.

'In the way that it was pretty much brand new, probably the newest thing in the house.' He started gathering the plates only to leave them in a pile in front of him. 'The Buckleys weren't flush with cash. Up to their necks in mortgage repayments after taking a bond out on the property a decade or so before. The fridge would have been a huge outlay and their pride and joy.'

'And ultimately their cause of death. A huge tragedy. And no thoughts that it was foul play, if the fridge was new?'

'Ah, Pad. Always a chip off the ole block. I excavated that idea right down to bedrock and with no skeletons in sight. We even took the fridge back to the lab, or what was left. There'll be a box of relevant bits and bobs somewhere unless someone's done a clear out.'

'What about Ciara's parents?'

'The mother wasn't well liked but then she kept herself to herself, which never goes down well in small communities. The husband was busy trying to put food on the table, too busy to make enemies or that's what his boss said. Everyone had a good word to say about him just as no one had anything nice to say about his missus.'

'And you don't remember anything else about their background?'

'Nothing that wouldn't be in the case notes. The investigation lost impetus when the jury returned a verdict of death by misadventure for the couple. I can't remember now whether the cause was put down as carbon monoxide poisoning or the roof caving in. It's so long ago.' He pushed away from the table and picked up the plates with one hand, the mugs in the other while Paddy followed with the teapot. 'The daughter really is lucky to be alive.'

If you can call losing your family lucky. Lorrie felt a burning at the back of her throat at the thought of never seeing her parents again, notwithstanding the bumps and potholes in their relationship. She hadn't been to see them in months. It didn't seem to matter so much whose fault that was. She'd plan something over the next few days.

'You said in your statement that Ciara headed downstairs after hearing a noise. Can you remember if she said anything about trying to rescue her parents?'

'No, there was nothing. We were lucky to get that much out of her. A random remark told to the fireman first on the scene. After, her mind was a complete blank. PTSD, with associated amnesia. The doctors were undecided if her memory of the incident would ever return.'

An interesting observation, which Lorrie jotted down in her notebook. If her memory had returned what else might she be able to add to the initial investigation into her parents' deaths?

'What about ID-ing the bodies after?' she said, her thoughts shifting to how Ciara could be related to both the woman in the pot and the woman in the house fire. If Irene was to be believed then Ciara's biological mother, and Barney and Mason's adoptive one, were one and the same. They didn't have enough information yet to either prove or disprove that nugget of wisdom. Was Paula Buckley even in the house when the roof collapsed? She could have set the fire herself before escaping out the back door to start a new life. Lorrie lifted her hand to her head, her brain starting to ache at the mental somersaults she was putting it through. The only thing she knew for certain was that Paula Buckley and Dympna Mulcahy were two different people. Joyce Cooke had told her Paula and Joseph had moved into the property in 1967, with their newborn daughter. Over in Dublin in 1967, Waldo and Dympna had been married a year.

'Funny, I was only thinking about that.' Jonah leant against the counter; his arms folded across his chest. 'The coroner couldn't make up his mind as to the cause of death. That old chicken and egg scenario about which came first. The tech wasn't sophisticated enough in those days to make an informed decision that wasn't fifty per cent guesswork and intuition combined. Luckily for us, although unlucky for the Buckleys, the collapsed roof prevented their bodies from being consumed in the flames, the slates acting as a barrier against the fire. Don't get too excited. There wasn't much left but probably enough to work on now.'

Lorrie glanced between them before stepping to the door, her phone in her hand. 'I'll just give Dr Mulholland the heads up while you're catching up with your da.'

'Dr Mulholland?'

'Speaking.'

'It's Lorrie.'

'Hi, Lorrie. What can I do for you?'

'I was wondering what the possibility of extracting DNA from a burns victim, buried forty years ago, would be?'

'Interesting question. I take it it's to do with the woman in the pot?'

'A side strand that we're trying to untangle in the hope it will lead to us eliminating her from the investigation, doctor.'

'So, pretty urgent then, and do call me Rusty. I can't offer any guarantees. DNA denatures pretty quickly when exposed to heat, but I might be able to do something, especially if I have access to the bones and/or the dentals.'

TWENTY-NINE

Thursday 7th September, 6 p.m.

Alana went home at six to thoughts of an empty evening stretching out in front of her. She didn't even have Wally to think about. William had offered to take him off her hands to walk the legs off him – his terminology – with the promise of dropping him off later.

It was crazy to think how quickly the mutt had ingratiated himself into her life. Twenty-four hours and she was already missing his investigative wet nose and accompanying doggy smell.

The apartment was quiet and with no welcome from Goose, who'd stalked off when she'd realised Wally wasn't with her.

Bloody great.

Alana wasn't an emotional sort. The guards had drummed that out of her within the first few weeks of joining, which in no way explained the prickly feeling behind her eyes. Billy hadn't been in touch and he wouldn't. From receiving a couple of texts a day, he'd gone completely silent on her. Whether it was a permanent ghosting, or the behaviour of a peeved little boy and all because she'd got his name wrong, was impossible to tell. Being busy was as good an excuse as any for her reluctance to examine her own feelings on the matter. There was the cat to feed, even though he was ignoring her, and a meal to cobble together one-handed. There was also the intercom to answer, her shoulders drooping at the sound of her buzzer.

It was Colm.

He arrived with bags bulging with food. 'I'm happy to just drop these off...'

He couldn't quite meet her gaze, barely crossing the threshold.

'Come in and take your coat off. Would you like a drink? There's tea, coffee or wine in the fridge?'

'I wasn't sure if it would be convenient.'

'As long as you don't mind dogs.'

'Dogs?'

'William and I have decided to take joint custody of a dog called Wally. It's a long story.'

'It sounds it. That's the lad who's on your team?'

'That's right. I was going to phone to say thank you for everything,' Alana said, changing the subject. William and Billy's relationship wasn't something she wanted to get into.

'A busy day?' he said from the kitchen part of the open-plan lounge where he'd started to unload the shopping.

'You could say that.' She watched as he placed all of her favourite foods in the fridge, ones that she could manage to cook and eat one-handed. 'I hope you're going to let me pay you for restocking my cupboards.'

'View it instead of flowers.'

Alana could well remember the days when he'd stroll in, a bunch of roses in one arm and a bottle of champagne in the other. Colm was the sort of man who only bought the best. As an esteemed psychiatrist, he could easily afford it but that wasn't the point. It was nice to be spoilt on occasion, but it all became a little trying day in, day out. He had standards she could never begin to meet.

'It would have to be one fancy bouquet to match that lot.' There was an uncomfortable beat of silence. 'I don't really fancy cooking so what about sharing a takeout but only on the proviso you let me pay as a thank you. I don't know what I would have done without...'

'That's what friends are for, Alana. I hope we can still be friends after... after everything that's happened.'

'I'd like that. Now, Chinese, Indian or pizza?' Alana said, swiftly changing the subject.

There was only Chardonnay to go with their beef madras instead of the red he favoured but he didn't utter a word, which was good because Alana wasn't in the mood for criticism. She'd decided to make her peace with him, but it would be on her terms.

Their conversation was curtailed by the intercom going and William breezing in with Wally.

'Well, I must be going.' Colm stood back from the table; the dishes in a pile ready to be stacked in the dishwasher. 'Leave you a chance to talk about work.'

'Who says we wanted to...?'

'Alana, how long have I known you?'

Alana felt she'd been caught red-handed, her clever ex-husband too clever by half. He'd been instrumental in helping them catch The Puppet Maker, and was someone sworn to a code of secrecy as stringent as their own. Colm had a fierce brain, and she had every intention of using it.

'Join us for a coffee?' She turned to William. 'You'll stay, won't you? I've kept you some food.'

The intricacies of the case didn't take long. Colm kept abreast of the newspapers. He knew about the woman in the pot and the death of Barney's brother in Kerry. What he didn't know was Irene's supposition that Jane, Barney and Mason's adoptive mother, and Ciara's biological mother, were one and the same.

'And you say there's no DNA apart from Jane's match to Ciara, when the girl's parents died in a fire back in 1981?'

'Lorrie is covering all the bases with Ciara's parents by rushing through a licence to exhume their bodies. Rusty thinks he might be able to extract useable DNA from the teeth or jaw. The hope is that it will point us in the right direction.'

'It's only dotting the i's and crossing the t's though, isn't it,' William said from his position on the floor beside Wally and Goose, his arm looped around the pair of them, an empty plate by his feet. 'Ciara's birth mother can't be in two places at once. What about Barney saying he didn't have anything belonging to his adoptive mother? Surely a search warrant is in order?'

'I know you're right.' Alana knew she was allowing her sympathies for the man to cloud her judgement. Barney could have easily been the one to place Jane in the pot before going on to murder his brother. That they didn't have a clue what his motive could be didn't mean there wasn't one.

'I'll drop Detective O'Hagan a line to check through Mason's stuff on the off chance he kept anything from those days, however unlikely it seems,' she said, grabbing her phone from the table, where it was starting up a fandango with the number of messages it was receiving.

Colm was a silent presence, his hands wrapped round his mug, his drink ignored, his gaze on the laminate flooring by his feet. His voice when he finally spoke was low, his words carefully considered. 'It's difficult for me to apply the concepts I use in addressing mental health concerns in children. Adults are a completely different ballgame, but I think we can all agree that these are carefully planned crimes, staged if you like and if they are staged, then to what purpose? Someone is setting a trail of clues and you're picking them up and trying to make them fit the narrative.' He settled his mug down, his expression grim.

'This person is dangerous, Alana, very dangerous indeed and you still have no idea what they're up to or the stakes involved but they've already committed two murders so I'm guessing that it's going to be high.'

Alana met his gaze before returning her attention to her phone, which was now ringing in her hand. Her stomach threatened to propel curry back up her neck at a speed which would make containment difficult as she scanned her messages.

She swallowed then swallowed again before speaking, her finger hovering over the flashing green answer button. 'It's three murders not two. There's been another one.'

THIRTY

Thursday 7th September, 7.45 p.m.

William was driving. Colm couldn't as he'd had a glass of wine as opposed to her couple of sips, all Alana would allow herself while staying within the boundaries of her pain medication. She'd asked him along, she wasn't sure why or what had made him accept. It wasn't a question she was prepared to ask as she checked her phone. Still no word from Billy.

Howth Harbour was striking in the glow from the setting sun. The sound of the yacht masts clinking in the wind that had picked up during the evening, the lights from the coast stretching into the harbour and beyond. There was no sign of Barney's boat, which was still in dry dock until Rogene and her team had finished with it, but that didn't mean there was no sign of its owner.

They headed as a pack towards Flynn, the one who'd placed the call and the one who could always be found hanging around boats when he wasn't on duty. He was standing in a huddle with another group of similarly garbed men, all dressed in white Helly Hanson sweatshirts with some kind of boat logo embroidered on the back but in his case with a towel round his shoulders and a pool of water collecting at his bare feet.

'What you got for us, Flynn?'

'Popped into the Yacht Club with my dad. Had only been there like five minutes when someone ran in shouting there was someone in the harbour. Thought he meant swimming and was unable to get out. It wouldn't be the first time someone has decided to go for a dip after getting tanked up but not face down.'

'No. And afterwards?'

'Managed to drag him onto the slipway.' He threw her a quick look. 'It was a tossup as to what would cause the least damage to any evidence, seawater or the slip. I've also alerted Rusty and Rogene, They're both on their way.'

'And you're sure it's Barney Mulcahy?'

'Rolled him over in case there was any chance of saving him.'

'Do you want me to take a quick look?' Colm interrupted. 'It's a long time since I've had to confirm a death, but the principle won't have changed.'

'Yes. Thank you.' Her gaze hovered between the two of them before shifting to the stream of cars screaming around the corner with no regard to either the time of night, or the speed limit. 'You remember Dr Colm Mack, Flynn. Show him what you've got while I go and speak to Rusty and Rog.'

William was hovering on the sideline, awkward, and uneasy. She'd have liked to send him home, but she needed him to drive when she went to break the news to Barney's wife. It would be easier to get a uniform to do the task, but there was a lot to be said for being present at such a time. As horrific as it sounded, Barney's wife had just shot up to the top of their suspect list.

Someone somewhere had managed to secure a tray of coffees along with a pile of sugar and one stirrer, which they all fell upon with an enthusiasm that far outweighed the humble offering. Barney had been confirmed dead at the scene and they were now hanging about watching as the paramedics stretchered his body to the ambulance to take him to Clonabee Hospital where Rusty would perform the post-mortem first thing tomorrow. She'd sent him home just as she had Colm, which only left Flynn and William hovering on the quay while Rogene supervised the removal. Alana would wait until that task was completed before heading over to visit the wife. The late time was unfortunate, but it wasn't something she was prepared to leave until the morning.

'Unlikely to be an accident.' William was first to speak, his cup cradled between his fingers, Wally pressed into his side. They'd thought about leaving him behind, but he'd made the decision for them by whining at the door.

'No, although you would have thought he'd have been able to make it to the harbour wall.'

'Probably couldn't swim,' Flynn replied, taking a cautious sip from the hot liquid.

'But he was a fisherman?'

'And like most fishermen around here, has probably never learnt to swim. Some think it's unlucky while the rest of them would prefer to die quickly instead of trying to save themselves, only to face the same outcome.'

Alana was astounded. 'And that's common knowledge, is it?'

'Absolutely. The same the world over. Don't you remember that initiative about ten years ago to try and improve safety, it was on the back of some tragedy or other where several fishermen lost their lives.'

'I don't know what to say.'

'There isn't a lot to say except if that's the case, and I don't believe for a minute that Flynn has got it wrong,' William added quickly, 'then Barney was a sitting duck, literally. All it would have needed was someone to follow him down here and push him in. It's not as if there's going to be that many people around this time of the evening or indeed this time of the year. I doubt there's even any CCTV to help us.'

Alana set her cup down on the tray, her good arm cradling her bad. It looked as if someone was trying to annihilate the whole of the Mulcahy family, which meant that Waldo and Deirdre were potential targets. A quick call to Leo was warranted in the hope that he'd see the sense in providing both with garda protection.

Deirdre Mulcahy opened the door before they'd even reached for the bell, a cigarette hanging from her mouth and the set expression of someone who knew something unpleasant was on the way.

Breaking bad news was a skill. It was also viewed as the shittiest of all the shitty jobs they had to complete. It ranked higher on the crapometer than a decomposed body or even a decapitation, both of which Alana had come across during her first week in the job.

'He's dead, isn't he?'

'Let's go inside out of the cold, Deirdre,' she replied, dependent on William to push her wheelchair over the threshold. She only spoke again once they were in the comfort of the kitchen, the sight of the empty mug and full ashtray testament to the unsettled evening she'd been having. With William instinctively making for the kettle and arranging fresh mugs and milk, Alana directed Deirdre into a chair and told her the news.

'I knew it. As soon as the bugger wasn't answering his phone, and it went straight to voicemail. He always answers. Knows how worried I get. Oh Gawd, what am I going to do now.' She reached for her packet of fags, fumbling to shake one out and then struggling to light it. 'Feck's sake!'

'Here, let me.' Alana gripped the lighter and managed to get a spark and then a flame. With the way the woman was drawing on the cigarette it wouldn't be long before she'd need another one, but chain smoking was the least of Deirdre Mulcahy's concerns currently. 'Is there anyone you'd like me to phone,' Alana asked, nodding her thanks to William as he set a tray of tea on the table.

'Like whom? We don't have any family. Barney was all I had.'

'What about a friend or a neighbour? I don't think you should be on your own,' Alana pressed. Everyone had somebody even if it was only an ex-husband to call in an emergency.

'I'll be fine. Going to have to get used to it now, aren't I?' She replaced the burnt-out cigarette with the mug William slid in front of her, her fingers wrapped around the handle. 'What happens now?'

'We've taken Barney back to the hospital. There'll be a post-mortem to find out what happened.' Alana paused a second before asking one of the most difficult questions of all. 'Do you think you'd be able to ID him for us? We can go on a blood sample but... I have seen him, Deirdre. It looks as if he's asleep.'

She nodded, biting her bottom lip to stop it trembling.

'Do you have any ideas as to what could have happened?'

'I know what happened,' Deirdre choked. 'Someone murdered him just like they murdered his brother. I told him he shouldn't have gone out tonight, that it would only end in tears.'

'And why did he?'

'He had a call. Someone told him they knew something about the woman in the pot and he was stupid enough to believe them.' Alana glanced across at William briefly. They hadn't found a mobile at the scene, either on his person or in his car. That didn't mean they wouldn't be able to locate it, but it would make it more difficult.

'Did he say anything else?'

'Only that he had to go over to Howth, and he'd be back within the hour.'

William stepped forward from where he'd been propping up the work surface. 'When Detective Mack last spoke to your husband, Mrs Mulcahy, he mentioned that he'd let us have that thing from his childhood he kept. It really is vital to the investigation.'

'What thing? I don't know what you're meaning?'

Alana was tempted to shut down that line of questioning until a later date. The woman was in no fit state to string two words together let alone think about her husband's childhood, but this was the oddest of cases and they needed all the help they could get.

'He told us there was something that his mother gave him. To be honest he was reluctant to tell us about it, I think maybe because of the sentimental meaning it held?'

'You can't be meaning the bear? A mangy ole thing he refused to chuck.'

'If it's something that his adoptive mother gave him, then yes.'

'Made it herself and it shows. Dreadful seamstress.' She pushed away from the table and made for the door. 'You're welcome to it. Anything to help. Made both boys one as a welcome home gift, not that it meant anything. Upped and walked out as soon as she realised how difficult it was.'

THIRTY-ONE

Thursday 7th September, 11 p.m.

It was eleven by the time Alana arrived home. Far too late to think about anything apart from bed but sleep was a long time in coming. They were no further forward in their efforts to identify Ciara's birth mother and fast running out of people to interview but she'd had complex cases before. Alana thrived on complex. What she couldn't seem to cope with was the sudden, irrational bag snatcher flashbacks she'd started to get and at the oddest of times. As soon as the door had closed on William, she'd been paralysed with fear, a fear that was as unwelcome as it was ungrounded. The doors were locked as were all the windows. There was no way for someone to get in unless she let them. She even had a door cam and intercom to vet callers. As a female copper living on her own, she had made sure her security arrangements were tight when she'd purchased the property.

Alana woke at six in the knowledge that she was done with bed for the night. By seven she was nursing a strong coffee, Eve's folder propped open on the table in front of her. Taking records off site was a clear breach of the station's GDPR policy and accompanied by the most stringent of reprimands but Alana didn't care about that. She'd like to know when she was meant to complete all the must do tasks assigned when there wasn't a spare moment in the day for the essentials like eating.

Eve's folder was thick, far thicker than hers or Paddy's but that was to be expected as the woman had moved around many times in her career. Alana started by jotting down a brief summary of her different moves only to stop at eight, her pen chucked aside in frustration. After an initial ten years in the same station Eve had got divorced and swapped jobs within the span of six months and had continued swapping jobs every two years since. There was a pile of letters of complaint from Eve about whichever team she happened to be working with at the time along with a pile of incendiary annual reviews from her senior managers with words like clever, unreliable, divisive and, in one instance, unpleasant to work with.

Alana raised her eyebrows at that one, her investigative nose twitching as she read over her scanty notes. What had happened sixteen years ago for Eve to end up the sad person she was today? There had to be something. It didn't take her long to trace back to the last job Eve had held for longer than a blink. The glowing reports and commendations. The inferences of a career satelliting to the top. Then nothing. No, not nothing. An uncontested divorce within weeks of returning from four months' sick leave following being assaulted on the job in Tipperary.

Not everything was included in staff records. It took a track back through the PULSE computer system and a search of the local newspapers to piece together the rest. A sting operation gone wrong and the vicious attack on the pregnant guard that had followed, resulting in her miscarrying her baby.

By the time her lift had arrived, she was waiting in the hall, her jacket over her arm and Eve's folder tucked down the bottom of her rucksack. Annoyance at the woman had been pushed aside by sympathy, not that Eve would appreciate the sentiment. The similarities in their history was something that couldn't be ignored, not that Alana would be able to act on her findings. The woman was a management nightmare. Suspecting the reason why wouldn't change that.

THIRTY-TWO

Friday 8th September, 9.30 a.m.

William undid his seatbelt, waiting for Paddy to do the same, his gaze on the old people's home. The white façade and fancy planters. The wheelchair-friendly entrance, which he now felt expert in recognising. The thick wooden door, pierced with a polished brass letter box.

While he loved his job, he didn't love all of it, which in no way explained why he'd volunteered to be the second guard when Paddy broke the news of Barney's death to his dad. It made sense to him to offer when Alana had asked. He'd met Waldo already so a familiar face might make it easier. William didn't have a clue really if it would make any difference, but he hoped that might be the case.

'I'm not sure I should let you see him. He's not that well. We're waiting for the doctor.' The nurse was the same. The pretty one with the red ponytail and bossy manner.

He blinked then blinked again at the thought, feeling a rush of heat explode up his neck and take up residence in his ears, an unfortunate trait that he would pay good money to see the back of. Another thought followed, one he could do without, so he ruthlessly pushed it aside.

'What's wrong with him exactly?' Paddy asked, rocking back on his heels.

William watched her frown, her nose wrinkling along with her brow.

'I'm not sure. He was well enough yesterday, even managed to play a hand of poker with some of the other men. A combination of his heart and his stomach when the problem is in his lungs. Most peculiar.'

'We'd still like to see him if you don't mind.'

Waldo wasn't so much sleeping as unconscious, his breathing a stertorous rasp, his skin flushed and dry, his lips an unhealthy shade of blue.

'He's worse, much worse.' Dora ran from the room, only to return shortly with another nurse. William and Paddy were both ignored while an oxygen mask was fitted, and a full range of observations recorded. William wasn't a medic, but it didn't take a medic to know that Waldo would be shortly joining his sons.

Paddy pulled out his mobile and started messaging. William glanced at him briefly before moving to the other side of the room to study the framed photos on the wall and the contents of the table below, his eyes skimming over the boxes and books with a frown before picking up Waldo's file and starting to leaf through it.

Dora had the presence of mind to call an ambulance instead of waiting for the doctor. They stood well back and watched as Waldo was slid across onto the trolley and escorted into the waiting vehicle. William beckoned to one of the paramedics and spoke to him briefly before following Paddy back into the care home.

'You still here?' Dora arrived back in the room and seemed surprised at their presence.

William stepped forward, a box of liquorice in his hand. 'What can you tell me about these?'

'Apart from the fact they're a box of sweets, you mean?'

'Apart from the fact they're a box of sweets, yes.' William didn't move his eyes. They might have flickered a little, but he managed to leash them, front and central just in time.

'Waldo likes sweets, always gets his visitors to bring in an assortment of chocolates and biscuits. Can wrap the hardest of geezers round his little finger, that one.'

'So, he didn't buy the liquorice himself then?'

'I'm not sure why you're so interested?' She glanced up at him, shorter by almost a foot and yet with a guileless stare that told him he wasn't the one in charge of the conversation. If he didn't get to the point soon, he knew Paddy would intervene.

'Liquorice in large quantities is known to have a detrimental effect on some people.' He didn't call her Dora. He didn't call her anything. He didn't quite have the nerve.

'Is it now? New one on me. Let me think.' She eyed the box, the nose wrinkling thing again making its appearance. He thought it charming. 'That's right, the befriending service. It was her who brought him the liquorice.'

'Her as in?'

She sighed, a heartfelt sigh that told him in no uncertain terms that she was completely bored with the conversation. 'We work with a local charity who offer a befriending service for those who don't get that many visitors. Waldo jumped at the chance so every week like clockwork someone comes from the charity for a chat and oftentimes they bring small gifts, usually edible.'

'And the name of his visitor?'

'Cassandra from Elder-Connect, Ireland. Been visiting for about a month, six weeks now. Nice enough except the one time someone called her Cassie by mistake. I thought she was going to poke their eyes out.'

'You don't happen to know her full name by any chance?'

'Hang on a mo.' They followed her across to the front desk, where a visitor register languished on a clipboard. 'Cassandra Brewin.'

William jotted the name down in his notebook. 'I'm guessing there's no CCTV by any chance?'

'Not a hope in hell with GDPR. If we were a locked unit then perhaps but we're not. Our residents have rights, you know.'

So do our victims but not so you'd notice.

'How do you feel about popping down to the station and meeting with one of our sketch artists?'

'If it's that important?' She glanced between them. 'I can see it is. Will have to be tomorrow now. I'm in charge and there's staff sickness.'

'Tomorrow will be fine. Here's my card if you think of anything else.' He opened his wallet and selected one before handing it to her, trying to ignore the way she examined both sides before popping it in her pocket.

'I can see you're going to be chasing after my job,' Paddy declared, ten minutes later. 'I'll have to watch my back the way you're going.'

'Pardon?'

They were in the car making their way to the station, William on his phone trying to track down the phone number of Elder-Connect, Ireland.

'Well done, William. I mean that. You really are shaping up to be a very good guard indeed and you know I don't give praise lightly.'

William didn't know what to say. In the same way Paddy had difficulty giving praise William had difficulty in accepting it. With an alcoholic for a mother, an estranged father and no friends, he had little experience of receiving rewards, verbal or otherwise.

'Thank you.'

He pressed dial only to choke at Paddy's next words, unfortunately just as the phone connected. 'I reckon that Dora nurse fancies you.'

'What! Oh, sorry. No, not you. I think it must be a bad line. Let's start again. I'm Detective William Slattery from the National Bureau of Criminal Investigation. I'd like to speak to someone about Elder-Connect's visits to Bobbins Care Home over in Donnybrook.'

'I can help you with that. I'm Jane Beaulieu, one of the managers. Is there a problem?'

'No, not as such, but we do need to get in touch with one of your volunteers and the dates when they visited. All the home could tell us was that her name was Cassandra Brewin.'

'Do you have a warrant, detective?'

William grimaced, hoping he'd managed to escape that little banana skin. 'I didn't think I'd need one, but it's easily obtained.'

'Drop into our head office when you've got it but, in the meantime, I am happy to confirm that we don't have any volunteers with that name working in our organisation.'

William ended the call. 'There's something odd about all this.'

'In what way?'

'How would this Cassandra Brewin know where to find Waldo? It's not as if his whereabouts would be on public record. The same goes for Mason's address. Barney would have been far easier to trace. Ask anyone hanging about Howth and they'd probably know his general whereabouts, but not the others.'

'So, she followed Barney, which led her to his dad, but what about Mason?'

'I don't know but it does give us a lead to follow,' Paddy said, turning off Poolbeg Way and into Clonabee Station before switching off the engine, his hands still resting on the steering wheel.

'Which one?'

'An ANPR one. No CCTV is only a minor irritant with the presence of number plate cameras. An analysis of the data from the cameras around Mason's property and then Barney's and Bobbins would be interesting, don't you think?'

'Not if you're asking me to do the donkey work, Paddy!'

'Hah. I like it when a guard is proactive. Flynn has already been looking into Barney's car and bank account, but he will probably still need a hand though?'

'Okay. Fine. Only if you promise not to mention that nurse again.'

'What nurse?'

THIRTY-THREE

Friday 8th September, 11 a.m.

'What the hell is the meaning of this?'

Leo slammed down the *Globe*, his hand clenching in anger. The incident room was reverberating with the emotion, so much so that Wally jumped to his feet and started to snarl, his sharp teeth gleaming between his gums.

Alana dropped her hand automatically to his head, her attention on the headline while she muttered soothing sounds under her breath.

'The Woman in the Pot. Her daughter reveals all. Turn to page four for the full story.'

'If I find that your boyfriend had a hand in this, believe me when I say that your time on the team will be very short lived indeed, Detective Mack.'

Alana wasn't listening, not really. She lifted her hand off Wally's head briefly to turn to page four and the two-page feature with a colour photograph of Ciara Buckley front and central. There were other pictures, one of black-haired Paula and Joseph Buckley on their wedding day, and a much younger Ciara with the same white-blonde hair tied in pigtails.

'Well, what have you got to say for yourself?'

'I'm not sure what you expect me to say other than Miss Buckley has obviously decided to cash in on her newfound notoriety.'

Alana was disappointed in a gut wrenching, why is everyone on the make, kind of way. But mostly she was disappointed that Ciara would be prepared to sell her story to the highest bidder. This was her family, her only link to finding out about her past. Tomorrow's chip wrappings but before that a whole lot of trouble if Leo honestly thought she was involved. She squinted down at the name of the reporter. Michael O'Finn, the name of Billy's top reporter, not that it made any difference to anything. There was no way she could prove her innocence either way. There was no way she should need to.

Wally had settled down again but with a watchful eye on Leo. Alana settled too, the paper neatly folded and pushed to one side, her decision made.

'If you honestly think I believe—'

'To be quite frank, *sir*, I don't care what you believe.' Alana pulled her keyboard closer, opened her non-urgent folder and changed the date of her resignation letter. 'Is there anything else, *sir*? I have work to do.'

'It's two o'clock. Showtime.'

The incident room was full, and with the addition of Ruan again dialling in on Teams. Alana had emailed him late last night about the teddy bear and had received a reply first thing. No bear. Hopefully it wouldn't be a problem with Barney's cuddly toy already in the hands of the SOCOs. The fact the bear was handmade offered a degree of hope out of keeping with the age and general appearance of the one-eyed, torn and decidedly grubby teddy.

'We have a lot to get through including some very worrying news from Paddy and William but first, Rusty – your report into Barney's PM.'

'No report. Far too early to find the time to type it up but it appears to be a straightforward case of drowning.' Rusty crossed one leg over the other, his trousers hitching to reveal a pair of black socks with pink and purple triangles. 'The basic tox screen has come back negative to the usual substances, and the contents of his alimentary tract are in keeping with his wife's menu of pepperoni pizza along with a gallon of sea water, which we found in the hyper-inflated lungs.'

Alana would have liked to ask more. Questions like would Barney have suffered and how long would it have taken, but she didn't. Muddying the waters with sentiment was best left for the pub after they'd solved his murder. Instead, she watched as Paddy made a note on the board next to the cause of the man's death.

While the team had been mostly out and about undertaking interviews, she'd spent the morning drilling down through the Mulcahy family history, looking for a motive, any piddly motive for the murder of the brothers and the woman they now suspected was their adoptive mother. The deaths were too much of a coincidence not to be related. She'd also taken the opportunity to rework the facts of the case on the three boards. It wasn't her best handiwork, but it didn't need to be. Accuracy over legibility.

'Thank you. Flynn, talk us through what happened when he was found?'

'There's not a lot to say outside of what you know already. I was in the area. There was a yacht race I was meant to be crewing for.' He shrugged away the fact he'd been too late to make it. 'I decided to pop into the club for a bit instead. We'd only been in about five minutes when someone came running in saying there was a body floating face down in the harbour. We fished him out—'

'As in you fished him out,' Alana interrupted. 'Don't go all coy on us, Flynn. Jumping into the Irish Sea is a feat of bravery whatever the time of year.'

'Yes, well.' He stopped to clear his throat. 'We fished him out and started CPR. Even put a defib on him but he was clearly dead. You arrived soon after, so you know the rest.'

'What about after that? I'm guessing you caught up with the person who found him?'

'An old woman out walking her dog. Says she didn't see anything and she's probably right. I reckon it happened a good half hour or so before that. What do you think, doc?'

'Sounds about right. His core temperature was thirty-four degrees when I got to him. Rapidly cooling but still reversible, if he could have been saved.'

'It should be thirty-seven, shouldn't it?' Paddy said.

'There or thereabouts.'

'And what about this morning, Flynn?' Alana prompted.

'I've been there since dawn knocking on doors.' Flynn shrugged a second time. 'No one saw a thing.'

'So, Barney gets a message on his phone to meet someone about our Jane Doe only for him to be pushed into the harbour.' Alana's gaze landed on Eve and where she was sitting back in her chair, her arms folded across her chest in contrast to Lorrie, Flynn and William who were busy taking notes, either on their laptop or notepad. 'Oh, what about CCTV and doorbell footage?' she added, her attention still on Eve and the way she picked up her phone and started swiping through her messages.

'Actually, yes. Remember, they had a problem with hooligans a few years back, so they opted for cameras along that stretch.' Flynn tapped his laptop. 'I've downloaded the footage from all four so we should get some kind of an idea as to what transpired.'

'And no sign of Barney's mobile?'

'Waiting for the diver to get back to me. It's not as easy as it sounds. The area is tidal, and the sea has lumped up overnight. I have contacted his provider though and they're going to try and track the signal to hopefully its last known whereabouts.'

'Good. The likelihood is the call to his phone was made from a burner, but people have been known to make stupid mistakes. Let's hope our perp is one of them. I'm going to ask you to lead on this one, Flynn. There are too many bodies for us to manage without a bit of delegating.' She turned to the room in general. 'William and I went to break the news to his wife. Poor woman. Tatty's been there all night. Not surprisingly, Deirdre is in a right state. We have obviously added her to the list of possible suspects, but I can't see it. The only positive is she admitted that Barney's adoptive mother made him and Mason a teddy bear. Most likely the reason why Rogene has yet to grace us with her presence. The hope is we'll get some lush DNA, our suspicion being that Dympna Mulcahy and Jane are one and the same.'

'And if they are the same? It's not as if you know what the mother was up to or why she was killed. It's all supposition currently.'

'As is detecting in general, Eve, or did you miss out on that part of the training?' Alana had just about had enough of Eve bleedin' Rohan, but she was stuck with her until she managed to get to the bottom of why the woman had asked to move to her team. There had to be a reason. 'We're building a case currently. We don't have all the blocks but, mark my words, we'll solve it a lot more easily without the sarcasm.' She turned to Paddy, letting air seep through her lungs and out again before speaking. Her pulse was thrumming in her ears as her heartbeat ratcheted up a notch. There weren't enough numbers to count to because ten in this instance wasn't going to be enough.

'What's happening with Barney's dad?'

'Admitted to Clonabee Hospital with suspected glycyrrhizin acid poisoning.' He glanced at Rusty. 'That's the right pronunciation, eh?'

'We'll make a doctor of you yet.'

Paddy gave a visible shudder. 'Not on your nelly!'

'And how is he?' Alana asked.

'Too early to say but at least we were able to point them in the right direction as to possible treatments.'

'No antidote, Rusty?'

'Not as such. It messes with the body's electrolytes so that's where they'll be focusing.'

'Okay. There's also nothing new on the Jane front.' Alana made a brief change to the first of the whiteboards before handing the tablet over to Paddy with a smile. 'And there won't be until we can ID her. I can't believe that a woman can go missing in Ireland for two weeks or more and no one notices her absence. What kind of world are we living in? No match from your forensic odontologist over in Tralee, Rusty?'

He shook his head. 'Identification is based on comparing antemortem and post-mortem data, easy enough these days with everything online but not so easy when it appears Jane didn't have much work done. Some fillings but when she was a child, which could have been anything up to seventy plus years ago. The likelihood of a dentist commuting records from that far back to electronic is negligible.'

Alana had already guessed that. The one thing about Rusty was he always messaged her as soon as he had something positive. With her confidence at rock bottom after Leo's blast, the last thing she was looking for was more dead ends. Add Eve to the mix and she was ready to hand in her notice and claim for disability pension. She scanned the room, glossing over Eve's smirk in favour of Lorrie's bent head.

'What's happening with the Buckley side of things, Lor?'

'That's where I've just come from.' She slid her chair back, pointing to her mud-streaked shoes and torn stockings. 'Remind me never to agree to attend an exhumation. It was the worst.'

'I can imagine.'

'Anyways Joseph and Paula Buckley are both on their way over to Dr Mulholland's pathology suite. Sorry, Rusty.' A comment he waved away with a small smile.

'Thank you. Eve tracked down Ciara's relatives but they had nothing new to add, that's right, isn't it?'

'Absolutely.'

Alana clenched her teeth at the shortness of the reply. 'And what about Ciara's background? What's she been up to in the intervening years?'

'Discharged from the burns unit aged sixteen and taken in by one of the doctors and her family. Sixteen was an age that she could have lived alone but it was felt that with the disruption to her home life and her education, living as part of a family would be beneficial.'

'That was good of the doctor. I gather we have the doctor's details, Eve? We will need to get in touch.'

'Of course! A Dr Louisa Laverty. It looks as if she's away currently, but I've left a message for her to contact me on her return.'

'Okay, and what about after Ciara left the doctor?'

'Left at eighteen and was helped to buy a house, remembering there was some money put in a trust from her parents' house when it was sold on,' Eve said, reading from an A4 piece of paper. 'Got a job at Roches Stores, over in Cork, working her way up to chief buyer until it closed in the mid-noughties. After, she trained as a psychotherapist and currently runs a small practice out of her house, along with another therapist.'

The background was comprehensive but a list of locations and job titles didn't really tell Alana anything about the woman, nothing that she could use to get a handle on the type of person she was. Damaged certainly with that medical history, probably emotionally as well as physically. There was also the issue of sending her DNA to one of those bone marrow registries when the uptake was primarily intended for people half her age. Alana made a scrawl on her pad to follow up on the email Ciara had forwarded her. 'Okay, I'd like you to have a peek at her financial situation please. Anything untoward, or monies either in or out not accounted for.' And then to Ruan: 'Anything new your end or any comments on what we've been discussing?'

'Nothing. We're concentrating on Mason's financials too. There's also the ANPR records you asked for, which I'll email over shortly. That's about it.'

'Perfect.' She turned to Flynn. 'What about Barney's bank account? Anything?'

'Nothing that I could see. Not much spare money but they didn't live outside of their means. No unusual activity with either deposits or withdrawals.'

'Okay. I'll leave you and William to run a comparison between the ANPR from Kerry and Waldo's care home as well as Barney's car. We really do need to find out how they tracked Mason down.'

'Actually...'

'What you got, William?'

'Sorry, I have an idea about that. I should have mentioned it earlier but well, with everything.'

He looked embarrassed, which prompted her to add, 'None of us know whether we're coming or going so don't worry about it.'

'Well, when we went to see Waldo in the home I happened upon his file.' He coughed briefly. 'There was a folder at the end of his bed table and I opened it. Didn't understand most of it if

I'm honest but it did include the contact details of all his next of kin, including Mason's, which I thought strange at the time. I would have mentioned it but with the man being taken away in the ambulance and everything...'

'It's alright, William. Thank you. Another box ticked.'

She turned back to the room. 'That's it for now unless anyone has anything to add?' She paused a second, taking the time to check that everyone seemed happy enough. 'No? Good. So, the key points are the ANPR records for any crossover, the Buckleys' post-mortem's, which Lorrie is coordinating, chasing up what happened over in Bobbins Care Home – that's you, William – and then the DNA from Barney's teddy, which I'll do. Eve, I'd like you to concentrate on who had the most to benefit from these murders, including Waldo Buckley in that. Look into the financials as well as someone bearing a grudge. Lastly, Flynn, I want you to find out everything you can about his missing wife. The police report should be a good place to start.' She took a minute to catch her breath. 'Right, we'd better get to it.'

THIRTY-FOUR

Friday 8th September, 3.05 p.m.

The Technical Bureau occupied the whole of the third floor of the building. A spacious area separated by glass partitions into their designated areas of specialism, from fingerprint and blood splatter analysis, to ballistics, firearms and a whole lot more besides.

Alana entered the department with caution, aware that her proficiency with the chair was at best incompetent. She'd already taken a lump out of the wall in the incident room, run over Mary's foot in reception, and that was by ten this morning. The sooner she could ditch the plaster and get back to using her own chair the better. It was still there in the incident room, folded behind her desk if she needed to head out urgently. The hope was they'd seen the last of the murders but the way the case was going there were no certainties anymore. Someone somewhere wanted the Mulcahy family wiped off the face of the earth and they were no further forward in understanding who or why. Thinking that the woman in the pot was key was very different to proving it.

Rogene was peering at her laptop, her hair obscuring part of her face, a chipped mug off to one side with *Welcome to Manilla* emblazoned across the front.

She knocked, then knocked again when Rogene didn't respond.

'I heard you the first time, Alana,' she said, lifting her head with a brief smile.

'Sorry, didn't want to disturb you.' Alana felt herself visibly relax now she was out of the incident room and away from that bloody woman, as she was starting to think of her instead of her given name. It wasn't like her to let someone get under her skin, but Eve was like a leech bleeding all her energy away and when she wasn't feeling one hundred per cent. That she thought she knew the reason for the woman's behaviour didn't help. There was no way of broaching the topic of her past.

'You alright?' Rogene was a friend, someone she'd clicked with the first time they'd met. They weren't the kind of friends to meet up socially – Rogene was as private as she was – but there was complete honesty and trust in their relationship as well as a huge dose of humour. Alana had brought Rog the mug as a cheeky present – who wants a souvenir mug from their hometown – at the same time she'd brought sport allergic Paddy a Chelsea one. In return they'd clubbed together to buy her a leprechaun-emblazoned teapot.

'Not really but I'll manage.'

'I have some painkillers in my bag?'

'Dosed up to the eyeballs. Any more and I won't be able to see straight but thank you. How are you getting on with the bear?'

'See for yourself.'

Rogene's office was multifunctional with a desk filled with the prerequisite laptop and printer on the right, and a workstation straight ahead, with an unpicked teddy littering the surface. 'I hope you're good with a needle and thread, Alana. There's no way I'm going to be able to get it back together.'

'I don't think the wife will mind if it leads us to finding out who his mother is, or was,' she qualified.

'Oh, definitely a was, I'm afraid. I can categorically tell you that your woman in the pot has the same DNA as Dympna Mulcahy.'

Alana sighed. Having your fears confirmed didn't change the size and shape of them or help in lessening the dread. What the hell was going on?

If someone was to ask her where the afternoon had vanished to, she wouldn't be able to tell them.

The office was as quiet as her mobile, now that the time was heading for half six. Still nothing from Billy and also nothing from Colm, but she had warned him not to phone as she'd be neck deep in the repercussions from Barney's death. It was a huge surprise that they were now managing to function as friends with their history, but she wasn't going to knock it. She also didn't have a minute to spare to think of either of them, she reminded herself, glancing at her watch before checking her messages for the umpteenth time.

Lorrie was over in Clonabee Hospital attending the Buckleys' post-mortem while Flynn had opted to work out of one of the empty rooms along the corridor to concentrate on the CCTV from Howth. Four cameras and an hour window to account for meant four hours of screen time, which he wanted to finish up tonight. William had accepted with good grace the brunt of the ANPR number plate records sent over by Ruan and had decided to start on them immediately only to be sidetracked by Wally whining at the door.

Alana shouldn't still be amazed at the dedication from her staff, who demonstrated over and over how committed they were, but she was. All apart from Eve who was again nearly standing by the door, bag in hand when the clock showed five. It was a tossup whether to have a word with her or Leo. The only part she was certain about was that words would have to be said to the bloody woman.

Paddy had only left five minutes ago to attend a midwife's appointment with Irene. He'd have stayed if Alana hadn't forced him out the door. She'd missed too many of her own life's highlights to allow the same sort of behaviour in her staff.

The sound of tap-tapping nails on the floor outside the office followed by a little woof of warning had her lifting her head to see Wally hurtling towards her.

'Had a good walk?'

'Just round the block. Did his big jobs too.'

"Great.' Not a conversation she'd ever imagined having but life held a surprise round every corner, some of which were pleasurable. 'That's a good boy, Wally.'

'I'll hang round for a bit until your taxi comes. Then I can drop Wal back at the same time. Still okay if I walk him in the morning?'

Alana knew he was only being polite. While some people could probably manage to walk their dog beside their mobility scooter, she was wise enough to know that wasn't her, yet.

'That would be perfect, thank you. What about checking in with the staff over at Bobbins to see how Waldo is doing? We could call direct, but you know what hospitals are like for managing information. I'll make us a coffee while you're at it. The taxi won't be here for another twenty minutes or so.'

'I can make the—'

'But you won't. I need to shift my lazy ass.'

'Okay. I'll pop it on loudspeaker. Will save me having to repeat it.'

'Good idea.' Alana swerved to the kettle and started assembling coffee, mugs and spoons, one ear tuned to the conversation happening over her shoulder.

'Bobbins.'

'Hello there, it's Detective William Slattery from Clonabee Station. I wanted to speak to someone about Waldo Mulcahy.'

There was a slight pause. 'It's Dora. I've just been in touch with the hospital. Waldo passed earlier on today.'

'I'm really sorry to hear that. You will still be able to come in tomorrow for the E-FIT picture... er... Dora?'

'Yes. Fine.' There was a slight pause. 'William is a nice name. I'm Theodora but that's not public knowledge. I only let my friends call me that.'

Alana felt like an eavesdropper suddenly, which didn't stop her from switching off the kettle within seconds of it boiling so she could hear every word.

William coughed – or was that a choking sound? It could have been either. 'Well, thank you again for...'

'Look, William, I know it's not the right time, when is it ever going to be the right time, but if you ever fancy a coffee, you know where to find me.'

'Yes, well, thank you for that. Goodbye.'

'Here's your drink. If you wouldn't mind carrying mine for me, please. Such awful news.' Alana was itching to mention Dora, but it was well beyond her remit as his manager. Rats!

'I'll let Dr Mulholland know.'

'Okay. We're certainly keeping him busy with the case. If we do find that it's glycyrrhizin acid poisoning, then we have a problem on our hands. With Jane proven to be Dympna that's the whole family wiped out.'

'Apart from Deirdre,' he said, sipping from his mug.

'Who we now have on round the clock surveillance in addition to Tatty almost moving in lock, stock and barrel,' Alana said, leafing through her in-tray and idly making three piles. To read now. To file for later, and bin. The bin pile was growing at twice the rate of the other two. There was also a couple of sheets she folded and placed in the top of her handbag. Evening reading while eating her tea.

'There's also Ciara to consider, isn't there?' he said, breaking a biscuit in two, a tiny sliver finding its way into Wally's waiting mouth.

'And wasn't she hacked off when I offered her garda protection earlier. Went on and on about me interfering with her human rights. She also wasn't happy with me picking her up on speaking to the *Globe*, but she can't have it all her own way.' Alana bit into the digestive biscuit, much to Wally's annoyance. 'If her life is under threat then we have a duty of care to provide protection to offset that possibility, no matter what she blags to the media. I'd far rather she hates me than the alternative of having to attend her funeral.' She finished the biscuit, stroking Wally's head in apology but she wasn't sure of the wisdom of giving him biscuits. 'So, between you, me and the dog, what do you think is going on, William?'

He pulled up a seat, stretching out his legs towards Wally, the tip of his right shoe gently rubbing the dog's belly. 'It's more a case of who's annoyed at the Mulcahy clan enough to want to wipe them out. If it's historic, and there's a chance that it will be due to their ages, then it's going to be even more difficult to explain.'

'And the CCTV is no help whatsoever.' Flynn walked into the room with an air of defeat, his shoulders hunched over a pile of images.

'To be fair, when is it ever? So, what you got? I take it no one you recognised?'

'As if I'm ever that lucky.'

Flynn placed the images down on her desk, one by one, William peering over her shoulder. '7.55 p.m. Barney pulls into a parking space and makes his way over to the harbour wall. It's not a great image but you can see it's him by the size and shape.'

Alana nodded for him to continue.

'Then 8.01 p.m. This next one is of someone walking towards him. The shape is all you get. Dressed head to toe in dark colours and with their head turned towards the sea and therefore away from the cameras.'

Alana squinted down at the image in frustration.

'Finally, 8.03. This one's a bit of a surprise, to me as well as to Barney.' Flynn tapped the side of the second image and the shadow on the right before placing the third image alongside, which clearly showed a figure mid stride from behind Barney, their arm outstretched.

There was a fourth image. Barney in the air, his arms reaching above his head. The two figures still visible just, on the edge of the image.

An accomplice.

THIRTY-FIVE

Friday 8th September, 7.05 p.m.

'Thank you for dropping Wally off, William. You're sure you won't come in for a drink before you head off?'

'I'm good, thanks. Ma will be waiting.'

'Okay. See you tomorrow then.' Alana closed the door, double checking the lock had clicked shut behind her. Taking nothing for granted was a new experience. The attack had hit her far more deeply than her broken bone would indicate. She never used to worry about being a disabled woman living alone until some random git had stolen her purse.

There was no news on that side of things, not that she'd had a minute to spare since it had happened. The guards might find him, but most likely they wouldn't. Assaulting an officer was serious stuff but not when the perp would have had no idea as to who he was attacking.

She placed her keys in the bowl on the table, her eyes on the ceramic dish she'd bought in Malaga for that purpose, her mind on the petty thief and what had made him target the car park. She'd thought it random until just now. It was Goose's plaintive *where's my dinner* miaow that had her discarding the idea as fanciful. The apartments were relatively upmarket. Easy pickings for someone who knew what they were about.

Dinner was a ready-made lasagne and a glass of wine, eaten on the table while she scrolled through the news headlines on her phone. The image of Billy Slattery fronting the entertainment section caused her to smile until she glanced at the woman by his side before shifting to the headlined article.

Billy Slattery, billionaire mogul of the Clonabee Globe,
partying the night away at Krystle's with unknown blonde
young enough to be his daughter.

She should have been surprised but wasn't. She should also be feeling disappointment and wondered why that wasn't the case. Alana wasn't a part of his society world, and she didn't want to be, but he'd been a good friend. No. she stabbed a large piece of lasagne and started to chew. He was still a good friend. She'd known what his baggage was when she'd met him. That the baggage now had a face didn't change a thing.

It didn't stop her from continuing to doom scroll through her phone, forking in lasagne in between mouthfuls of wine. If she didn't taste either was neither here nor there. With the plate soaking in the sink, the animals settled and another wine poured, she returned to the table and her laptop, forcing herself to concentrate on work. There was more than enough for her to be going on with, although not a great deal she could do from the comfort of her lounge.

Not liking someone and not trusting them had no common ground with Alana. She'd come across colleagues and acquaintances like her former boss and media grass, Ox Reilly, that were both unlikeable and untrustworthy but that had been a decision she'd formed over the two years of working with him. Eve was new to her and yet there was something both disagreeable and unreliable about the woman. That she'd decided to double check on the work of another highly experienced officer instead of sitting in front of the television was unheard of but there it was.

With her laptop open and logged onto PULSE, she entered the unique generated code belonging to the case to pull up the relevant files before glancing at the A4 folded piece of paper she'd rescued from her inbox earlier and the list of Ciara's relatives. If someone was to ask her why the list was of interest, she wouldn't have been able to answer them. Call it a copper's nose. The sixth sense that all was not as it should be, but without any idea as to why. Maybe a healthy tinge of sympathy for the fourteen-year-old being seemingly abandoned by her relatives at a time when she would have needed them the most – following the deaths of the only people she had ever known as parents.

Alana approached the list of names and telephone numbers with trepidation. Forty-two years was a long time for anyone to remember anything of significance, some small element that might open the case wide. She couldn't even admit to a crime having been committed back in the 1980s. All they had was the mystery of why the woman Ciara thought to be her birth mother was in two places at once. In the bottom of Barney Mulcahy's pots and layered in Paula Buckley's coffin. They might know more after Paula's post-mortem but there were a lot of ifs surrounding the extraction of a useable source of DNA from fire damaged bones. With that thought, Alana reached for her phone, decision made.

'Hello, could I speak to Kent Buckley?'

'Speaking.'

'Hi there. I'm Detective Alana Mack from the National Bureau of Criminal Investigation.'

'We only spoke to you lot earlier.'

Yes, well. This is a follow up call to see if you'd thought any more about the circumstances surrounding...' Alana checked

Eve's brief notes. 'Your brother's death and the arrangements made for his daughter following.'

'See, we weren't in touch at the time. Not with us living in Cavan. The girl was welcome enough here but was also adamant she didn't want to leave Cork. Not a lot we could do with her being of age when they finally discharged her.'

'Okay, fair enough. And has she ever been in touch since?'

'Nothing. And after us making the trip a few times to see her.'

'One more thing. I'm sorry if I'm repeating myself and I can appreciate that it was a long time ago, but can you remember anything about Paula's pregnancy? Anything that you thought odd at the time?'

'As I told the other officer, we weren't that close.'

The second and third call followed the same pattern. The only thing they proved was that Eve was good at her job, asking all the right questions even if her documentation didn't reflect that. A quick glance at her watch told Alana it was a little after nine. Later than she normally liked to contact people unless it was urgent, and checking up on Eve couldn't in any way be classified as anything other than an over-the-top, authoritarian style of management. Not urgent or even important.

The start of the next call followed the same format except that now she was speaking to Collette Welsh over in Connemara, Paula Buckley's sister and Ciara's aunt.

'Yes, nothing to worry about. Only a follow-up call. Were you and your sister close, Mrs Welsh?'

'Close enough until she upped and married Joseph without a by your leave.' The sound of a hearty sniff down the line conveyed her thoughts on the subject of Joseph Buckley, a subject Alana decided to unravel as best she could. Eve's notes on this last call were far from comprehensive.

'It's always unfortunate when that happens.'

'A cabbie when she could have had anyone. Had to work all the hours just to make ends meet.'

'Were they in debt that you know of?' Alana had a list of all their borrowings in front of her but wanted to hear her take on what she was looking at.

'No idea.' The answer was curt, on the cusp of rude and, if Alana was right, it was also a lie.

'I'm afraid that was the case, Mrs Welsh. Your sister and her husband had to remortgage their house. In fact, they would have probably lost it if they hadn't died suddenly.'

'Well, as I said, Joseph didn't earn much.'

'Again, that's not quite accurate. Our investigation into their finances show that he had a decent enough salary, sufficient to cover most borrowings but not the ten thousand euros they forked out fourteen years before they died. A huge outlay in those days, which begs the question what it could have been for?'

Jonah Quigg had been thorough but had come up against a thick, brick wall when he'd tried to answer that question. It was one Alana intended to dismantle brick by brick even if it meant she had to travel to Connemara to do it.

'I don't know anything about that and why is it of interest and after all this time too? It's disrespectful, that's what it is.' The tone had changed. Icy as opposed to cautious.

Alana had a choice. Wait until tomorrow when she might have the medical proof she needed that Paula had never carried a child to term or to follow her nose, which was starting to twitch in anticipation not least because of the discrepancy between Joseph and Paula's black hair in contrast to Ciara's white blonde.

'We have reason to believe that your sister never gave birth to Ciara, Mrs Welsh. That, in fact Ciara was the reason for the ten thousand euros and the second mortgage. Your sister was older than you and there are numerous entries in her medical record about the number of miscarriages she had before Ciara's birth. Why was your niece's birth registered in the district of Western County Galway instead of Cork, Mrs Welsh? In fact, the district that you're currently living in.'

The call ended shortly after but not before Alana had advised her that they'd be sending a garda over tomorrow to get a witness statement.

After, she sat in the growing silence, the noise from outside trickling away like sand as evening switched to night. The room was dark apart from the dim light cast from the lamp in the corner, the only noise the occasional snuffle from Wally, Goose curled into his side.

Alana didn't blame Eve for failing to dig up the dirt. It had been a tricky interview led by instinct and a growing anger at what had befallen the family. Someone somewhere was responsible for their deaths. It still wasn't clear who, but a picture was forming, something they could work on. A couple desperate for a child, an older couple who wouldn't have fit the stringent parameters set out by Ireland's adoption authority.

The black market in Irish babies was something she'd heard about during her training, a scandal that ripped the hearts out of young Irish women, their offspring torn from their grasp, a practice in which doctors, nurses and even priests were complicit. Locking the women away in Magdalene laundries was only the tip of the iceberg, rip away the top layer to find the true tragedy hidden beneath. Children brought up in ignorance of their birthplace and background, their mothers treated no better than animals and, in some cases far worse.

The case was coming full circle, a case which started with the discovery of Dympna Mulcahy's bones in the bottom of Barney's crab pot. A woman who'd given birth to Ciara at eighteen only to marry Waldo two years later, a man fifteen years her senior. Was it significant that Barney had been born the same year as Ciara, and that they'd decided to adopt two boys instead of a daughter? All questions impossible to answer with Waldo's death but Alana suspected she knew at least part of Dympna's story. She made a note to ask Flynn about the original missing person's report filed by Waldo, not that she thought it would tell her anything. Just something else crossed off the list.

Alana wasn't a mother, but she'd been pregnant, a pregnancy that had been abruptly terminated with her accident. That had been nearly three years ago. A date that was indelibly inked on her mind. Parents never forgot such things and Dympna wouldn't have. Alana might never know why Dympna had walked out but she could imagine the isolation she'd gone through during her pregnancy. The bonding issues with the baby. The abuse. The physical and mental anguish at the hands of the nuns.

If her phone hadn't decided at that moment to ping through a message from Rusty, Alana might very well have found herself lying on the sofa in the morning with the biggest crick in her neck.

'Sorry, not sure if you're still awake but I stayed to rush through the DNA on the Buckleys' bones. They're not a match, Alana. Paula and Joseph have no blood ties to Ciara. I guessed that would be the case as soon as I checked Paula's pelvis for signs of childbirth.'

Sleep was short lived when it finally arrived, and populated with women living in workhouse like conditions, their swollen bellies taut under their raggedy, lopsided dresses, any trace of their beauty masked by their collective air of disappointment and poverty. At four she was sitting in front of her laptop, a mug of strong coffee by her side, an idea hovering as she pulled up the birth certificates of the Mulcahy family. The adopted brothers and their father. And finally, their adopted mother. Dympna Mulcahy, née Fanning.

They'd learnt a valuable lesson during the Dart Attacker murders, which was the public's lack of originality when it came to choosing a pseudonym, whether that was writers or arch criminals. Why google a new name when there was a ready supply of surnames in your own family tree begging for a mention?

Dympna Fanning. An unusual enough name but it was there, hidden away in her passport and driver's licence application forms along with her PPS (social security card) and local property tax records. If Alana was right, and for once she didn't for a second doubt that she could be wrong, then Dympna Mulcahy had walked out on her husband and boys only to revert back to her maiden name. She now had all her details including her address. All she needed was William to turn up and act as her driver to see if she was right.

Alana twisted her mouth at the disingenuous thought as she made for the fridge and the vacuum pack of rashers lurking at the back. William was a good copper as well as an intuitive one. All it took was a glance at Wally waiting patiently by the door for his morning walk for her to appreciate the lad's worth. There wasn't much she could do in the way of appreciation apart from make him a bacon sandwich.

THIRTY-SIX

Saturday 9th September, 8.35 a.m.

While William was out with Wally, Alana was able to expand her facts on Dympna Fanning, not that there was much on PULSE. Only a few parking tickets. The location of her home on Google Maps along with a photo of her lifted from her passport came next. A dainty, well preserved blonde with hair swept back off her face and the kind of earrings that looked like nothing but cost a fortune. Alana spent considerable seconds on the photo, a picture she recognised but she couldn't for the life of her remember where from. There were no signs in either her smooth skin and straight nose to indicate why she'd walked out of her home with only the clothes on her back, never to be seen or heard from again. That is until she'd turned up four decades later in the bottom of her adopted son's crab pot after stuffing her face full of liquorice and at around the same time her other son was being stuffed inside his mattress. Bizarre didn't cover it.

Dympna Fanning lived on Dublin's southside in the primarily suburban area of Rathfarnham. The journey from Kilmacud took seventeen minutes, which was plenty of time to message Paddy to tell him where she was going and what she was up to, as well as arrange to meet one of the garda working out of Butterfield Avenue, the location of Rathfarnham's nearest police station. It was all very well stepping onto someone else's patch, something else entirely to mop up the fallout from not informing them first. Her relationship with Leo was rocky enough for her not to want to upset it any more than she had to. Alana understood the local coppers were in a far better position to drill down through the layers of the woman's life than they were, but that wasn't how she did things. Local information couldn't outweigh the importance of insider knowledge. She'd been present at the scene of three of the murders, which weighted the argument that her presence was essential to this initial visit.

Alana wasn't in a good mood, but she felt lighter than she had in days. She was convinced they were approaching a breakthrough. Everything was going to plan, from the way Wally was happy to stay in the car stretched out along the back seat, to the quick journey in rush hour, aided and abetted by the fact they were travelling against the traffic going into town for once. Doubts only started to creep in when she caught sight of the sweeping driveway leading up to Glenmalure House from behind the security of an impressive-looking pair of electric wrought-iron gates. Dympna's home was set in extensive, manicured gardens and all to the backdrop of the Castle Golf Club with the Wicklow Mountains beyond.

'Go ring the bell, William. There's every chance I could be wrong.' Closely followed by 'What the hell!' Her explosion was as heartfelt as it was confused, at the sight of a squad car pulling up behind them and flashing their lights.

They'd sent the big guns, was her first thought. Her second was lost in the fuss surrounding introductions to the senior detective working the patch.

'And you say that you think Ms Fanning may be dead, Detective Mack?'

'Call me Alana. It's not certain. More like an informed guess that we'll need a DNA sample to confirm, or the woman herself.' She waited for William to join them, the gate resolutely shut. 'She doesn't appear to be in, so any idea how we'll be able to access the property?' she asked, weighing up Detective Brett Browne from the security of her position on the pavement outside the gates. Brett was of medium height with a slight beer belly and stick thin arms and legs, none of which was relevant. If he was helpful as opposed to one of the obstructive, by-the-letter sorts of blokes she frequently came up against then he could sprout horns and she wouldn't bat an eyelid.

'In hand, Alana – call me Brett – I messaged the security team that manage the property. They should be with us any second.'

'You know the woman?' She was careful in her choice of tense. Suspecting something was very different to having the proof.

'Not personally, no. I only know of her.' He smiled, which changed his face into a myriad of wrinkles. 'You must have heard of Fanning Clean Team?'

Alana blinked. Everyone had heard of the Fanning Clean Team. The bright pink vans were to Dublin what the black hackney cabs were to London or the yellow ones to New York. She'd even heard a little of the history of the woman now that Brett had helped her join the dots, but her memory was patchy. Something she'd read in some magazine or newspaper years ago.

'That Fanning! I had no idea.' She swept her gaze over the property again before turning back to him. 'Where there's muck there's brass... or something.'

He repeated the smile. 'Or something. Started working for herself out of a bedsit in Ballymun after she left home. Within a year she'd taken on two employees, within five she'd opened offices in Dublin and the rest is history. Only retired last year.'

'You seem to know a lot about her.'

He shrugged. 'My ma was Dympna's accountant at one point. Has always worked within the law,' he added, the sentence ending on a question, one she was happy to avoid answering with the security van drawing up to the gates.

Inside, the house was palatial but then with the Fanning fortune behind it, it was going to be. However, Alana wasn't there to admire the tasteful wall coverings and soft furnishings. Her brief was far more important than a bit of golden chintz and hand-printed paper in duck-egg blue. With her gloves safely snapped into place she ran a finger across the slight trace of dust on the coffee table, her attention drawn to the sprinkling of marks on the oriental rug in front of the sofa. The kitchen was country rustic with no dishes in the sink. Nothing to indicate if the owner was absent for five minutes or two weeks. The fridge held a different story. Milk as solid as a block of cheese. Lettuce turned to soup. One lonely steak a greyish blue. William and Brett had gone ahead but it didn't take them long to return with the same story. Everything empty, deserted. No sign of the owner. No sign of anyone.

'Found anything?' Brett said, swivelling his keys between his fingers as they headed back outside and towards the garages.

'Nothing that stands out. She lives here by herself?'

'Spends a lot of time travelling since selling the business. There's normally a housekeeping team that comes in daily, but she phoned them on the 14th of August to take the next three weeks off before doing the same with the security team. She has the top package with the company, which includes monitoring of everyone who enters and leaves the property.'

Alana glanced up at the security cameras by the gate before scanning the high wall perimeter. 'This the only way in?'

'Yup. Unless you're into climbing walls and there are these

things.' He pointed to the cameras targeting the gates. 'Covers all of it.'

'Impressive.'

'She can afford it.' Alana watched as he pressed the remote to the garage, the doors lifting open without a creak. The large empty double garage apart from a couple of recycling bins provided by the council.

'No cars?'

'She can't drive. Employs one of those chauffeur companies to ferry her round as and when.'

'Interesting. We'll have to check which firm she...'

'I've got something!'

Alana turned to where William was standing by the bins, a couple of clear bags by his feet, a squashed box of liquorice pressed against the side.

THIRTY-SEVEN

Sunday 27th August 1967, 10 a.m.

The day started out just like every other Sunday. There was no rushing over to the neighbouring farm to help look after the children, but Sunday was her day off, her only day off until she started her nurse training in September.

Sundays for Dympna always started with a lie-in. Come September she'd still only get one day off a week but every second Sunday too.

Such luxury, she thought, snuggling deeper under the pile of blankets only to poke her nose out at the sound of her mother hollering up the stairs.

'Dympna, haul yourself out of bed and go fetch me some spuds. We have Father Eugene coming for lunch and I'll be needing a hand.'

'F'ing hell.' And then in a much louder voice. 'Ten minutes.' Swears in the house meant the back of her pa's hand on whichever part of her he came across first. He wasn't fussy.

She rolled over and stared at her bedside clock, her belly starting to growl. 'Shut up, you. I'm not feeding you again until much later or me fav jeans won't zip.' That was another thing and one of the reasons she was so keen to leave home. All the big meals they insisted she needed. If she ate any more, she'd turn into a barrel and Ethan wouldn't look at her.

Ethan. Her on-off boyfriend, who was currently back on again much to the annoyance of her best friend, Finnula, who fancied him for herself. Fat chance of that with her braces and freckles. No, Ethan was all hers although...

'Dympna!'

'Coming.'

She slid out of bed and into her waiting slippers before reaching for her fluffy pink dressing gown, the one her parents had given her for Christmas, and which was starting to feel tight. A quick shower. She refused to go anywhere without a shower despite the ribbing her parents gave her for wasting the hot water. She also refused to look in the mirror, which for a pretty girl was unusual. But to look into the mirror meant that you had to like what you were about to see and the rolls of thickening flesh gathering round her middle where her tiny waist should have been, wasn't it. If she didn't know any better, she'd think she was up the duff.

That would certainly put the cat among the chickens, but it couldn't be the case. She'd have laughed but there was nothing to laugh about as she struggled into her jeans, pressing her belly in, the roll of fat shifting to the top of the band. The zip closed. The small fact she couldn't breathe was only a minor irritant.

The kitchen smelt of baking and the remains of a breakfast fry-up, the full works including her ma's speciality fried bread, and potato cakes.

Her mother was standing in front of the sink with her back to her, her spine ramrod straight, which meant she'd done something to upset her. Either that or she was worried about the priest's visit.

'Morning, Ma.'

The reply was a grunt. So, something she'd done then, which meant pouring her own tea from the pot in the middle of the table and taking her mug with her along with the black bucket and the spade propped up by the door, exchanging her slippers for a pair of wellies first.

The day was glorious, the sun already high in the sky, the free-range chickens pecking at the dirt, the two cats, Timmy and Tango, asleep under the shade of her ma's hydrangea bushes.

Dympna thought of that last day often, the happiness that spread right to her toes as she lifted her face to the warmth of the sun before making her way over the little, wooden bridge to the bottom field below where her da had planted that year's crop of potatoes, the spade banging against her wellies, the air full of birdsong.

She would have done anything she could to change that day, to alter what had happened next. She'd never felt quite as happy since.

Father Eugene's black Ford Escort was parked in the drive on her return, the heavy bucket almost causing her to bend double.

Ma won't like that he's early. Where is she anyway and where's Da? And what is he doing with my suitcase?

THIRTY-EIGHT

Saturday 9th September, 10.25 a.m.

Alana took a one-floor detour instead of following William to the incident room and headed for Leo's office.

With his secretary not at her desk, she knocked and waited before being ushered into what appeared to be a madhouse.

'Morning, Leo.' She struggled not to grin at him sitting on the floor surrounded by scraps of paper, what appeared to be all his pens and two black-haired identikit toddlers with his eyes looking back at her in surprise. 'I'm sorry, I didn't know you were occupied.'

'I'm not.' He looked tousled and grumpy, his tie in disarray along with his hair and a nick on his chin from where he must have cut himself shaving. 'Girls, stay there a bit. I'm just going to speak to Alana.'

''Kay.'

'I take it they're yours?'

'Nanny doesn't work on a Saturday but I have too much on to stay at home.'

So, he is normal then. She filed the information away as

good to know, along with his usual habit of swimming at Kilmacud bathing pools first thing on a Saturday and how he took his coffee, not that she was about to make him one.

'Not a problem. After all, there's not much difference between a pooch parlour and a creche, is there?'

Alana often thought her worst feature was her inability to put a leash on her gob, but she couldn't help herself. 'Actually, that's a thought. I wouldn't offer normally as I have no experience of young children but if you need us to mind them for a short while, Wally would make the perfect distraction.' She was lying about the experience part. Her best friend had twins of a similar age even though she rarely got to see them during the middle of an investigation.

His smile was sheepish. 'I don't object to dogs. It was just the shock.'

Alana ignored that. There was nothing wrong with a bit of chit-chat to smooth over the wrinkles of a working relationship, but time was pressing, and it was the one thing she didn't have to waste.

'Potentially we have a huge problem heading our way.'

She'd been on her phone googling Dympna Fanning on their journey back. The woman's meteoric rise from the gutter and all by hard work instead of off the back of others. A shining example of what it was to be a good person and to ask for nothing in return. The woman was a local legend for helping others get back on their feet through the offer of employment and somewhere to stay. The abused and dependant. The poor and oppressed. It didn't matter to her what the story was, only that she was able to help break the pattern. There was nothing on her background, not a whisper before her stay in Ballymun. No family to interview. No school friends keen to dish the dirt. No husband, former or otherwise, wanting a slice of her very fancy pile of bricks. And that's where Alana's thoughts derailed onto a completely different track because, of course, there was no way Waldo wouldn't have recognised his wife. She'd known during the interview that there was something off kilter with the conversation, that he was lying but she hadn't been able to narrow it down. His wife had walked out, leaving him with two nippers while she went off to become a millionaire philanthropist and he'd never said a word. Either he'd loved her absolutely and unconditionally, or she'd paid him off. Another slant to the case that she'd have to get someone to investigate.

'Not what I want to hear first thing on a Saturday morning when I'm meant to be still in bed.' He rested his elbows on the table, offering her his full attention. 'I take it it's to do with the case?'

'We're pretty certain we've identified the woman in the pot as Dympna Fanning, as in...'

'The megawatt philanthropist loved by all women across Ireland and beyond?'

'That's the one.'

'Boll...' He pulled a face at the near slip, his gaze flickering to the two girls who were now watching them instead of working on their drawings.

'Exactly. I'll leave any outfall to you, shall I?' she said, making for the door.

William hadn't just rounded up the team for an impromptu catch-up. He'd also fed Wally, who was now asleep under his desk, and made her a coffee into the bargain. That boy was a keeper.

'Morning, everyone, and sorry for the late arrival but I'm pretty confident that we now have an ID for Jane, which I'm sure you'll agree is as good an excuse as any for my tardiness.' That got everyone's attention, including Eve's, who looked up from her laptop, her mouth compressed into a thin line. Alana would have liked for her to be pleased but that was probably too much to ask of the woman.

'Confident as in?' Paddy asked, fiddling with the cuffs of his rolled-up sleeves.

'As in I'm waiting for Rogene to match the DNA found at Dympna Fanning's house to that of our Jane. We knew last night that Jane and Dympna Mulcahy were one and the same because of Barney's teddy bear, it was only a short leap to check out her maiden name and voila.'

'Hold on a minute.' Lorrie shifted back in her chair, her laptop for once ignored. 'You mean the Dympna Fanning who...?'

'Yup. The one and only. William and I have just returned from her palatial residence over in Rathfarnham, where we had an enlightening conversation with the security team employed to guard the premises, as well as a Detective Brett Browne from the local nick. Dympna phoned to cancel the usual checks on the 14th of August, a little over two weeks ago. Said she was going on an extended break and to pare it back while she was away. Nothing untoward in that. Something she's done many a time in the past.' Alana took a sip from her mug before settling it on her desk and picking up the biscuit William had placed beside it. 'I also contacted Fanning's Clean Team and spoke to the senior manager. When Dympna retired she became a non-executive director, which comes with round-the-clock house-keeping staff on site, a service she always cancels when she goes away on her travels. That's right, you guessed it. She cancelled it for three weeks on the same day she did the security team.'

'And who's to say she didn't go?' Eve interjected, her expression and demeanour unchanged.

'No one, but neither did they confirm otherwise and that's the problem. No postcard from any of the far-flung places she liked to visit. No emails to check in with the Clean Team. I'm still waiting to hear back from her bank but what are the bets she hasn't accessed her account since her disappearing. There is more though.' Alana broke her biscuit in two and bit into it before continuing, using her little finger to wipe away any crumbs from around her mouth. 'Sadly, reinterviewing Waldo is now out of the question. He died yesterday from what we suspect might be glycyrrhizin acid poisoning. Dr Mulholland will be performing the PM sometime later on today,' she added, biting down on the second piece of biscuit.

'It's a bit of a leap from where she came from.' Flynn held up a piece of discoloured paper. 'The original misper report filed by Waldo. I've uploaded it onto the system and sent you all a copy, not that it tells us anything. Pretty straightforward for someone who obviously wasn't.'

'Quite. Thank you.'

'We still don't have any kind of a motive for her murder, do we?' Flynn continued, fiddling with slipping the report into a plastic wallet.

'That's a difficult one. It's easy to see how she might have been a target for many disgruntled partners and husbands in her quest to right the balance between the sexes but to take out everyone that's related to her does seem a little extreme.'

'What about Ciara?'

Alana glanced at Eve. 'As in she's Dympna's daughter? Unlikely as she only found out about that relationship when we told her, but a good call. We now have a date we can work with to check on her whereabouts, if I can leave that with you? William and I have already arranged for round-the-clock protection for both her and Deirdre Mulcahy. Oh.' She paused a second, moving the various pieces of the case around in her mind to her satisfaction before continuing. 'I did a bit more digging into the Buckleys' background last night and came across something interesting. Their lives were in Cork, which begs the question why Paula went back to Connemara to register her daughter's birth. There's also the reason why they had to take out a second mortgage the same year. Ten thousand euros is a lot of money, a huge amount in those days. Far more than the cost of a new car, home improvements and the holiday of a lifetime, so what did they spend it on?' Alana repositioned her right arm across her stomach, taking a moment to stretch out her fingers like she'd been told to. 'And before anyone mentions IVF, remember that it was still in its infancy in 1981, with only fifteen live births recorded globally of which I doubt Ciara was one. I checked last night! Paula also didn't have any signs in her pelvic girdle that she'd ever given birth so that line is a complete non-starter.'

'You do know this is going to be huge,' Paddy said, waving his mobile in the air. 'Fanning was on first-name terms with the Taoiseach and the President. There's even a picture of her at a reception held at Steward's Lodge earlier on in the year, along with the great and the good from Dáil Éireann. She appears to have been a frequent visitor.'

'And the reason I have just come from DS Barry's office,' Alana said, glancing down at the incoming text from Billy, which she ignored. 'We don't know all the details, but what we do know is that Dympna Fanning gave birth at eighteen to a baby girl, Ciara, who ended up being illegally adopted by Joseph and Paula Buckley. Within two years, she'd married Waldo Mulcahy, a man fifteen years her senior, who was unable to give her children, the one thing she craved. Within a year, after the couple had adopted Barney and Mason, she'd upped and walked out, moved into a flat in Ballymun and reinvented herself as Dympna Fanning.' Alana scanned the room. 'We know the middle of the story and the ending. Now it's time to go back to the woman's beginning.'

THIRTY-NINE

Sunday 27th August 1967

'Where are you taking me? What have I done!'

Dympna was hoarse from repeating the words, but she'd continue saying them until she got a response. 'Please. Tell me!'

All Father Eugene had said when he'd manhandled her into the car was that her sins had found her out and wasn't it a blessing her good parents had decided to show her the error of her ways.

What sins? She'd done nothing.

She finally gave up, her tears drying on her cheeks as she huddled into the corner of the car, her jeans cutting into her sides. She wasn't about to open the button in front of him. Father Eugene might be a man of the cloth, as her da called him, but he was a man, wasn't he, just like Ethan. Ethan who was pressuring her into having sex when all she was prepared to do was play round a bit.

The monotony of the journey compounded by the warmth of the car caused her to shut her eyes against the glare of the road and the heat shimmering off the tarmac.

'Wake up. We're here.'

He was already out of the car and pulling open the boot by the time she shook the sleep from her mind, the thought of how agile he was for someone so fat lost at the first sight of Dunmore Manor, the name etched into brick to the left of the ornate doorway. A large house with sixteen windows glinting in the morning sun and a set of stone steps leading up to the front door.

'You carry it.'

'What?'

He'd left the case by her feet and was now making for the entrance, his hands outstretched in greeting to the woman filling the doorway, a tall, thin woman with a cruel mouth and a crucifix draped around her neck. A nun.

Dympna looked from the case to the couple staring back at her, her mouth slightly open in surprise as she grabbed the handle. There really was no other choice.

'Mavis, show Dympna where she's to sleep and provide her with a uniform.' The nun finally met her gaze, her bony hand relieving her of her case. 'I'm Sister Agnes Rose. Personal belongings are forbidden at the Manor.'

The biggest shock for Dympna was the size of Mavis's swollen belly pushing against the thin blue fabric of her smock, the hem uneven at the front due to the pull on the material. She tried not to stare, her eyes rounded at the sight of the young girl's swollen ankles streaked with thick, blue veins, her feet thrust into leather sandals. Only a young girl, younger than her.

She followed her along the passage and down a set of steep stone steps into what must be the basement. It was certainly cold enough to never get the sun. The room in front of her was like something from a Charles Dickens novel or was it *Jane Eyre* she was thinking of. She couldn't remember now. The narrow beds and thin, grey blankets. The bare floorboards and barred windows. The wooden crucifix hanging on the wall beside the door.

Dympna turned to face Mavis, her mind full of so many questions, the sharp stab in her side causing her to glance down in alarm, the questions forgotten.

'Kicking youse, is he? The lil' blighter.'

FORTY

Saturday 9th September, 6.05 p.m.

The story broke on the Six One News, with a picture of Dympna Fanning filling the screen. The report was full of words like unconfirmed and suspected, unsubstantiated and alleged, but the damage had been done without the need for Rogene to lift a finger with regards to matching Dympna's DNA to that of Barney's teddy or Jane's bones. Alana had received notification of the DNA match at five to six, too late for anyone in media circles to know anything about it but that didn't stop the suppositions and rumours spreading like warm margarine. The *Clonabee Globe* would be full of it tomorrow. Their online version had already jumped on the gravy train with a preliminary article on the life of the woman. The full obituary was planned as a four-page colour spread later in the week. She had yet to answer Billy's text. There was no ulterior motive behind her decision for ghosting him unless lack of time and priority setting could be viewed in such terms.

'Might as well turn it off now the lead story has finished.'

Paddy made good his words by picking up the remote and pressing the red button.

Everyone was still in the office, including Eve, which was a surprise. Leo had dropped in mid-afternoon to give them the heads up about the leading news item, his children nowhere in sight. Any interference on his part to stem the story would be quickly termed suppression and was best left alone: managing the media was a game no one in the gardai could afford to lose. Alana still hadn't made her mind up about him. Most days he annoyed the hell out of her but taking the pressure off by dealing with the press was a huge thing in his favour.

The afternoon had been frustrating in contrast to the excitement of earlier, spent mopping up all the information they could find about Dympna Fanning of which there was reams. The woman seemed to have as many enemies as she did friends, as well as a history of a few of the more belligerent types trying to take the law into their own hands. It was good that she'd been wealthy, she'd needed it to pay the exorbitant legal fees in taking out injunctions and restraining orders against anyone who'd tried to cross her. After whittling it down by removing those in prison, already dead or electronically tagged, they'd come up with six men and one woman to add to the list of potential suspects. People who Dympna had upset during her quest to offer women and their children a safe haven along with the means to support themselves.

The killer was someone special, someone who'd decided to murder Dympna along with her family. That required a degree of hatred they rarely saw. Serial killers chose indiscriminately. Yes, there were certain patterns to their behaviour. Patterns they followed like murdering within their own race and the taking of trophies. These victims were different, all handpicked with the only common denominator the fact they were in some way related to Dympna Fanning. That they'd managed to eliminate Ciara from the suspect list had been a relief with the news from Eve that the woman had been in the middle of a ten-day stretch in the Balearics on and around the 14th of August.

Alana's head was throbbing along with her hand, but she still had twenty minutes before she could take another tablet, her attention shifting from her screen to the box of pills, which she'd propped next to her mug.

Get on with your bloody work. You've still got twenty-five minutes before the wheelchair taxi arrives to drop you home.

'I'm happy to stay. Follow with your chair and bring Wally along after his walk.'

Alana glanced over and down at where William was making a fuss of the dog. 'Not tonight but thank you. I really do need to try and W-A-L-K him myself,' she replied, the word spelt out for the sake of the long, inquiring face glancing between them, his tongue overtaking one side of his jaw.

'Okay, but I'll be round first thing to help.'

Alana hijacked her pending laugh, sending it on a detour back down her neck. 'I'm onto you, William. This is all about you and Wally and nothing to do with trying to help me out. Now, off with you before I change my mind.' She waved him away, taking a moment to watch them herd out of the room, Eve dragging up the rear, her spine as stiff as a cat who'd spied a mouse.

The board beckoned but she didn't have the energy, time or writing power to do more than send a screenshot to her laptop before popping the device in her bag for later. The plan was for something homemade instead of the ready meals she'd been surviving on, and that was still the agenda. Something spicy with lots of veg to make up for the junk she'd been eating recently.

'Thank you. Yes, I'm fine, really. Tomorrow for seven thirty? Brilliant. See you then.'

The taxi driver had escorted her to the door and waited for her to enter before turning back to his vehicle. Finding someone with a wheelchair accessible taxi who also happened to be a dog lover had been the win of the year.

'Come on, Wally. Let's get you and Goose fed first before...' Wally eyed her expectantly, causing her to laugh. 'You silly fella.'

Alana wasn't a great cook. She was alright at the basics but anything outside of a bacon roll and steak was a challenge, which had made Colm take over the kitchen within days of her moving in. Her meals were also dependent on what was in the fridge and the freezer. With the makings of a stir-fry assembled and ready to throw in the wok, she grabbed her mobile and keys before attaching Wally's lead to his collar and slipping out into the car park.

'Five minutes is your limit.'

The evening was still and quiet, the incessant rain of earlier leaving a star-filled sky but with a touch of chill in the air which had her regretting she hadn't thought to add a jacket, hat, scarf and gloves to her ensemble but it was only a brief thought, her mind full of the case and what might have happened to Dympna for her to have ended up in one of Barney's pots.

She'd manoeuvred the chair to the pavement that skirted the building, conveniently lit by a set of very interesting lamp-posts requiring intense investigating, a glimmer of a smile on her lips as she watched Wally's antics. A brief respite before she propped open her laptop and worked while she ate. A bad habit but one impossible to break. There was no work-life balance. It was all work and that's how she liked it. Malaga was great, a necessary break but it wasn't real life. It wasn't her life. Work was her life and now it appeared Wally and Goose were too. She didn't pause to think about Billy. She'd probably message him later, but it wasn't going to be a priority. She'd also message Colm...

The attack when it came was out of nowhere.

Hands clawing onto her shoulders, digging deep as they tried to drag her out of the chair, pulling and wrenching muscle from bone.

'What the... HELP. HELP!' she shrieked, her brain finally engaging with her vocal cords. There was nothing she could do. The only thing stopping him from pulling her out of the chair was the seatbelt wrapped round her stomach and securing her back into the seat.

The bark was loud and sharp, quickly followed by a low rumble, a guttural sound. A growl. A snap. Then a beat of silence before a loud scream wrenched through the quiet of the night.

'What the fuck. Get off. GET OFF!'

'Attack, Wally. Attack.'

So many things happened that it was impossible to separate them. A car pulling to a screeching halt. The door slamming back on its hinges as someone ran towards her, shouting and waving his arms. Billy.

The sound of running feet as people spilled out from the apartment block clutching onto an array of hastily picked up weapons from a hockey stick to a rolling pin and, for some reason, a violin.

Her attacker managed to rip free and break into a sprint in the opposite direction before leaping over the back wall and disappearing into the night.

The second of silence, just the one. A second where she found her breath, her lungs heaving in air. The realisation that it was over and, with the realisation, a flood of tears she didn't try to contain.

FORTY-ONE

Saturday 9th September, 8.55 p.m.

The guards had been and gone. The neighbours, some of whom she'd never set eyes on before, were all safely ensconced back behind their front doors. Wally was chomping on the chicken pieces she'd defrosted to go into her stir-fry while Billy was still on his phone after ordering a Chinese. She didn't demur. All trace of appetite had disappeared along with her nerve, but she knew she had to eat just as she knew he meant well. That all she wanted to do was curl up into a tiny ball was something she tucked away in the corner of her mind along with all the other things she never got to do like running on the beach with the wind in her hair and the sand slamming against her toes. Instead, she had Billy fussing over her like an old mother hen while Rogene sat at the table, her emergency Tech Bureau kit spread out on a sterile paper sheet in front of her while she processed the evidence before rushing it back to the lab.

Wally was the hero in all of this. Wally and Billy, who'd both sent the rapscallion on his way with fear in his heart and a large strip of denim missing from the seat of his jeans. Alana hoped that Wally had scared the shit out of him, along with Billy who was built like a tank. He was also a total pussycat who wouldn't have the first clue in how to use his fists, but the little tyke wasn't to know that.

She rested back on the sofa, a rug she didn't want draped across her knees, Goose pressed into her side. Goose, the most single-minded of animals who always put her own comfort first. Goose, who hadn't left her since she'd arrived back. Alana hadn't been either a cat or a dog person until recently. Brought up in poverty, her mother had struggled to put food on the table. Animals were a luxury they couldn't afford. Her view on that had completed an about-turn. Animals were a necessity and one she now obviously couldn't do without. She remembered that she'd joked to Leo about Wally being a working dog. Nothing could be closer to the truth.

Leo. Rats! Thinking of her boss, in even the loosest of terms, was a reminder of the promise she'd made about never putting herself at a disadvantage by the choices she made.

'Pass me my phone, would you, Billy. Cheers.' If she didn't tell him about the attack before he heard it through the grapevine, she'd be toast.

> It's Alana. Just come up against the little shit again – the one who broke my arm. He was even dressed the same! I'm fine. The guards from Dundrum have just left. I have Rog here to process some DNA left at the scene. Just so you know, I'm recommending Wally for a National Bravery Award.

She'd barely placed her mobile down when it pinged back his reply.

> Are you okay? Shouldn't you be in hospital or something? Take tomorrow off. That's an order, Alana. I'd come over if it wasn't for the girls.

What? No!

Any blurring of professional boundaries was to be discouraged as far as she was concerned. And as for taking tomorrow off... He could go whistle.

I'm fine.

She pressed send then put her phone down before thinking again, picking it up and messaging Paddy a brief update. Their two-way communication system only worked when they both kept the flow of conversation going.

'Right. I'll be off. Leave you to have an early night unless there's anything you need me to do before I go?' Rogene gathered her supplies, replaced them in the lidded box and snapped the top closed.

'What about sharing our Chinese?' Billy said, his hands full of brimming carrier bags.

'That was quick?'

'Told them I'd pay them double at the door if they speeded the order through.'

'You would!' Alana smiled across at Rogene. 'Go on, stay. You can't have managed to eat yet with... today's schedule.' She'd nearly mentioned Rathfarnham, which meant she was more tired than she thought.

'Okay, fine. As I'm being double teamed by the two of you.'

It was only later, after Billy had left that Alana realised he'd never once mentioned the one thing at the forefront of all their minds. The death of Dympna Fanning.

'Time for a coffee now we're on our own, Rog? I know it will mean a late one for you but...'

'I'll make it, you stay there. Doctor's orders.'

Alana laughed at her abrupt response and not her use of the

title. Rogene was one of the most matter-of-fact people she'd ever met. Her full focus was on the job and not the twiddly bits that had secured her a position on the NBCI, like her doctorate in forensic science. Being surrounded by intelligent people was liberating as well as daunting but Alana was sensible enough to realise they were all part of the same team. A good one.

'Are you sure you're alright, Alana?' Rogene placed the tray on the table in front of her before settling down on the chair opposite.

'As right as I'll ever be,' she said, collecting her mug and wrapping her good hand around the pottery for warmth. She felt stone cold, but it was probably shock setting in.

'And you're sure it was the same man as before?'

That was a question she'd like to answer with a few degrees more certainty than she was feeling. The guard had asked her the same and she'd been positive, but now she'd had more time to think about it.

'I think so.' She didn't need to close her eyes to have the man's image pressed against her irises. Tall and skinny, dressed in black, and with some kind of ski mask or balaclava type face covering hiding his features, but then what modern day criminal wore anything else. It was a uniform. A uniform she never wanted to see again.

'At least there's a good chance we'll be able to identify him if he's on the system. That was some chunk Wally took out of his rear end. In fact, I'm thinking I might get a dog myself.'

Alana smiled across at her, taking a quick sip from her drink before meeting her gaze over the rim of her mug. 'So, anything from Fanning's house then?'

'Lots of DNA if that's what you mean but it's all going to be either from Fanning or her housekeeping staff I reckon. I spent a good hour going through the details of her security plan with the firm she hires. Fanning was as secretive as they come – Brett's words not mine. Apart from the carefully vetted team from the cleaning company she rarely had visitors or entertained. The house was a status symbol, but a complete waste of money in his eyes because she rarely showed it off.'

'So, an intensely private person, which would fit in with her background, what we know of it.'

Rogene nodded. 'She lived alone and holidayed alone. Quite sad really.'

Alana wasn't so sure. There were a lot of people who put Dympna Fanning on a pedestal, but it was a pedestal of her own making. She'd made the choice to champion the disadvantaged, but in doing so had made herself a target for all sorts of wackos and weirdos. 'I have a meeting planned with her father tomorrow but I'm not putting much store in it being helpful.'

'It's a miracle he's still alive, surely. Must be a good age?'

'Ninety-nine and still living alone.'

'Yikes.' Rogene started to stand. 'I'm going to make myself scarce so. Give you the opportunity to have a good night's sleep, and make sure you keep your mobile with you, that is unless you'd like to come back and stay at mine. You do realise that you're now a target?'

FORTY-TWO

Monday 27th November 1967, 6 a.m.

Days started early at Dunmore Manor, or it seemed that way to Dympna. Watches weren't allowed just as calendars were banned, which didn't prevent her from scoring the side of her bed with the edge of her spoon when she was meant to be saying her prayers. Religion was of no use to someone in her position.

Three months to the day since she'd last seen her parents and her brother. Three months since they'd arranged to exile her in the middle of Kilkenny with a group of nightmarish nuns with less compassion than the wart on the side of Sister Agnes Rose's nose.

She had no friends here, none of the comradery she might have expected with a group of similarly aged girls, but that was hardly surprising as she wasn't like them. Oh, she was pregnant. There was no refuting the baby in her belly but how it got there was another thing because she'd never. She wouldn't. A bit of kissing and the like. It was nothing but apparently nothing was enough. She'd been mocked for her virgin pregnancy stance and then she'd been ignored.

Mavis, the girl who had shown her around that first day had disappeared within a week of her arrival and no one would tell her where she'd gone even if they knew. For some reason Dympna felt they were as surprised as she was by Mavis's absence, surprised and scared. Giving birth wasn't an escape route, far from it. It changed nothing, so where had she gone? What had happened to her?

She was in the laundry darning sheets when the pain hit. Darning was the only concession when they neared their time. Darning and embroidery but she'd always been shit at that. They had to work the same long hours from dawn until dusk but at least they could sit while they were doing it.

The lack of comradery continued almost as soon as the first gasp escaped her lips.

'Sister. Sister. Dympna has started.'

The birthing room was on the ground floor and a completely different set-up to the basement. Starched sheets, probably the same sheets they had to scrub clean before hanging out to dry and pressing into razor-sharp creases. Even the smell was different, none of the musky dampness of the lower floors. This was clinical, reminiscent of the times she'd had to visit the hospital.

The pain was unbearable and with no relief apart from a wet flannel to her forehead. She wanted her ma more than anything then, and would have welcomed her back into her life with open arms at any point during her labour. After was different. After, when they'd ripped the baby from her arms on the pretext of bathing her only to whisk her away in a waiting taxi. After, she never thought about the woman who had given her life with anything other than malevolence. Her da was as callous but he'd never experienced the beauty of giving birth like her mother had. The washing away of the pain, and the memory of that pain with the sound of her baby's cry. As her milk dried, and the days passed, the seasons speeding up on a tide of repetition, she never once broke her stance on forgiveness. To forgive meant being able to understand and she knew she'd never reach the place where she could understand how her mother had done that to her.

FORTY-THREE

Sunday 10th September, 8.25 a.m.

'You look terrible, Al, if you don't mind me saying?'

'And even if I did mind, Paddy, you'd say it anyway.' She laughed, but it was a pretty miserable attempt at humour.

Paddy wasn't wrong in his comments about her looks. The only positive she could see was that she looked the way she felt. When she'd peeled off her blouse before bed, the full extent of the bruising across her shoulders and around her waist from the seatbelt and where he'd tried to drag her out of the chair, was a shock. She'd been feeling quite well all things considered up to that point.

'You know me, as honest as the day is long.'

'Sometimes it's better to tell the odd porky, like now for instance. In fact, I'll share a tip with you. Never tell a woman she's looking less than perfect unless you've got a death wish.'

'Fair point. It's probably also irrelevant in comparison to how you're feeling. How are you feeling?'

'Like shit, but thanks for asking. Also full of extra-strong painkillers because of my arm, so there are small mercies to be had. I can't feel anything from the neck down and, as you know, I haven't been able to feel anything from my toes up for years.'

'Alana!' He was struggling not to laugh, which meant he was exactly where she wanted him. Not about to sympathise with something he could do nothing about.

'Tell me again about Graham Fanning, Pad?' She opted for a change in subject. Laughing off her disability had become a habit; it was easier to joke than to field a whole pile of questions she wasn't prepared to answer.

'Well, as you know, he's in his late nineties. Has lived alone since the death of his wife. There was also a son, Lee, but he passed away when he was in his forties. Fanning has a small farm outside Clondalkin. Used to rear cattle but not in recent years.'

'That's quite a bit of information.'

'Not really. Birth certificate. Marriage certificate. Death certificates. Tax and housing records. Only the usual. I have no idea what we'll find when we arrive. Any idea how you want to play it?'

'As in good cop, bad cop? Nah, let's just play it by ear for a change.'

Graham lived on a thirty-four-acre farm on the outskirts of Clondalkin, a suburban town ten kilometres west of Dublin city, known best for its round tower and, latterly the location of Microsoft, Google and Amazon data factories. Alana wasn't a history buff or a geography one, but she liked to read up on areas before she visited them, albeit via Wikipedia.

There was a feeling of dilapidation and decay when they drove over the cattle grid in front of the farm, the ground made up of impacted soil where the weeds had already encroached. The barn buttressing the house, warped and rotting. The small, single-storey farmhouse in desperate need of a paint. A dog ran out to greet them, some kind of sheepdog cross running down the drive and yelping his head off, scattering the few chickens pecking at the ground.

'Stop that, Harrison. Heel.'

The man in the doorway had once been tall. He was still tall but with rounded shoulders and the posture of someone fighting the battle with old age, a battle he wasn't going to win.

'You'd best come in.'

Graham Fanning didn't bother with the normal introductions. He knew who they were and what they were after, the rest was irrelevant. Alana glanced over her shoulder at Paddy as he negotiated the wheelchair across the small stoop. There was no hall, instead the front door opened into a large kitchen with traditional wooden cupboards and a Rayburn positioned in a recess at one end of the room.

They sat around the scrubbed pine table, a large earthenware pot of tea and three chipped mugs along with the carton of milk in the centre. Graham poured out the dark brew, his hands gnarled with arthritis, the backs peppered with brown liver spots. So far, the conversation had been limited to *thank you for agreeing to see us* and *take a seat*.

'As you know, we're here about your daughter,' Alana said.

'I don't have a daughter.'

His statement was final, irrevocable. Tragic. Of course he had a daughter. He was just choosing to deny it.

'Your wife gave birth to a baby on the 1st of March 1949, a little girl who you called Dympna,' Alana continued, ignoring the way the man's hands were curling into fists. 'Dympna attended St Anne's until she was seventeen. When she left, she worked as a nanny while she waited to be old enough to train as a nurse. In the summer of '67, aged eighteen, she disappeared off the scene only to reappear four years later living in a tenement flat over in Ballymun. All of those things are facts, Mr Fanning, and therefore irrefutable and impossible to deny.' She paused a second. 'I am also very sorry to inform you that your daughter passed away a couple of weeks ago.'

'My daughter died when she was eighteen, detective.'

'I'm sorry, sir,' Paddy said, his voice soft, his words and demeanour one of respect. 'Whatever you might like to think, that's not the case. We're not here to go over the old ground of your relationship with your child but we would like your help in trying to find the person who murdered her. It's not right that they should get away with it.'

Alana watched as Graham ran his hands over his balding head before scrubbing them down his face, his eyes rheumy and bloodshot. 'I promised my wife when we sent her away that I'd never mention her name again and I've made good on that all these years. We told my son she'd died in an accident and that's what we told the neighbours too.'

'But surely, what about a death certificate? What about visiting her grave? I don't understand how you could have got away with it.' Alana was rarely surprised about the way some people lived their lives, now she was quite frankly flabbergasted.

He smiled, taking it for praise at how clever they'd been when there were no accolades to be had in what he'd done. 'Easy enough. We pretended she was going to stay with a cousin of mine in France, which was where the accident happened shortly after she arrived.'

It was getting worse and worse. What accident? Alana didn't ask. That wasn't why they were there.

'And instead, you sent your daughter to one of the Magdalene laundries to have your grandchild, only for the babe to be sold to the highest bidder after.'

His face was rigid, his gaze unwavering. 'That wasn't how it happened. We invited the priest over to discuss the issue. He was the one who took her away, there and then. He told us not to ask where he was taking her to, and we never did.'

'And your daughter never got in touch in all those years.'

'Why would she. She was dead. She is dead.'

'What about when she became famous, sir?' Paddy asked. 'I can't believe you and your wife wouldn't have realised the connection between your daughter and the Fanning Clean Team.'

'And you think fame and fortune could wipe the slate clean? Once a tawdry tart, always one.'

The conversation was finished as far as Alana was concerned and for Paddy, too, the way he pushed back his chair and started thanking the man for his help, such that it was, the words laboured, forced out of his mouth.

'Hold on a minute.' Alana looked up from where she was slipping the left brake, while Paddy leaned over to help her with the right.

'Yes?'

'You said there was a child. Where are they? At least tell me that.'

Alana paused briefly, her hand fumbling in her pocket for one of her business cards, the tear escaping down his cheek far more convincing than his words.

'Dympna gave birth to a daughter, but because of GDPR we aren't at liberty to share anything further. However, I'm happy to pass on your details to her, with your consent of course?'

Alana strapped herself in and waited for Paddy to do the same before speaking. 'How much do you reckon the farm is worth, then?'

'What?'

'As in prime real estate situated thirty minutes outside of Dublin and in an area scheduled for urban expansion?'

'You've been reading that drivel on Wiki again, haven't you? You do know it's all lies. Totally unregulated drivel.'

'It also said there's a round tower,' Alana replied, tapping her fingernail on the windscreen at the sight of the tall, roundish tower up ahead. 'But, back to my question. How much?'

'Millions probably. Would need to come with planning permission but easily enough obtained if you cross the right palm with the right amount of silver.'

'And what about Dympna's home?'

He flicked her a glance. 'She bought it for three million ten years ago so ten, fifteen perhaps, more or less.'

'And who's going to inherit now they're all dead, or nearly dead?' she said, picking up her phone and looking through her contacts.

'God, Al, we're not going to have any coppers left on the streets if they're all out guarding the Fannings and Mulcahys.'

'Can't be helped. He's elderly and therefore vulnerable.'

'But inheritance law doesn't work like that. Always down or across, never up.'

'Up if everyone else is off the menu and if there's no one, where does it go then?'

'To the state.' Paddy glanced at her briefly before returning to the road ahead. 'Well, in that case maybe we should add ourselves to the suspect list because I can't see Graham having bumped off anyone.'

FORTY-FOUR

Friday 2nd March 1968

The truth was Dympna was lonely. There was no one for her to talk to. The other girls had singled her out as a liar and any new girls were told to avoid her as soon as they entered the building. Twenty-seven weeks was a long time without conversation. Any longer and she'd have to ask to move bed as she was running out of carving room. She'd taken to talking to herself when no one else was around, but someone had heard her. They took to calling her Dotty, even the nuns. It got so bad that she didn't think of herself as Dympna anymore, Dympna had died along with any hope she had of a future outside of Dunmore Manor.

It didn't help her relationship with the other inmates that her body had sprung back into its pre-pregnancy state almost straight away, her waist a mere handspan, her skin and hair belying the poor diet they were made to suffer. While the other girls seemed to age overnight, she maintained her youthful vigour and irrepressible optimism.

At some point she'd find the opportunity to leave the place. She had to believe that or give up.

The opportunity presented itself in the first week of March when a new driver started on the laundry run. The Manor supplied all kinds of organisations with their laundry services from hospitals and care homes to schools and private residents. The nuns were able to undercut all the local firms and why wouldn't they. They didn't have any wages to pay. But for the system to work they also had to employ drivers for their vans. Male drivers like Waldo Mulcahy.

Dympna spied him out the corner of her eye when she was hanging the sheets on the line, her hands fixed on the task, her mind noting the time by the height of the sun and the lengthening shadows on the ground. Nice enough from what she could see. Laughing and joking with one of the nuns, one of the nicer nuns. There were one or two. A simple man. A man who could be swayed. She remembered enough from her time on the outside to know how to do the swaying.

It didn't take much after she'd made her decision. A teased blonde curl that just so happened to escape the tight bands they had to wear to keep their hair in order. Pinching her cheeks, and biting her lips blood red, moments before she knew he was expected. A shy smile and half-formed wink as soon as the nun's back was turned. Little tricks, which escalated to the odd whispered word or two, fingers brushing against the underside of the bundle of sheets as laundry was exchanged. The hint of future passions when nothing could be further from her mind. It was all about the escape.

It took a month, a whole month of tricks and ploys to help him make up his mind, and a sick nun for her to put her plan into action. Sister Ignatius, the nun in charge of the laundry deliveries, was never sick, which made her sudden collapse a shock to the whole order. Dympna had nothing to do with the woman's illness but that didn't prevent her from taking full advantage of the opportunity by slipping into the back of the van and hiding behind the bags of laundry while the other nuns were hovering around Sister Ignatius's prostrate body.

The first thing Waldo knew about his stowaway was when he parked for the night and by then it was too late.

FORTY-FIVE

Sunday 10th September, 10.45 a.m.

'The super told me to send you right up if I happened to see you.'

'I'll add him to the list. Thanks for looking after my chair,' she said, taking a moment to swap seats before making for the lift. It was all very well Paddy having to push her around when they were out and about, but she preferred a bit of independence in the office.

'Morning, Rog. Thought I'd pop up and see how you're doing with Dympna's house search?'

'And not forgetting the lovely bit of DNA from that bloke's backside, eh, Alana. He won't be wearing those jeans again in a hurry,' she said with a cackle, swivelling in her chair and taking a moment to cast her gaze over her. She didn't comment on her looks, unlike Paddy. 'Fancy a coffee? I was just about to top mine up.'

'Perfect.'

'You doing okay, after yesterday's little escapade?'

'Oh, so so. Bruises on my bruises. You know how it is.'

'No. not really. Remember, I only get to go in after all the fun's happened, and not during,' she said, handing her a mug before retaking her seat. 'It's bound to take its toll.'

'I'll be fine, really, or I will be after I catch the little git. Any matches on the DNA?'

'Still waiting to hear back. There's been a bit of a backlog recently.'

'Which has primarily been down to me. I know.' The coffee was hot, strong and laden with sugar, just the way she liked it. She was halfway down the mug when she had an idea, one so obvious that she'd kick herself if she'd been able to. 'Do me a favour and cross check the DNA from those jeans with Dympna's home.'

'Why? What are you thinking?'

'I'm not sure and that's the problem.' Alana placed her mug down and pulled her hair back. She'd thought it random. No, she'd hoped that was the case but it had stopped being random with the second attack. Someone had assaulted her with the intent to harm her, perhaps permanently.

'So, what about our Dympna then?' she finally said, brushing aside the idea until she had time to examine it further.

'The recycling was the most interesting part, with the empty boxes of liquorice, proving Rusty's theory about the type of poison used.' She turned to her laptop and logged in. 'I contacted the Clean Team first thing. Had a good chat with the housekeeper usually assigned. We know about Dympna liking to keep a low profile. Not surprising with the amount of people wanting her head on a platter for upsetting their plans by her providing an escape route for their so-called partners. However, what we didn't realise was the low profile involved not only keeping out of the public's way but also the use of disguises when she did venture past her front door.'

'You're having me on.'

'I wish I wasn't! Tracking her movements in the weeks up to

her death is going to be virtually impossible. Here, check these out.' Rogene took her mug from her, instead handing her photo after photo of the fanciest dressing room Alana had ever seen. 'Dympna liked playing dress-up. I lost count of the outfits and shoes she owned but it's the full wigs and hairpieces that were the real surprise.'

Alana flipped through the images. The professional-looking wigs in all the colours from blonde to purple, brown to black. There was another rack full of glasses and enough pots, tubes and bottles to open a beautician.

'Looks like a serious set-up.'

'I think she would have had help to source it like the make-up department at the Gaiety or Abbey Theatre,' she said, arranging the pictures into a neat pile before slipping them back into their plastic wallet.

'But there were cameras all over the place. The most security I've seen in a private residence, so what would be the point? It's all very well being private, but the paparazzi would still have been able to track her comings and goings with those long lenses they use.'

'Not if you have a secret entrance.'

Alana lifted her head from where she'd been checking for messages, her mouth forming a small O-shape. 'You're joking?'

'Nope. Only wish I was because...'

'Because, Rogene, a secret entrance that isn't secret is the most dangerous entrance of all.'

'But why would she have needed a secret entrance at all? I don't get it, Alana. Not with all the security she had.'

'She'd been targeted before, remember.' Alana checked her watch suddenly. 'Rats, we'll have to pick up on this after I've met with his lordship.'

She was still puzzling over the intricacies of the case when she made her way through the open door into Leo's office five minutes later.

'You wanted to see...' Closely followed by. 'Wally, what are you doing here?' The sight of Wally lying on his back while two little girls rubbed his belly had her forget her manners in their entirety.

'Ah, yes, well, William said it would be alright while you were out the office.'

He stood back from his desk and was now in front of her, a deep frown darkening his forehead. 'More to the point, what are you doing *in the office*? I expressly told you that...'

'Stop. Just Stop.' She lifted her hand, not prepared to take any more nonsense from the man, her eyes skittering to the suddenly interested girls briefly as she redacted her reply to remove any words that even brushed over a swear. 'I'm fine, absolutely fine and all thanks to Wally. If it wasn't for him, yes, of course, I'd take some time off but there's no need, really.' She made an urgent retreat to the door. 'So, unless there's anything else?'

Alana knew she was on safe territory with both girls looking between them with rounded eyes. If he wanted to say something to her either about the case or her management style, the current hot topics, then he wouldn't want to do it in front of his daughters. She watched him open his mouth only to close it, then open it again.

'Er, how long can I keep the dog?'

Alana was still giggling when she arrived in the office, a giggle that died in her throat at the sight of Paddy walking towards her, his mobile clutched in his hand, his face doing that proverbial grey-as-a-ghost thing. She didn't have to ask him what the problem was, the words were popping out left, right and centre like bullets from a gun.

'That was the paramedics over in Clondalkin. Graham Fanning asked them to phone us before collapsing. He's on the way to the hospital, in a serious but stable condition.'

'What! We only left like forty-five minutes ago.'

'Apparently some tyke on a bike rocked up with a can of petrol and a wodge of newspaper. Graham came out when he smelt burning. He tried to defend himself, Alana. A ninety-nine-year-old against a yob. The git attacked him with his own walking stick before scarpering when the dog came on the scene.'

'Good for Harrison. What about the house?'

Paddy rocked his hand sideways. 'Too early to tell. It was set in the barn, which was tinder dry. There's two fire crew on the scene and another on the way. He's been taken to Tallaght Hospital. It's the nearest and, due to his age...'

Paddy didn't have to say any more. It was enough.

'Arrange for a guard at the door, Pad. We had one on the way anyway for protection so just divert them. No one enters the room without our say so first, got it?'

Alana switched her attention to the board and the information they'd been adding, layer upon layer of clues and ideas, possible leads and potential suspects. She needed more, something to tie it all together. Her idea about money and inheritance was a good one but she wasn't there yet. What she needed was thinking time away from the incident room.

'I'll be in my office if you need me. If someone could cadge me a sandwich on their way back from lunch. Oh, and round up the usual suspects for our two o'clock. We should have all the DNA back and the results of Waldo's PM, although I'm thinking it will only be a tick box exercise. What do you think about asking your dad to attend? I know it's not something we normally do but when has this case ever been normal.'

FORTY-SIX

Sunday 10th September, 2 p.m.

Paddy had surpassed himself. The Incident Room was more packed than Alana had ever seen it, which was a good thing. It did make it difficult to negotiate an assortment of feet, which were clearly asking to be run over but she managed to reach the front with no obvious toe squashing or shin bashing yelps to be heard above the din – she'd have to try harder next time.

Before starting, she spent a moment scanning the sea of faces, which included all the usual reprobates in addition to Paddy's dad, Brett Browne from the Rathfarnham Station and a slim, grey-haired elderly woman she didn't recognise, chatting away to Rusty as if they were firm friends. Paddy had also set up Ruan on Teams, right next to the sandwich sitting in the middle of her desk. She'd miss Paddy's friendly face if he decided to leave when the case was over. If it was ever over. She also must try to remember to eat her lunch.

'Right, a quick round of names so we're clear who's who. I'm Alana Mack, SIO of the Clonabee branch of the NBCI.' She picked up the tablet and handed it to Paddy while the room raced through the introductions, only lifting her head when the last person spoke, a voice she didn't recognise.

'Dr Louisa Laverty, consultant in burns and plastic surgery, retired. Thank you for inviting me.'

And clever of Paddy to think to add you to the list and at such short notice.

'You're very welcome.' She decided to omit the usual confidentiality rider. Rusty was a good judge of character and his relaxed demeanour in the fellow doctor's presence was good enough for her as to the woman's integrity over the sharing of highly sensitive information.

'Okay, thanks everyone for turning out, particularly as it's a Sunday. We've a lot to get through so let's get started. Anyone in a rush to get away and want to go first?' she added, scanning the room a second time. 'No? Good. Let's begin with you, Rusty, and Waldo Mulcahy's PM.'

Rusty leant back in his chair, hooking one leg over the other. 'In short, a replica of his wife's murder all apart from the being placed in the pot part. Mr Mulcahy was an ill man with stage-four mesothelioma. Asbestos poisoning,' he qualified. 'It wouldn't have taken much liquorice to push his already enlarged heart over the edge.'

'Thank you, doctor.' Alana turned to Rogene who was sporting a new pair of glasses with red frames. 'Which leads me very nicely onto your findings over at Dympna's house, Rog. A secret tunnel no less. All very Enid Blyton and the Famous Five, is it not?'

'More like Agatha Christie!' Rogene parried. 'Dympna bought Glenmalure House ten years ago on the suggestion of her accountant. A smart investment but also somewhere she could hide away in relative safety. When the neighbouring house came on the market within weeks of her purchase the idea of an escape hatch formulated, and she bought that one too. She purchased both properties under the cover of a company based in the Cayman Islands, so her name didn't appear on the title deeds. According to her accountant it was nothing to do with tax avoidance, more a way of protecting herself under a cloak of anonymity and pretty standard practice among the mega wealthy with the increased threat of kidnapping plots and what have you.'

'Then the builders wouldn't have known who they were working for?' Paddy said.

'That's right. Only someone rich and paranoid enough to think to excavate through tonnes of bedrock under the boundary wall and come up the other side with barely a cobweb or a scratch.' Rogene propped her glasses on top of her head, her hands steepled in front of her. 'An ingenious plan but again a stupid one. If she could escape, it meant that someone could just as easily enter. We know she must have been watched and for an extensive period. It wouldn't have been that difficult to put two and two together and come up with the right answer.'

'But they don't appear anywhere on the CCTV we harvested from the property?' Alana was puzzled, which made her annoyed. They'd checked through the camera reports from the security firm and there was nothing reported as untoward.

'Oh, I think you'll find that they're there,' Ruan piped up, his voice sounding tinny and disjointed over the video call.

'Sorry, what was that?' Alana reached out her good hand to tilt the laptop so that she was facing the screen.

'Remember when the killer was spotted by the neighbour, who thought it was Mason Clare heading out for a swim?'

'But it wasn't. It couldn't have been because he was already dead! Thank you.' Alana caught Rogene's eye. 'Let's discount the reports and go through all the footage again but this time no assuming that all the images of Dympna are her, disguise or not. The woman doesn't have a double that we know of so it's going to be impossible for anyone to replicate her exactly, even if it's only down to their gait or type of footwear – why is it that criminals always forget about their feet? That way we might be able to narrow the time frame as to when she died but, more importantly where and how to track down her murderer.'

'I'm on it.'

'Thank you. While we're on the subject of feet, what about that footprint from Barney's boat?'

'Another dead end, I'm afraid,' Rogene replied. 'A size-nine mass produced wellington boot sold in garden centres the length of the country. Impossible to narrow it down any further.'

'Annoying but not unsuspected. And there's still no trace of Dympna's phone?'

'Nope. I've had our electronic expert on it. Switched off on the 14th of August, the same date she contacted both the security company and the Clean Team. It hasn't been switched back on since. We've narrowed the last known location to her bedroom but that's it.'

'Okay, thank you.' Alana turned to William. 'How did you get on with looking into the charity worker's spurious visits to Waldo?'

'Definitely not known to the charity and with no CCTV.' He shrugged. 'I've been in touch with Waldo's nurse though. Nurse Theodora Crombie visited the station earlier to meet with one of the E-FIT technicians.' He held up a computer-generated image of a black-haired woman with distinctive teeth and large, horn-rimmed glasses before getting to his feet and passing copies round. 'Dora... the nurse, said the woman was plainly dressed, nothing that she remembered specifically.'

'Height? Weight?'

'Both average.'

'Hmm.' An average woman with distinctive glasses dominating her features or disguising them. 'Anything else?'

'There's an ANPR camera on the road outside. I'm getting a

printout of all the vehicles in case we need it for comparison purposes.'

'Good thinking.' Alana paused a second, watching as Paddy updated the relevant board while she thought back to her own visit to the care home.

If it had been her, how would she have travelled? Would she have chanced on the home not having cameras or would she have made a fundamental mistake in trying to avoid detection?

'There's a bus stop right outside I seem to remember,' she finally said, eyeing William as he went to retake his seat.

'You think she would have taken public transport? But why?' He looked astounded.

'Because it meant she'd be leaving a key element in crime detection tucked away safely behind garage doors. Remember, this was an intelligent crime. Leaving the car would certainly be something I'd have considered, but only fleetingly.' She grinned but it was only a brief Cheshire cat rearrangement of her lips and teeth. 'As a way of avoiding detection it's a pretty stupid one...'

'Since Bus Éireann buses decked out all their vehicles with CCTV.'

The talk of ANPR reminded her of one of the outstanding elements. Thanks to William, they knew how the killer had obtained Mason's address but not how they'd stalked him. They must have followed him extensively to find out his daily living habits.

She glanced at the board briefly. 'Flynn, any joy in triangulating the number plates that Ruan supplied from Mason's property with either Howth or the care home?'

'No crossover. William and I were thinking they might have hired a car so that's where we've been concentrating our efforts but no names of note so far, remembering that they could have hired it anywhere. Lots of two-bit companies dotted round as well as the national ones.'

'Okay, thank you. Probably to be expected.'

Alana's attention shifted to Louisa Laverty and where she was whispering something to Rusty. A timely reminder that Dympna Fanning's life had both started and ended in tragedy. It was only the middle act where she'd managed to find some happiness, if only by helping others but paying the ultimate price for the privilege. Losing her privacy and ultimately her life.

'Dr Laverty...'

'Louisa, please.'

'Louisa. As you've been hearing, we have a bit of a convoluted problem on our hands and one which you must be wondering about.'

'Rusty has been filling me in on the blanks.'

'Good. So, you know that Ciara Buckley is relevant in that Dympna Fanning was her birth mother, the Buckleys only her adopted ones.'

'We had no idea.'

'No, no one had, not even Ciara, until we managed to link mother with daughter via their DNA.' Alana shifted her bad arm slightly, her mind running back over what Ciara had said and the copy of the email she'd forwarded from the blood donor register. Without that little piece of luck, it could have been weeks before they'd finally identified Dympna and as for forging the link between mother and daughter. Perhaps never. 'It was very good of you to agree to foster her after her period in hospital.'

'I'm not sure goodness came into it. The girl needed somewhere and moving in with a medic who was able to help with her specialist needs seemed the obvious choice at the time.'

'We've met with Ciara. She showed us the scars she sustained when she raced down the stairs to rescue the dog. Did she ever say why she neglected to wake her parents at the same time?' Paddy asked.

As a question it was a good one, the hovering elephant in the room.

'Ciara certainly had a great deal of survivor's guilt, which we tried to work through during counselling sessions with our resident psychologist.' Louisa toyed with her bracelet, a thin thread of gold on her left wrist. There were no rings, wedding or otherwise. 'Fourteen is a difficult age at the best of times. For a young girl on the cusp of womanhood to be faced with such life changing injuries on top of PSTD, in relation to prioritising her animal over her parents, it was almost catastrophic. It took her almost a year to come to terms with the reality of the roof collapsing and what would have almost certainly happened to her if she had attempted to save them.'

'And what was she like after she was discharged?' Alana said. 'She was with you two years, right?'

Louisa was composed, her expression relaxed, her hands on her lap, her slender fingers loosely linked up to that point. The question caused a frown along with a dropping of her gaze. Of all the answers so far, this was the one Alana was suddenly the most interested in.

'Ciara was a troubled girl when she arrived at the unit for the reasons I've just mentioned. Intelligent but with a hard edge if you like. No matter what we did or didn't do, it was never right. Perhaps we were at fault.' She spread her hands briefly. 'Whatever the reason, when she left us, she was still the same troubled youngster only now disguised in the body of a woman.'

'You helped her sort out the purchase of her house?'

'I think one of the only reasons she decided to move in with us was to navigate the lawyers and the release of her parents' estate.' Her voice held a raw undertone of emotion. 'Even at sixteen she was the sort to manage on her own.'

She didn't sound as if she'd liked Ciara all that much, which posed a whole string of questions but not the sort Alana was prepared to ask in front of a room full of professionals.

'You said we?' Alana's gaze flickered to her bare hands and back to her face.

'I'm a widow.'

'Oh. I'm sorry to hear that.' A platitude but necessary before she moved on.

Alana glanced at the board, which was in desperate need of a rework, again, her mind on Louisa until she forced herself to concentrate back on the room. 'What about the liquorice? We know how Waldo got his but there's still Dympna to consider.' She smiled across at William who always seemed to need that little extra slice of encouragement. 'That's you again, right?'

'Right.' His answer was dour but at least it matched his expression. 'She used to order her food online from Tesco's. The housekeeper told me she detested shopping with a passion unless it was for clothes and the like. There was also the security issue of having to visit a large superstore like the one in Rathfarnham shopping centre.'

'Which in no way explains why she ordered liquorice.'

'No although she did have a sweet tooth but for chocolate, particularly Butlers.'

'Don't we all,' Lorrie interrupted, drawing a laugh at the thought of Ireland's luxury brand of confectionery. They were too busy for banter, but the case was so horrific that a little humour was bound to seep through the cracks and crevices of their tightly controlled environment.

'And?' Alana prompted.

'And checking through her online orders with the company...' He glanced up briefly from where he was looking at his notepad. 'There were six liquorice substitutions in the weeks leading up to her death. I've been in touch with her GP and given the state of her heart that would have been enough to tip her fibrillation into disarray.'

Bingo!

'Can you clarify how substitutions work please, for those of us who don't do online food shops?' she asked, trying not to get her hopes up too much, an impossible task with the thought of an arrest gleaning neon bright.

'If something isn't in stock then the company uses their discretion by exchanging it for a similar product.'

'You'd have thought chocolate for chocolate instead of other sweeties, especially marmite ones like liquorice and what's it with the lack of Butlers or is there an Ireland-wide shortage?'

'That's the thing. I spoke with one of the confectionery buyers for the store and popular as they are, there's rarely a stock issue except perhaps at Easter and Christmas. They couldn't understand the substitution and have set up an internal enquiry on the back of it.' He swallowed, his Adam's apple jumping round his neck. 'Obviously I didn't tell them the relevance, with the media currently out of this loop but it's not going to take much for them to make the connection.'

'We can't worry about that. What we need to worry about is if this is the lead we need to ID the killer. I want that employee's name.'

FORTY-SEVEN

Sunday 10th September, 8 p.m.

'Are you sure Gaby doesn't mind? I don't even have a bottle to give her.'

'Enough now, Alana. You know me and Gaby don't go in for any of those trappings. Good food and good company are what it's about and...' Rusty paused a second to reverse into his drive before picking up the thread of the conversation. 'Louisa will be there too. I thought it would be an ideal time to continue the conversation. An interesting woman if ever there was one.'

Alana had been downing a couple of painkillers with a slug of cold coffee when Rusty's call had come through. Now, instead of having to decide between an evening with Billy or Colm, who'd both offered to feed her as well as act guardian, she found herself on the way to Maretimo Gardens, Rusty and Gaby's stunning home with private access to Blackrock Beach.

'I gathered that. You seem to know her well?' Alana said, arranging her legs in preparation for her wheelchair, Wally peering over her shoulder.

'One of my lecturers at Trinity and more recently someone I've kept in touch with as part of my work.'

'Oh, of course.' There were parts of Rusty's job that Alana never dared to delve into. How he did it, how any doctor did their job, was a mystery she'd never be able to solve. Having to work on the fringes was bad enough.

Gaby and Lara, their three-year-old adopted daughter, were waiting by the front door. Connor, Rusty's teen and chip off the block, was away at some math Olympiad in Belfast.

'Doggy!'

Lara raced out of the door before standing in front of Wally, stock-still, her face a picture of happiness, which was just as well as it looked like Wally was equally smitten, his tail almost wagging off in his excitement.

'Gawd, there'll be no stopping her now. She's been after a dog for months.' Gaby bent down and hugged Alana, careful to avoid the arm. 'I hear you've been in the wars.'

'You should have seen the other fella, except for the little fact he ran away before I could get started.'

'Hah, never change! Come inside, out the cold. There's a gin waiting and our new cat to meet. She's a sweetheart.'

'And it looks like a dog is imminent.' Rusty rolled his eyes at the sight of his daughter grabbing Wally's lead and walking him into the house. 'Five minutes, Lara, then bed,' he added, his voice changing from friend to father in an instant.

There were no formalities in the Mulholland household, there wasn't even a dining room as Gaby had given it over to Lara's playroom within days of moving into the property. Supper was in the large kitchen cum breakfast room, which led onto a patio and the garden and sea beyond, but it was too chilly to do more than draw the thick, heavy curtains against the twinkling backdrop of lights from Howth on the skyline.

With Lara finally in bed and the table cleared, they traipsed into the lounge and the homely arrangement of sofas and comfy chairs around the wood burner, the walls decorated with large modern artwork, a photo of Lara's birth parents taking centre stage.

Alana examined the photo with a smile. There'd never been any attempt to hide Lara's history. It was something Gaby and Rusty had been open about from the day she could understand such things, which made what had happened to Ciara even more stark. That she'd gone through life unaware of her parentage, her only living relative a very elderly man currently recovering from major trauma over in Tallaght Hospital, was unimaginably cruel. But there was no one to blame. Certainly not her birth mother who'd been carted off to one of those reviled mother and baby homes when she'd fallen pregnant. Alana couldn't conceive what it must have felt like for eighteen-year-old Dympna to have given up her baby, but she'd finally been able to make some sort of sense out of the events that had followed.

Dympna would have been scarred in all the ways possible and, with the way the Irish system worked, she would have had no way of knowing what had happened to her daughter. The secrets of those dark days in Irish history were only starting to come to light with recent changes to the law so there would have been no avenue to follow. A ready-made family was a stop-gap, only that. A knee-jerk marriage to a man fifteen years older, and two replacement children. It was never going to work.

'More gin, Alana?'

'No, best not or you'll have to put me into bed after dropping me home.'

'Can be arranged.'

'Hah, no, really. While it's tempting, I have a busy day tomorrow, a hangover would make it an impossible one.' Alana replied, going through the motions of polite discourse while she tried to pin down a thought hovering just out of reach. She blinked in annoyance, hoping she'd be able to remember what it was sometime later, which was often the case.

'Another merlot, Louisa?' Rusty asked.

'No but a coffee would be lovely, if one's going spare.'

Gaby went to stand, only to stop at Rusty's sharp tut. 'No way, woman. That's my job.'

Gaby had confided earlier that at eight months pregnant, he barely allowed her to lift a finger let alone make coffee when he was around. The relief when he was at work so she could get on with her life was enormous, which had them all breaking into laughter much to Rusty's annoyance when he arrived back downstairs from saying goodnight to Lara.

As soon as he left the room with the empty coffee pot, she turned to Alana and Louisa, a wicked gleam in her eye.

'So, what's happening with Operation Enigma? He's stopped updating me. Thinks I'll go into early labour, and he won't remember what to do.'

Alana grinned. Confidentiality between spouses was one thing but not when Gaby had signed the same clauses in her contract with regards to disclosure, albeit in Welsh instead of the Gaelic one she'd been presented with, luckily translated.

'More bodies. Many more and I'll run out of fingers to count them on.'

'And all related to Dympna Fanning?' She had the grace to look guilty for a second. 'He's also stopped bringing the Globe home, so I've been forced to read it online instead.' She slid a quick, suspicious glance at the door only to land on Wally and where he was grunting in front of the fire. 'Carry on.'

'We were thinking that it might be to do with inheritance but if we lose anyone else the only people to inherit will be the state.'

'What about Ciara?' Louisa knocked back the last of her wine and settled the long-stemmed glass on the coffee table.

'What about her?'

'Surely she's in the ideal position being as she's Fanning's daughter?'

'But she wasn't aware of that until we told her as well as being away during the window when we believe her mother was killed.' Alana's reply was automatic, her mind switching from park to drive in a blink at what she considered an unusual comment from someone who knew Ciara better than all of them put together.

'An accomplice?' Rusty entered the room and the conversation, both hands laden with a tray, four mugs and a plate of biscuits.

'While she's sunning herself in the Balearics and earning her alibi to boot. It's certainly a possibility but we've had a peek at her bank account and there doesn't seem to be anything untoward.' Alana switched back to Louisa. 'You really think there's a possibility of Ciara being involved?'

'I think living with her and her tall tales has maybe skewed my judgement somewhat.'

'You found her out in lies?'

'All the time. Ciara couldn't tell the truth even if the lie was staring us in the face.' She accepted her drink from Rusty and cradled the mug between her fingers. 'What if she managed to find out about her parentage before the fire? What then? A brand-new fridge, so new it was barely out of its wrapping. Saving a dog before her parents only to ignore the dog afterwards as if he'd never existed. It didn't make sense then and it makes less now when put up against everything that has happened since. There's also the little question of where her partner is because I can't see she doesn't have one. Maybe not a husband but there's bound to be a boyfriend knocking around. Ciara liked her men. If she hadn't decided to leave when she was eighteen, I would have instigated it myself.' Louisa picked a biscuit and took a moment to examine it before taking a small bite. 'Then again, I haven't seen her for forty years. A lot could have changed since then.'

Alana lifted her mug, the warmth leaching into her fingers in the same way Louisa's words leached into her thoughts, nudging and shifting everything she knew about the case and changing the slant. There would have been no documentation from Ciara's birth, no records for her to find, but parents talked. All it would have taken was an overheard conversation for a smart girl like Ciara to join the dots. The clues were there already. A quick comparison between her slight frame and colouring that seemed to come straight from a Scandinavian colour palate for all the bolts to slide into place and the screws to tighten. There was the best friend's statement to follow up on too. The one who took the dog. What was her name again. Jacinta Cooke. That was it. What would she remember after all this time, if anything?

With the mug almost empty, Alana knew it was time to think about leaving not least because she needed to get home to draw up what was fast becoming an expanded list for the morning. There was CCTV from Bus Éireann for a start. The CCTV from Dympna's home too. Jacinta Cooke's testimony and that of Lucas Pounder, Ciara's business partner. Showing Waldo's nurse a photo of Ciara. The Tesco chocolate fiasco was still a problem as was the little fact that it was impossible for Ciara to be in two places at once, if the CCTV images from Dympna's home proved to be that of her daughter...

Wally jumped up suddenly, drawing the gaze of everyone in the room, initially in jest.

'Oh, look. Must be past his bedtime.'

'Wonder if a flea has jumped.'

'My dog doesn't have passengers.'

Wally stood to attention, his ears flattened against his head, his eyes fixed on the door, his tongue for once restrained in his mouth, a deep, low growl in his throat before running across the room and scrabbling to get out, the smoke detector in the hall suddenly beeping into action.

The joking stopped as quickly as it started, the atmosphere changing in a blink from laughing relaxed to mildly concerned to anxiety as eyes fixed and minds caught up. Rusty grabbed the poker and Alana replaced her mug with her mobile while Gaby started to stand, the struggle at having to heave her swollen belly drawing a muttered curse but no one was listening. Louisa stayed where she was, a statue, her attention glued to the door, almost separate from the scene unfolding in front of her.

'What the devil.' Rusty reached for the door only to stop. The sight of smoke seeping through the frame had him tapping the handle only to draw it back in alarm, his gaze instinctively reaching and holding on to Gaby's, one thought filling everyone's mind.

Lara.

FORTY-EIGHT

Sunday 10th September, 10.10 p.m.

'You can't.'

'I can and I will, Gaby.' Rusty never called his wife anything other than Gabriella, which was testament to what he was going through if the sight of the smoke starting to fill the room wasn't enough. There was only one way to rescue Lara and that was through the smoke-filled hall.

'Here.' Alana made for the still half full coffee pot, doused her scarf before ringing it out with no regards for the shower of hot drops, her broken bone ignored as she pushed through the pain. 'Wrap it round your mouth. Sorry, it's all we've got. Go. I'll sort out Gaby.'

There was no time for words or looks, or even prayers. That train had pulled out of the station at the first sight of smoke.

'Stay, Wally. Good boy.'

Alana watched as Rusty slipped through the door, the sight of flames licking the walls one she'd take to her grave, her phone pressed to her ear. Only sixty seconds had passed since Wally had alerted them, the longest sixty seconds she'd ever been through, yet.

'Hello, 999. Which service do you need?'

Louisa hadn't moved or spoken after the initial flea joke. Alana didn't know the woman outside of today's dealings, but she felt extreme sorrow at the sight of someone clearly in shock. Of all of them she was the one who'd spent her life coping with the aftermath of fire. The only one who knew the true implications of what Rusty was trying to do and Alana didn't have a moment to comfort her. There was a pregnant woman to consider.

'Gaby, we need something by the door to stop the smoke. Any ideas?'

'The throw on the back of the sofa. I'll do it.'

Alana watched as Gaby did just that, her face grey with fear, her hands shaking with the effort. There was nothing she could do for her except try and keep her focused.

'What about collecting a few things, Gabs. Pictures and the like just in case?' Then to Louisa: 'There isn't a second to lose in getting you and the animals out. Any more smoke in here and we won't be able to open the window,' she added, glancing at where the cat was sitting on the sill. 'I don't want any of that backdraft shit, which is what we'll get if we leave it any longer.' She didn't wait for a reply, there wasn't one. There also wasn't any other choice. The window was narrow, too narrow for a heavily pregnant woman or a paralysed detective to negotiate. She only hoped the jump wouldn't be too much for the elderly woman.

Louisa had the sense not to argue. She picked up Wally's lead without a word and hurried to the ledge before easing the window open the smallest of gaps, just small enough for the cat to weave through before opening it a little bit more and pushing out the reluctant dog. She followed him in an awkward jump that had her landing on her bottom.

Alana slammed the window closed and continued watching a second as Louisa managed to coral Wally and drag him after her, his neck lifted and his feet digging in, but she was stronger than she looked.

Some sixth sense told her that Gaby had joined her side, a pile of pictures lined up beside them. Their hands linked, their fingers a crushing pressure, their attention on the road outside long after the duo had disappeared from view. Of the cat there was no sign.

Four minutes had gone. How much longer? Alana stopped breathing a second, her ear tuned in for sounds. Silence. A crash from the hall, causing her to glance over her shoulder. A bang. Silence. The smell of smoke leaking through the barrier, the air taking on a misty hue, the tickle at the back of her throat causing her to cough. She glanced towards the window and back again. Nothing yet.

Dear God. Don't let them be much longer.

Five minutes and it was difficult enough to breathe let alone see, the room full of acrid smoke, a cough on each breath, neither of them able to reach the clearer air by their feet. The wail of fire engines screamed in the distance pierced by the even louder sound of Gaby's scream as Alana turned towards her in horror.

Gaby clenching her belly, a puddle of liquid gathering between her feet.

FORTY-NINE

Sunday 10th September, 10.15 p.m.

'No. I'm not going anywhere without my husband and daughter, even if.' Alana watched Gaby heave air into her lungs, her voice resembling that of a forty-a-day, lifelong smoker, her eyes damp along with her cheeks. 'Even if...'

They were by the first ambulance, the sight of broken glass from where the firemen had smashed the window glistening like stars on the grass, the neighbours filtering out of their front doors in a variety of leisure and bedwear.

'The firemen are doing what they can, love.' Alana glanced at her watch before turning back to the burning building. Nine minutes and forty-six seconds had passed but it didn't take a genius to see that the fire had taken hold in every room, the flames licking up the windows in search of fuel. Wardrobes. Beds. Cots. Toys. Flesh. Fire didn't differentiate and the reason why Alana had added a new smoke detector to her shopping list earlier in the week.

'There. On the roof! Get a ladder.'

The shout came out of nowhere then everywhere. Alana

angled her head, her eyes scrunching to see through the smoke, the flames rising over the building and beyond.

A fireman on the crest of the roof clutching a bundle to his chest.

She blinked then blinked again before managing to say in the most reassuring voice she could muster, 'There, you see, love. They're fine just like we knew they would be.'

Alana felt Gaby tightening her grip as they tracked the fire crew working in tandem to rescue Rusty and Lara before the roof caved in. Roofs caved in. People got trapped below. She suddenly wished the knowledge away. Blissful ignorance was the only defence in such situations.

She remained on the side of the road while Gaby, Rusty and Lara were reunited, hanging slightly back from the hustle and bustle of the paramedics, fire crews and neighbours. A solitary figure with a face set in stone, her fingers clutching onto her phone, Wally sitting patiently by her side, Louisa long gone. She'd left as soon as she knew Rusty and Lara were safe.

Any of the onlookers might have thought Alana in a daze but nothing could be further from the truth. The likelihood was someone had followed her. It wasn't difficult. After the two attacks she'd suffered, she was on the top of someone's hit list and the only person who knew where she was going that evening was Rusty. The chances were the person was still here and, if that was the case she was in the ideal position to make a note of all the faces gathered at the scene.

'We're about to head off. If you're sure you don't need anything?' the paramedic asked, the one she recognised from when she'd been attacked the second time, which made it a little awkward. It wasn't as if she could put her recent misfortunes down to bad luck or plain clumsiness. Someone was trying to kill her, which begged the question why. The answer was even more interesting. Because she was getting too close.

'I'm fine but thanks for asking.'

Alana felt finc. Well, not as fine as she could be but fine enough to avoid being shipped off to hospital. She'd had enough of hospitals.

Paddy pulled onto the kerb and flung his car door open, not bothering to shut it. She hoped he'd remembered the handbrake. That would be all they needed.

'Jeez, I can't leave you for a minute, Al. What do you call this then?'

'This, Paddy, my ole friend, is a disaster.'

And with that the tears came, a great, big torrent.

Paddy looked left, then right before rummaging in his pocket and pulling out a handful of tissues and thrusting them at her while Wally did his bit by nuzzling into her side.

'Here, they're clean.'

'Thank you.' She blew her nose, sniffed, hiccupped once then raised her hand to check her face. Crying for her was the real deal with snot and saliva in copious amounts but it also ended as quickly as it started, leaving red eyes, a red nose and a feeling of relief.

'Rusty and Gaby and...?'

'Lara and the baby are doing good,' she completed, the soggy tissues now in a heap on her lap, her fingers playing with Wally's ears.

'But I thought Gaby wasn't due until next month?'

'She wasn't. Went into labour early so baby is on the way but doing well by all accounts with heart beats and what have you. They're going to try and stop the labour if they can. Something to do with the lungs, I think.'

'Thank God for that. And you, you're alright.' He stepped back to look at her. 'Apart from looking like you've crawled backwards out of a chimney.'

'I'm fine. Just take me home, Pad. Please.'

They were halfway along the road when she shouted STOP, the subsequent emergency braking almost driving her into the windscreen.

'What the hell!' Paddy exploded, his hands clenched around the steering wheel, his sideways glance saying it all.

Alana would have patted his arm in apology if she had a hand to pat with. Instead, she pointed. 'There, on the wall. Look. That's Gaby's cat. I'm sure she'd appreciate it if we rescued it. Her. I think it's a her.'

It was at that precise moment she wished she'd bothered to ask its name.

FIFTY

Monday 11th September, 8 a.m.

Alana and Paddy were in the office by eight as were William and Wally.

Wally's presence meant the incident room was pervaded by the faint odour of smoke, something she'd had to explain to William in great depth on the journey into work. She'd decided to leave the powered chair at home. The walls weren't up to her driving skills, and she'd got over her issues of having to ask someone to push her. If Gaby could manage with the sight of her husband and daughter on the roof, then she could manage to swallow what little pride she had left.

She was a paraplegic. So what!

'I know we only have an hour before the briefing but I have news. Good news for a change. Gaby gave birth about an hour ago and, by all accounts mother and baby are doing better than expected. Rusty sends his apologies for the briefing.' She looked up at that, her eyes shimmering. 'I know, right! I told him to get his priorities right for once.'

'Boy or girl?'

Alana felt her jaw drop. 'I forgot to ask, Pad. I also don't know the weight or name, or anything. What am I like!'

'You're busy. Don't beat yourself up about it.' Paddy started fiddling with the tablet, the only prompt she needed to get down to business.

'Okay, I'll message him later. Right, we now have an attempted murder to add to the list, five attempted murders to be exact so we're not hanging round on this one. I want Ciara brought in for questioning, Pad, but in the meantime, we have some background to sort. Firstly, where are we with the Tesco angle, specifically, the git who substituted a box of Butlers finest chocs for one of liquorice. Clearly there's a bribery issue and I want the name of that toad five minutes ago. That's you, William.'

'I'm waiting for Tesco's to get back to me.'

'Tell them if we don't hear from them we'll get the legal team involved. After, I want you to chase up on Ciara's convenient trip to the Balearics because, unless she has a bleedin' Tardis or a magic carpet then she can't be in the frame here.' She paused a second, rummaging through the pile of papers on her desk before pulling out a handful of paper. 'Ah, here it is. If you can check with the Hotel Esperanza. There seems to be a discrepancy with the information they forwarded about her stay. There's also her boyfriend to weed out. Okay, so she says she's single, but Dr Laverty also says not to believe a word she says. We could check up on her business partner for a start. Does this Lucas Pounder just share the workplace or the whole building, including her bed? We know she couldn't have carried out the crimes by herself. Driving a boat and laying pots is a two-person job if you don't know what you're doing and there were two people caught on CCTV over in Howth when Barney died.'

'You think it's her then?'

'It doesn't matter what I think, it's what I can prove and for that I need your help.'

She glanced up at the image of Dympna that Paddy had added next to Mason, Waldo and Barney.

'Like mother, like daughter in build and colouring except for their height difference but, remember back to when we interviewed Ciara, Pad, and the heeled boots she was wearing? I'll bet a fiver that the images from Bus Éireann outside the care home and the ones taken from Dymphna's home around the date of her disappearance are both wearing heels. We were led down the garden path by the woman and I think we all know why. Money and revenge.' She checked her watch and reached for her phone. 'While you're doing that I'd best let the guvnor know what's what.'

The call didn't last long. Seconds in fact, and a few seconds after Leo hurled into the room, his chest heaving for the effort it must have taken to fling himself down the stairs.

Alana smiled. 'Sorry, Leo. I didn't mean to interrupt...'

He shook his head. 'Just stop, alright. What are you trying to do here, Alana, because I'd really like to know?'

'Excuse me?'

'You heard. That's three attempts on your life and yet you're still in the office when you know someone is out to get you. On a death wish, is that it?'

Alana was flabbergasted at his response. 'I'm doing my job, Leo, and one you're keeping me from,' she replied, her mood darkening by the second.

'You need to go home and let Paddy take charge. I'll arrange for a guard to be stationed outside your apartment, and that's final.'

He turned to go. Her next words stopped him.

'What are the reasons for the suspension because I'm not resigning, and you have no cause to sack me.'

'Suspend you! I'm trying to keep you alive, woman.'

'Which I'm managing to do quite well by myself but thank you for your concern. If there isn't anything else, I have work to do. Oh, and please don't refer to me as "woman" in that tone. I don't like it. It's detective or Alana. Take your pick.'

He banged the door so hard on the way out that the glass shook in its frame. William and Paddy stayed at their desks, heads down but unable to quite conceal the broad grins overtaking their face.

'Right, which one of you fine chaps is going to make me a coffee? Extra strong and with lots of sugar if you please. I have a case to build.'

FIFTY-ONE

Monday 11th September, 11 a.m.

'I hope this is important. I have clients booked.'

'I'm sure they'll be able to reschedule, Miss Buckley.' Alana reached out a hand to flick on the cameras before reciting the date, time and the people present.

'You're recording me! I never gave you permission to...'

'Your permission isn't needed as per the Criminal Justice Act, but I am happy to provide you with a copy of the recording if you so wish. Would you like a copy, Miss Buckley?' Alana watched as Ciara swatted the comment aside like an irritating fly.

'Just get on with it.'

'Thank you. In case you haven't heard, your grandfather has recovered sufficiently to go to a nursing home for a few days.'

'I... I don't...' Ciara picked up one of the paper cups set out in front of her before reaching for the jug of water. 'Did he ask about me?'

'He'd like to make contact with you if that's what you mean?'

'Perhaps I could visit him?'

'Of course. I'll find out where he is before you leave.'

Alana was in a difficult position. William had tracked down the Tesco worker, who'd substituted the chocolates as one Manuel Pinto from Portugal only to learn that he'd already returned to the Algarve leaving a fictitious address and a pile of debts. She had all the dates and times of the murders in front of her. It would be interesting to see what Ciara made of them.

'About your trip to the Balearics. What were the exact dates again?'

'The 10th to the 20th of August.'

Paddy tapped the printout he'd placed on the table before drawing in his chair. 'I have the flight details here, which corroborate that.'

'Then why did you need to...?'

'I also have the flight details of a Ciara Buckley and a Lucas Pounder on a TUI from Ibiza Airport on the 12th of August and returning on the 19th,' Paddy continued. 'In addition, we've been in touch with your hotel and obtained a copy of your bill, which doesn't include any additional purchases between those two dates. What's going on, Miss Buckley?'

'We had an urgent need to get home.'

'Must have been urgent to interrupt your summer holidays?'

'I don't have to explain my reasons.'

Alana let that go for now. 'We have some more dates to run past you. Where were you on the evening of the 3rd of September, just gone? Take a moment if you need to check your diary.'

'And why is this relevant?' Ciara sat back in her chair, her arms folded, her bottom lip protruding like a petulant child used to getting her own way.

'We don't have to explain our reasons,' Alana said, paraphrasing Ciara's own words back to her. 'Detective Quigg, please repeat the question for Miss Buckley.'

'I don't need it repeating. I was at home like I am every night. I don't go out of an evening, detective.'

'And do you have anyone who can corroborate that?'

She shook her head.

'No boyfriend or significant other?'

'I answered that question previously. It's unlikely to have changed in a couple of days.'

'And what about the Tuesday just gone?'

'Same answer as before.'

'Okay. And some dates during the day. The 22nd and 29th of August and the 5th of September, all Tuesdays between 2 and 3 p.m.,' Alana said, checking her notepad for the details of Cassandra's visits to Waldo's care home and the liquorice deliveries.

'I'll need to check my calendar for that.'

'That's fine. We're happy to wait.'

'My desk calendar, detective. I don't keep that information on me.' Ciara leant forward in her chair, her face contorted into a sort of smile, which made Alana think she'd read up on body language. As a psychotherapist she probably knew the manual inside out. 'Look, what are you trying to get at? That I was somewhere where I clearly wasn't? Something to do with my birth mother's death?' Her smile widened. 'Unless you have any proof, I don't see you can keep me here asking a lot of silly questions when my answer is going to be the same. I'm not under arrest, am I? You'd have read me my rights and instructed me about engaging a lawyer to prevent any miscarriages of justice, and you haven't.'

And that was the problem. Circumstantial evidence wasn't the kind that held up in court. They couldn't get a conviction based on her being unable to prove she wasn't in the same place and time as any of the murders. It didn't work like that. What they needed was irrefutable proof that she had been present and, with no DNA and no witness testimony apart from the likes of Mason's neighbour, that was something they didn't have.

'No, you're not under arrest, Miss Buckley.' Alana made sure to leave a slight pause at the end of her reply before continuing. 'You are free to go but I would ask that you don't leave the country. You know, in case we have some more questions. Now, your father's address...'

'Well, that was a complete waste of time,' Alana said shortly after, the sound of Ciara's heeled boots fading into the distance.

'Oh, I wouldn't go as far as to say that. All it means is that we're going to have to work a little harder to get a conviction.'

'We need to have something we can arrest her for first.'

'And we'll find it,' Paddy said, his voice terse as he started pushing her towards the lift. 'I'm not sure the wisdom in giving her the address of Graham's care home though.'

'Oh, don't you worry about that. Graham Fanning will be fine,' she replied, taking the opportunity to draft an email. 'We're going to nail Ciara's scummy boots to the floor of her cell before throwing away the key, Pad.'

It was one of those unusual coincidences that had placed Graham Fanning in the same care home as Waldo, although not so unusual considering beds in the social care sector were under an unprecedented demand. It was something that Alana intended to take full advantage of.

She glanced over her words before clicking send.

Drop everything. I have a little job for you. No questions. I'm not in the mood to answer them. Here's what I want you to do...

FIFTY-TWO

Monday 11th September, 1.15 p.m.

They were all in the doldrums, including Wally who was eyeing the carrier bag beside him with all the disdain he could muster at the sight of the jumbo size bottle of doggy shampoo. If Alana didn't know better she'd say that he could read. In fact, she was sure of it. He was certainly giving the white bottle more attention than its plain packaging warranted.

Of William there was no sign, which was probably adding to Wally's dejection. He'd left the office straight after dropping off the dog and the carrier.

Her phone pinged through a message from Dympna's solicitor confirming that he was available for a call at five. She was about to respond when Eve sidled up.

'Alana, can I have a word?'

'Of course.' Alana glanced briefly at her watch with a frown before nodding to the spare chair. 'Here okay, or do you want to take it to my office?'

'Here is fine.' She sank onto the seat, her fingers starting to pluck at her skirt.

Eve had been different after learning about Ciara's return trip in the middle of her supposed holiday. Oh, not in the way she presented herself as someone with a mega chip on their shoulder, or even in the way she set about her work. The woman would always be on the far right of abrupt but there was room for allowances to be made if she was good at her job. No, there was something in the way she carried herself, the set of her shoulders and the fading of her ruddy-cheeked complexion that was different. Alana could guess at the reason but guessing only gave her the opportunity to be wrong and she wasn't in the mood for any more disappointments with the case stalling.

'Look, I'm sorry, alright. I made a mistake about the airline...'

'A mistake any of us could have made, Eve, and one that you would have found eventually if the clues hadn't been leading us astray.'

'But—'

Alana interrupted, her voice soft. 'There's no point in beating yourself up about it. It's over and done with. Now, let's continue working together in trying to pin these atrocious crimes on the right person?'

'But I don't make mistakes.'

Alana would have joked at that if she'd been speaking to anyone else. Everyone made mistakes, she'd made great big doozies in her time and not all of them that she'd ever admit to in public. But Eve wouldn't appreciate the humour. She was different and, as her manager she had to accept that if only for a quiet life. Leo was right that the team lacked someone more mature. She could only hope Eve was the right individual to fill that gap.

'And this will make you even better at your job than you are already.'

'I think I have something.'

They both turned to Paddy and where he was waving a sheet of paper above his head. Alana managed a relieved smile.

'Spill.'

'I've just been on the citizen's information website. It says, and I quote, "The Birth Information and Tracing Act 2022 was signed into law on 30th June 2022. This Act gives adopted people, people who were boarded out, or born in a Mother and Baby, or County Home Institution, or people who had their births illegally registered, the right to their birth certificate."' He lifted his head to add. 'The act also gave the same rights to the mothers.'

Alana might have an arm that throbbed, the start of a headache and worries about William but there was nothing wrong with the way her neurones were suddenly snapping to attention, Olympians each and every one. 'You're thinking Ciara knew about Dympna being her mother and used joining the bone marrow register as a way to hide that fact? A simple way of getting her DNA into the public domain.'

He nodded. 'And this little piece of paper proves it. Dympna contacted the Birth Information and Tracing Service in the autumn of 2022 and was subsequently issued with the name of Ciara's adoptive parents. I always had my suspicions about the bone marrow register as most places have a severe age cut-off point.'

'So, what would be the benefit of her joining? Okay. Dympna is provided with the names of the people who bought her daughter off the nuns. We can only assume that she quickly ascertained what happened to them, not difficult as the fire was extensively reported in the Irish media.' Alana thought back to the newspaper articles that William had passed on to her after their Wednesday briefing, particularly the exposé that had detailed both Ciara's name and that of the burns unit. Dympna would have had Ciara Buckley's details and, as she'd never married and ran a business under her name, she would have found tracing her daughter simple.

'In effect, Dympna signed her own death warrant by her need to connect with her child. What's the world coming to? At least now we have the proof to do something about our suspicions. I'd like you to arrange an arrest warrant, Eve.' She turned to face Paddy. 'You're with me, Paddy. I just hope we're not too late.'

'Why. Where are we going?'

'I'll tell you in the car. Come on, get pushing.' She tapped her wheelchair. 'There's no time to lose.'

'You set up William in Graham Fanning's place. Alana, you muppet.'

Alana felt bad enough without having her second in command picking her up. What had seemed a good idea in the spur of the moment now felt like a stupid rookie mistake and one that put her team at unnecessary risk.

'You think I'm that foolish? No, don't answer that.' She would have cracked a joke but there was nothing to laugh about. 'Graham is safe enough and Waldo's care home were more than happy to help after what happened to him.'

'Even so. It's a huge risk. What if something goes wrong?'

'I know but don't keep going on about it, eh, Pad. Just concentrate on putting your foot down and, anyway, I sent Flynn in as backup.'

'Flynn?' She felt Paddy's shrewd gaze flicker in her direction but decided to ignore it. 'Flynn as in our Flynn? He's not exactly backup material, is he?'

'You leave Flynn alone. We can't all be built like James bloody Bond. That lad has hidden talents. Just look at the way he jumped in after Barney. If we don't give them a chance to succeed, then they'll give up trying.' She didn't mention the scanty instructions she'd messaged him in preparation for his debut role of hiding behind the curtains. In spite of Paddy's pessimism she was sure Flynn was up to the task even if it was all hidden underneath his sober exterior.

'I take it you haven't told Leo then?'

'Well, no, he wouldn't have agreed to...'

'I'm sure he wouldn't! Okay.' Paddy held his hands up before slapping them down on the steering wheel. 'I'll support you but if it goes wrong...'

There was no need for him to finish the sentence. If it went wrong, she'd take the full weight of the blame on her sturdy shoulders.

FIFTY-THREE

Monday 11th September, 2.45 p.m.

It was hot and sticky, the room overheated and with an underlying whiff of stale piss no matter which way William moved his head. He'd tried breathing through his mouth, but he could only manage that for a short time before reverting to his nose, his preferred option. He was also desperate for a pee, and he had been for the last two hours.

Bloody hell, stop thinking about peeing or you're going to wet the bed and where will that get you. In the same place as the poor ole sod who'd vacated the bed.

Yes, he was lying in someone else's bed, some poor incontinent geezer who'd offered to give up his mattress when Dora had asked him. She'd changed the sheets, and the duvet. She'd made that point three times on the way to the second-floor room. One of their superior rooms with an en suite, an en suite he couldn't avail himself of even if he was about to soil the bed.

STOP THINKING ABOUT IT!

It was warm, far too warm in the home. With the duvet over his head, with only a small breathing hole to prevent him from dying from suffocation, or poisoning from stale pee, he was starting to feel drowsy. Not quite asleep but definitely on the verge when a sudden knock on the door roused him from his slumber.

'Hello, okay if I come in? You have a visitor.' Then more quietly, the voice barely audible under the mound of duvet, 'Aw, look at that. He's asleep. Best not disturb him.'

'Maybe if I sit beside him for a while. He might appreciate the company. Ninety-nine, you say. Poor ole bloke. What a thing.'

'Well, if you're sure, Cassandra. I'll be outside if you need me. Just holler.'

'Course I will. You're a gem, Dora. An absolute gem.'

The door clicked shut, the silence surrounding him, blanketing out everything except the thoughts racing round his mind. Was Flynn still there? William wasn't convinced in Alana's decision to have him as backup. He was a nice enough bloke but not known for his assertiveness. What if he'd dropped off to sleep? There'd been no conversation since they'd arrived. He could be dead for all he knew or bunked off for a cuppa with Dora. Either way, it might be him up against a madwoman.

The continued silence was off putting. The fear of what was about to happen set his teeth on edge and his heart thumping. If it thumped any louder she'd be bound to hear it. Alana had told him that, with no proof except circumstantial, they needed definitive evidence they had the right person in the frame, which meant an attack of some sort.

A knife. A gun. No, not a gun. Too noisy.

'You stupid old man, why couldn't you have died the first time?'

One second, he was considering they'd got it wrong, that this Cassandra person was the real deal, the next his head was pressed into the mattress, a pillow rammed over his mouth.

Ah. I didn't think of suffocation. Figures after Mason though.

'God, you stink. I hate you for what you did. For what they all did.'

'Stop. You've got it all wrong.' He tried to speak but the words came out in a guttural mumble. Then he stopped trying to do anything other than fighting her off.

Ciara Buckley, for all her slight frame and feminine appearance, was as strong as a proverbial ox, her arms refusing to give an inch despite her years.

William only realised the true extent of the trouble he was in when he remembered both his arms were trapped under the duvet, her full length stretching over him to prevent him from resisting.

Really! He was going to let a scrawny mass murderess kill him? But that's how it was beginning to look as his oxygen levels started to deplete and the world closed in.

FIFTY-FOUR

Monday 11th September, 2.50 p.m.

'We did exactly as you asked,' Dora said, escorting Alana to the lift, a narrow affair, which Paddy had wheeled her to before jogging towards the stairs. 'A second-floor room with a curtain wide enough for someone to hide behind. Mr Cullen was very accommodating. There hasn't been this much excitement in the home since Ireland won the rugby.'

'That was obliging of him.'

'He's a very obliging man. I've popped him in the lounge in front of the television. He likes a good war movie.'

Alana let her witter on. A nice enough woman but Mr Cullen's taste in programmes held little interest.

'You're sure it was Cassandra?' Alana interrupted, waiting for the lift doors to peel apart, the smell of some chemical cleaner causing her nostrils to quiver. These places all smelt the same, a hospital smell that dragged her back to her mother's bedside, her schoolbag by her feet, her mother's skeletal fingers cooling under her palm.

Alana blinked back the image, choosing her wide-eyed

reflection with its remnant of Spanish tan staring back at her in preference to the painful past.

'Yes. The very same. I showed her in seconds before you arrived and closed the door just like William told me.' There was a brief pause. 'He'll be alright, won't he?'

Alana suddenly switched to Dora's reflection and the worried expression pulling at her mouth. If she could have managed a smile, a reassuring gesture to make the woman feel better, to make her feel the guards had it all under control. But they didn't. Not now.

What have I done?

She had too much on her mind to provide a suitably calming answer. She'd based her decision on her determination to catch the killer but without being in possession of the facts. They now had the proof needed to take Ciara to trial. The paper trail of Dympna's dealings with the Birth Information and Tracing Service was irrefutable. The sketchy details would need filling in but there were enough people around who'd been in a similar position to help highlight the way. An Irish blot that had been hidden from view far too long.

The lift reached its destination with a final squeak before the doors began opening, the sound of shouting now filling the corridor, and a red-faced Paddy racing past.

FIFTY-FIVE

Monday 11th September, 2.55 p.m.

'What the hell! Get off him, I tell you,' Flynn shouted, the words muffled through wads of pillow stuffing, closely followed by the more muted noise of a scuffle and the sound of a thud and a scream, a woman's scream.

Good, hope she's broken something. Even if she sues it will have been worth it.

William lay there a second, then two, trying to get air into his lungs, the pillow snatched from his face by an irate hand.

'Sorry. I thought I should video it on my phone. By the time I realised what was happening...' Closely followed by, 'Paddy, am I glad to see you.'

William managed a grunt, running his hands down his face where everything appeared to be in order, before turning to where Flynn was now sitting on the floor. Well, to be fair he wasn't so much sitting on the floor as on top of Ciara as he looped a pair of handcuffs around her wrists.

'Well done, William and Flynn,' Alana said from the doorway, as Dora ran to his side.

'Yes, well done. Gawd. I've never seen the like. Wait till I tell Mr Cullen what's been happening in his bedroom. Not a patch on *The Guns of Navarone*, that's for sure.'

William was starting to feel decidedly shaky around the knees. If she'd had a knife or a gun. He didn't want to think along those lines, but he couldn't seem to stop himself.

'Gawd, I think he's going to faint.' Dora took his arm and forced him into the nearest chair, her hand on his head. 'Head between your knees, laddo. I'll get you a cuppa in a sec. As soon as the guards come and remove this piece of trash.'

He wasn't about to faint, was he? Pee himself more like but the deep breathing she was now getting him to do was at least helping to divert one particular disaster. He wouldn't leave until he'd watched them escort Ciara Buckley out.

William blinked, as the screaming started up again in earnest. Ciara screamed and screamed as if it was going out of fashion.

Ah, the insanity plea. Good luck with that. You lost that chance when you decided to only knock off those people related to you.

Paddy started to speak, his voice barely audible over the din. 'Ciara Buckley, I am arresting you for the murders of Dympna Fanning, Waldo Mulcahy, Barney Mulcahy and Mason Clare, and the attempted murder of Graham Fanning, Dr and Mrs Mulholland, Lara Mulholland, Dr Laverty and Detective Mack. You are not obliged to say anything unless you wish to do so but anything you say may be taken down in writing and may be used in evidence.'

Dora whistled. 'Gee whiz. That's a lot of people, so it is.'

FIFTY-SIX

Monday 11th September, 5.55 p.m.

In between the bursts of screaming Ciara had miraculously managed to find sufficient internal strength from somewhere to get lawyered up on the way to the station. It was a tossup as to whether she'd be offering an insanity plea or whether she had another plan tucked up her sleeve. Either way, Alana took the added precaution to prime herself with a double espresso and another dose of painkillers.

She nodded to Ciara's lawyer briefly while Paddy pushed her into place before taking his seat beside her. The cameras were on and the statement sheet set out in preparation.

'Afternoon, Mr Matthews. Miss Buckley. Let's get started.'

'I have only had a brief consult with my client, detective,' he said, placing his mobile on the table along with a pile of forms, his hand on top. 'Before you get started I'd like to ask for a delay, and I will also be pushing for bail.'

Good luck with that.

Alana smiled, sounding bored. 'While you're writing out your forms, we'll get cracking on finding out why your client is up for four counts of murder and six of attempted.' She paused a second, looking puzzled before tilting her head at Paddy, her gaze snagging his with the briefest twitch of her upper eyelid. 'Change that to seven. We've forgotten poor ole William.'

She turned back to the lawyer, in time to note his startled expression. Catching criminals was the hard bit. Banging them to rights came with its own set of difficulties but, as a rule, Alana much preferred that part of the process. It also came with a reduced risk of getting injured.

'This is a serious charge sheet, Mr Matthews, and, contrary to anything Miss Buckley might have told you, we do have sufficient evidence to take this to trial. Any further questions before I start?'

'No.' The no was abrupt and slightly startled. Alana quite liked Keith Matthews but he was way out of his league with Ciara Buckley, something he must be beginning to realise.

'Good. Now, Miss Buckley, when did you first decide to murder your parents?'

'Which ones?' She crossed one leg over the other, swinging her foot backwards and forwards, the patent leather boot catching the light.

Alana switched her attention from the boot and back to Ciara's face, brushing aside any thought as to the woman's mental state. A full confession was rare. Everyone took to lying like a national sport these days making it impossible to weed out the truth.

'Let's start with Paula and Joseph Buckley and the unfortunate fire that appeared to start in their new fridge.'

Ciara leant back, the faint redness under her left cheek the only sign of her recent altercation. 'The fire that I barely escaped from?'

'Yes. The fire where you rescued your dog instead of your parents and subsequently made no effort to ask what had happened to him,' Alana said, flicking through her sheet of pages. 'You were good friends with your next-door neighbour's daughter, Jacinta Cooke. Figures as you were similar ages. She always wondered why you never agreed to let her visit. After all, she ended up taking your dog.'

'No comment.'

'When exactly did you learn they weren't your parents, Miss Buckley?' Alana continued, placing a photo of Ciara and her parents on the table between them, the image the same one all the newspapers had used on their front pages, the differences in their colouring clear to see.

'I didn't, or at least, not until you told me.'

'Really?' Alana watched Paddy make a note. 'You might be interested to learn that Jacinta remembers it differently.' She tucked the statement back into the pile before retrieving a second document and pushing it across the table. 'Moving on. In October 2022, Dympna Fanning made an application to the Birth Information and Tracing Service and was subsequently issued with the name of her daughter. You, Miss Buckley. In December of the same year she hired her usual chauffeur to take her to Cork.' Alana layered a third document on top. 'I put it to you that you recognised Dympna Fanning from her frequent appearances in the press and television. Only the week before her visit to Cork your mother was invited to a reception at Steward's Lodge along with the Taoiseach and the President. Her image was everywhere.'

'Coincidental. I don't watch television or read the papers.' She brushed aside the papers, scattering them on the floor.

Alana ignored the childish behaviour, taking it as proof that the woman was starting to feel the pressure build.

'We've also been tracking back through your mother's bank accounts, and have confirmed she stayed in Bandon for two nights, in December 2022. Interestingly the hotel has provided us with a detailed breakdown of her expenditure, which includes all the meals consumed in the restaurant.' Alana waved the bill instead of handing it over. 'Tell me about Lucas Pounder, your business partner?'

'No comment.'

Alana turned to Keith briefly, who was looking like a rabbit in headlights, his usually firm jaw unravelling along with his impeccably knotted tie and carefully arranged hair.

'We are in the process of interviewing Mr Pounder as well as obtaining samples of his DNA for comparison purposes. There's a little question of the petrol can used to start two recent fires in addition to a sample of denim fabric rescued from my dog's mouth.' Alana felt like smiling but there was nothing to smile about in the room. 'When did you first learn about your mother's problem with her heart, Miss Buckley?'

'I didn't.'

'And you didn't perform an internet search on ways to murder someone with a heart condition? Before you answer, please remember that our team of analysts have your phone and the password.'

'No comment.'

'And, finally...' Alana opened the folder and started to place a series of stills from the CCTV footage harvested from both the bus and Dympna's house. 'You wouldn't happen to recognise this person, would you? Look closely, particularly at the boots, which appear to be very similar to the ones you're wearing today. In fact, I'd go so far as to say identical.'

FIFTY-SEVEN

Monday 11th September, 9.15 p.m.

'It's time for the pub, so it is, Alana.'

'I second that, Pad,' William said, returning from walking Wally. 'While Flynn thirds it, don't you, Flynn?'

'Suppose.'

'It can't be!' Alana glanced at her watch. 'Last time I looked it was five.'

'Go figure, but with Ciara and her partner in crime in the process of being shown the delights of our custodial suite there's very little we can do until the morning,' Paddy said, slipping on his jacket and picking up his keys and phone. 'I never expected Pounder to squeal like a pig when we explained the difference between being an accessory after the fact and that of a murdering bastard. They're both going to be put away for a very long time.'

'We always knew she didn't act alone. There's the boat and manhandling Dympna into the pot for a start, and the little question of who did this to me.' Alana lifted up her broken arm.

'It will be interesting to see if Mr Pounder's DNA is the same as the one we rescued from Wally.' She took a second to pat the dog's head.

'There's also the little matter of the plastic wrap pulled from Mason's bin. A partial palm print no less.' Paddy waved his phone in the air. 'Just had a message in from Ruan about it.'

'Really? All the proof we need and more besides. I wonder what made them think they could get away with it. If something did happen to me, something incapacitating, another guard would have easily taken over my workload.'

'Lucas isn't on the system and neither is Ciara. Amateurs both,' Paddy said, taking charge of her chair. 'Got everything? Keys? Mobile? Dog lead? Kitchen sink? And no one could ever replace you. Alana.' He dropped his voice to a whisper for her ears only. 'Occasionally I might think along those lines but it's all about priorities and mine is keeping you in post so that I don't have to cope with all the managerial shite that goes with the job.'

Alana didn't know what to say. They were a team, a good one. She'd been dreading the day she'd lose him. It was bound to come but not yet.

'Thank you.'

'You do look tired, Al, if you don't mind me saying. Great looking but still tired,' he qualified quickly. 'I'm happy to drop you off first if you like? Up to you.'

'No, I'll join you but only for one.'

'I wonder if Leo would like to...?'

Leo! She'd forgotten all about him. *Rats!*

She'd messaged him earlier, a brief update as to where they were and what they were at but since then it had been bedlam. Literally. She was also aware of the deep sighs coming from the team desperate to celebrate their win. Even Wally appeared to be in on it with his noisy yap.

'I know! Give me a minute or we'll all get the sack. You know what his lordship is like.'

She picked up her phone.

'Hi, Leo. Sorry, I promised to call you back. Buckley is being bedded downstairs for the night so there's nothing else to do this evening.'

'Heading for the pub?'

She frowned at the phone and where she'd placed it on loudspeaker. 'Yes, actually.'

'Good, I'll meet you there. I'm buying.'

Alana had suddenly fallen into a parallel universe where Leo was the type to join their merry band on the odd occasions they chose to go for a drink. To the best of her knowledge he didn't know where their usual pub was or even what her usual drink was but there was nothing she could say other than agree before ending the call, her phone back on her lap.

'We've got company.'

'We heard! Drinks on the boss. Couldn't be better. Might it be a good opportunity to submit our overtime?' Paddy said. 'Another lost weekend.'

'Hah. You can try!'

'Dora said she might join us if that's okay?' William added.

Yes! She would have thumped the air if she didn't think it would embarrass him.

'The more the merrier. Irene too if she doesn't object to spending time with a whole pile of drunk coppers.'

'She'll love it. You don't mind if we don't ask Billy, as it seems to be growing into a party? It's just...'

'Billy and I are and will only ever be friends, Pad,' she said, annoyed he'd chosen to raise it but pleased it was out in the open in front of William. 'He's also on the opposite side of the fence so no, he won't be invited and before you ask, neither will Colm, alright. As sad as it sounds, you guys are my family now.'

'Hah, I wouldn't go there, Al, or we'll all be watching our backs as well as our fronts in case you decide to do a Ciara on us.'

'And our heads,' William said, his tone mournful.

'That is in very poor taste, both of you.'

She smiled, then grinned before starting to chuckle.

There was nothing they could do about the past so there was little point in dwelling on it. She was lucky she'd learnt that early on in her career. Many coppers only found it out at the bottom of a whiskey bottle. When the bodies were released, she'd be sure to attend every funeral in order to pay her respects but tonight, in good old Irish tradition, they'd hold the wake before the burial. It would also be an opportunity for her to share a little titbit of news from Dympna's solicitor and the contents of her will, which was solely to the benefit of the largest fostering and adoption charity in Ireland.

Even if she'd been successful in evading capture, Ciara Buckley wouldn't have received a penny.

She reached for her jacket only to catch sight of Eve making for the door. Sneaking out if her lack of eye contact was anything to go by.

'Wait up, Eve.'

'What?'

'Join us for a celebratory drink?'

'I don't think so.' Eve flicked her a brief glance before adding, 'Thanks for asking though.'

'No need to thank me. You're an important part of the team. I know we started off on the wrong foot, but I hope that's been rectified.' Alana worked on stuffing papers into her desk drawer, with no regard to how she'd find them in the morning. 'You've been instrumental in helping catch Buckley and Pounder but what's the betting that tomorrow we'll have another equally tough case thrown at us. We might as well enjoy ourselves while we can.'

She could see the woman was starting to weaken so decided to go in for the kill.

'Also, there is the added advantage that his lordship is buying. Now, what's the most expensive bar in Dublin? One proviso. It must accept dogs.'

A LETTER FROM THE AUTHOR

Dear Reader,

I hope you enjoyed *Cage of Bones*, the third in my Detective Alana Mack series, although each book is a standalone.

If you'd like to join other readers in being the first to know about all future books I write, just click the link below for my personal email newsletter. You'll get bonus content and get occasional updates and insights from my writing life. I'd be delighted if you choose to sign up.

www.stormpublishing.co/jenny-obrien

If you enjoyed *Cage of Bones* and could spare a few moments to leave a review that would be hugely appreciated. Even a short review can make all the difference in encouraging a reader to discover my books for the first time. Thank you so much!

The idea for *Cage of Bones* came about by the merging of three unconnected facts. I am what I term a blank page writer, which means I start a book with very little idea about how it is going to end, as opposed to someone who plots the story out from beginning to end. Another word for it is Pantzer, as in writing by the seat of your pants. It's a scary place to be but it also seems to be the only way I can write.

In *Cage of Bones* I had the start, or that fishy chapter one if you like. I was a few weeks into the book when I read an article about the changes to the adoption rules in Ireland, and the opening in 2022 of what had been up to then sealed files. A few weeks later I happened upon an Interpol article about Bonaparte.

Fishing, changes to adoption rules and Bonaparte. That's how *Cage of Bones* came about.

Thank you for reading.

Jenny.

ACKNOWLEDGEMENTS

I can't believe I'm here again. This is the part of writing a book I struggle with the most. I'm bound to miss someone out.

As always, the dedication first. I have been known to pull crab pots in my time so writing a book about crab fishing was always a given. Easy research! Micky is a keen potter, Jane his lovely wife.

Thank you to my agent, Nicola Barr, from the Bent Agency, to help turn a very short idea about a man pulling his pots into *Cage of Bones*. I'm lucky to have an amazing editor in Claire Bord, who gets what I'm trying to put down on paper. Also, thanks go to Oliver Rhodes, Alexandra Holmes, Naomi Knox, Anna McKerrow, Elke Desanghere, Chris Lucraft and all at Storm along with Dushi Horti and Shirley Khan. A strong team of talented professionals. I couldn't ask for better editors if I tried.

Harry Steadman, you are a genius.

Michele Moran, your voice! Thank you. You have brought Alana and her team to life. Thank you.

All writers have a fellow muse. Someone to bounce ideas off. Someone to share the highs and lows of this amazing, madcap industry. That's you, Valerie Keogh. Thank you!

Also, thanks to fellow writers Pam Lecky, Jane Mosse, Luisa Jones, Susie Lynes and Sam Tonge.

Character names. Sometimes I include real people. Keith Matthews is a good swimming friend, one of the kindest most generous people you could meet. Those of you who have read my Gaby Darin series might remember I murdered his wife in one of the books? Barbara has yet to forgive me!

I raffled the name of Rusty's sidekick pathologist last year. Thank you to Chris Sharp for the winning bid and naming the good doc Gabby Quinn.

Kari, you made it through the edits this time!

Thank you, CHOG. If you know, you know.

I have a small group of fans who have been with me since the beginning in a 'they found me' way, rather than the other way round. In no particular order, thanks to Beverley, Michele, Maureen, Diane, Elaine, Susan, Lesley, Tracy, Amanda, Sarah, Sharon, Pauline, Jo, Daniela, Carol, Madeleine, Tracey, Terri, Maggie, Lynda, Hayley and Donna. Also, Maureen, please remind me about your address change in time for your December card, thank you.

We lost one of the group recently. *Dear Adele Blair, you will never be forgotten.*

Wally! I nearly forgot the most important character. When I decided to include a dog in the series, way back in October 2023, I ran a little poll on Twitter (X) for a name. Maggie Way was the winner with Wally. I think he might steal the show from Goose. Maybe. Maybe not.

Final thanks go to my husband, and our three children. We're getting there. Tell me when we actually arrive. Buns for tea!

If you've managed to get this far, I hope you have enjoyed the book. If you can leave a review that would be great. If you can't, just sharing your reading experience with your friends would help, and do look out for my next, which I am halfway through writing. A deviation as I felt I needed a little break from crime. An historical mystery set in Guernsey, my home for the last thirty-six years. A violin features. More shortly.

Thank you for choosing *Cage of Bones*.

Printed in Great Britain
by Amazon